# I DO OR DYE TRYING

## AIMEE NICOLE WALKER

*I Do, or Dye Trying*
(Curl Up and DYE Mysteries, #4)
Copyright © 2017 Aimee Nicole Walker

ISBN: 978-0-9974225-7-3

aimeenicolewalker@blogspot.com

This is a work of fiction. Names, characters, places, and incidents either are the product of the author's imagination or are used fictitiously, and any resemblance to the actual person, living or dead, business establishments, events, or locales is entirely coincidental.

Cover photograph and interior photos © Wander Aguiar – www.wanderaguiar.com
Cover art © Jay Aheer of Simply Defined Art – www.jayscoversbydesign.com
Editing provided by Pam Ebeler of Undivided Editing – www.undividedediting.com
Proofreading provided by Judy Zweifel of Judy's Proofreading – www.judysproofreading.com
Interior Design and Formatting provided by Stacey Ryan Blake of Champagne Formats
– www.champagneformats.com

**This book contains sexually explicit material and is only intended for adult readers.**

Copyright and Trademark Acknowledgments
The author acknowledges the copyrights and trademarked status and trademark owners of the following trademarks and copyrights mentioned in this work of fiction.
Copyrights and Trademarks:
Word of Warcraft – Blizzard Entertainment
Miami Vice – Universal Television, NBC
Friends – Warner Bros Television, NBC
Netflix
Coca Cola
Ninja Coffee Bar
20/20 – ABC
60 Minutes – CBS
Dateline – NBC
Rhett and Scarlett – Gone with the Wind
"Try" – P!nk
Walmart
The Twilight Zone – CBS
Skype
"A Tale of Two Cities" – Charles Dickens
"Can't Get Enough of Your Love, Babe" – Barry White
Cincinnati Reds
Atlanta Braves
Mary Poppins – Walt Disney Company
"Marry Me" – Train
"Somewhere Over the Rainbow" – Wizard of Oz
"What a Wonderful World" – Louis Armstrong
"It Takes Two" – Rob Base and DJ EZ Rock
"Because you Loved Me" – Celine Dion
Coach
"Simple Love Song" – Anuhea
Miss Congeniality – Warner Bros

Other Books by Aimee Nicole Walker

*Only You*

**The Fated Hearts Series**
*Chasing Mr. Wright, Book 1*
*Rhythm of Us, Book 2*
*Surrender Your Heart, Book 3*
*Perfect Fit, Book 4*
*Return to Me, Book 5*
*Always You, Book 6*
*Any Means Necessary, Book 7*

**Curl Up and Dye Mysteries**
*Fatal Reaction (Series Prequel found on author's blog)*
*Dyeing to be Loved*
*Something to Dye For*
*Dyed and Gone to Heaven*

*Undisputed* – coauthored with Nicholas Bella

# DEDICATION

To my Dye Hards,
You brighten my world every single day, and I cherish the
friendships we've made. Thank you for being a part of my life!

# ONE

## Gabriel Wyatt

Josh and I had the most amazing week in the Bahamas to celebrate his birthday and our future. We spent our time swimming, sunbathing, eating, and making love. I soaked in every second we had alone because we both knew things would get crazy once we returned home.

Broadman's pretrial hearings were scheduled to start, we also had a wedding to plan, and a mini-mansion to buy. The changes to our lives were huge and overwhelming, but so fucking amazing. I couldn't wait to start our new life together and raise a family. In fact, we treated Josh's birthday vacation like it might be the last time we got to go away alone as a couple for a very long time. I thought trips to Disney might be in our future instead of a romantic getaway for two. Some couples were lucky enough to do both, and I thought it should be our goal also.

"That was the most amazing week I've ever had," Josh said as I pulled down our street. "Thank you for so many wonderful birthday surprises." He was talking about the little gifts I gave him daily to celebrate him taking another trip around the sun. Those were nothing compared to the surprise I had for him at home. I knew the moment he saw his special gift.

"Oh! My! GOD!" He squealed and danced in his seat as I pulled in the driveway. The car hadn't even come to a complete stop before he jumped out and ran to his Princess. "Racing stripes! You bought me racing stripes!" There was more dancing followed by a kiss fit for a hero. I seriously debated painting some temporary racing stripes down the front of my body to see what kind of reaction I would get from him. "You shouldn't have spent so much money, but damn I'm so in love with them." He ran his finger lightly over one of the silver stripes.

"I've seen the way you lust after Emory's stripes, or at least I hope it was just the damn stripes," I grumbled.

"Shut up," Josh said, slapping me playfully on my arm. "Oh, speaking of Emory, here he comes. I bet he wants to talk about my new stripes."

I could tell by the expression on Emory's face when he neared us that he wasn't there to admire the stripes. In fact, I was positive that I didn't want to hear whatever Emory had to say.

"I've had a vision," he said somberly. "I know why I'm here in Blissville."

I automatically reached for Josh and pulled him close. I didn't have to be a psychic to know that it was bad news. "Why are you

2

here, Emory?" I asked him.

"Someone's looking for you, Gabe. A man." He replied so solemnly that it was almost funny.

"Should I be worried?" Josh quipped, never one to miss an opportunity to snark. I looked down into his hazel eyes and was surprised that I saw concern there instead of the humor I expected. I remembered how unsettled Josh was about Emory's appearance in our lives and how hard he worked to convince himself that everything was going to be okay.

"Honestly," Emory said then paused for effect, "yes."

"Whoa," Josh said softly, every ounce of happiness he'd felt moments before was gone. I knew I needed to act fast to get it back.

"Emory, do you know anything more specific than a man is looking for me. I mean, that could be anything. What makes you think we should be worried?" I asked our friend.

"It's hard to explain," he said, but he could tell by the expression on my face that he was going to need to try. "There was an aura of danger in my vision."

"A feeling?" I asked. I wanted—no, I needed—something more concrete than a feeling. I was a cop and worked on facts, not premonitions.

"More than that," Emory said in frustration. I could tell he was struggling to find a way to explain things to me. "Sometimes my visions have colors around the edges, and sometimes colors surround the person in the vision. I saw a red aura, which can be several things, among them is anger, resentment, and even danger. This man—or whatever he represents—could be dangerous to you."

"Did you get a good look at his face?" Josh asked. "Believe it or not, we have a sketch artist on the task force."

"I remember," Emory said. "Your work with the artist brought a killer to your door—the same man whose negative energy I sensed in my house when I first moved in."

"Well, did you see his face?" Josh asked, urging Emory to

answer his question. I was curious to hear the answer myself.

"It wasn't a clear vision of the man; it seldom works that way. Hell, if it did I could prevent…" His words broke off as a look of complete devastation washed over him. I wondered if he was talking about his husband's death, but hadn't I read that his abilities started *after* River died? I also noticed he spoke in future tense—not past— like he wanted to prevent something that hadn't happened yet, but knew he couldn't. "Never mind," he said, shaking his head. "What I see are fragmented pieces of events like snapshots, and sometimes they're nothing more than vague impressions. In your case," he nodded to me, "I saw an outline of a tall man appearing before you and his aura was so dark black that…"

"I thought you said it was red," Josh said, cutting him off.

"Gabe's aura was red," Emory clarified patiently. "The stranger's aura was black, which usually indicates the inability to forgive, repressed anger, and bitterness."

"Emory, why don't we go upstairs and talk about this," I suggested. "You can tell me exactly what you saw."

"Yeah, okay," he said, but his tone indicated that he'd rather not. "I guess the least I can do is grab a suitcase."

"You're reading my mind again," Josh told him, trying to inject some humor into the situation.

Once upstairs in our apartment above the salon, Emory sat sipping a can of Coke that Josh handed him while we greeted our fur and feather babies. Adrian had sent a text when we were on our way home that said he'd drop Buddy off, so that he could be waiting for us when we arrived. He couldn't decide if he was happy to see us or pissed because we left him in the first place. Someone abandoned him once, and I always worried he felt left behind when Josh and I left him for an extended time.

"You're such a good boy," I assured him as I rubbed his belly. "Best boy in the world."

"Bite me, asshole! Bite me!" Savage squawked as he flapped his wings angrily and rocked his little swing back and forth. "Asshole!"

"Somebody's jealous," Josh said, nodding his head toward the bird. "Let me take over here while you calm the bird down."

I rose to my feet and walked over to the cage while Diva wove in and out of my legs. "Did you miss me, Savage? I missed you." Savage settled down as soon as I opened his cage. "Have you been a good boy, Dirty Bird?" I stroked my finger over his soft blue feathers.

"Big Daddy's home! Little Daddy's home!" *Finally!* I'd been trying to teach him to call Josh that for weeks!

"*Little Daddy*?" Josh asked.

I turned to face Josh, who had Jazzy sitting on his shoulders, while he rubbed Buddy's belly. "I don't know where he learns these things, Sunshine. I honestly don't." I turned back to face our bird who bopped his head like he was jamming to music that only he could hear, which made me wonder if I could teach him to dance to music to entertain our guests. "Daddies are home, Dirty Bird."

"Dirty Bird!" Savage repeated.

Emory's chuckle reminded me that a more serious discussion needed to take place. I stroked over Savage one last time before I closed his cage then braced myself to hear whatever Emory had to say. He looked nervous where before he looked afraid. Was he worried that I wouldn't believe him? While I couldn't say that I was hanging onto his every word, I wasn't going to ignore him either.

"Okay," I said, taking a seat on the sofa. "Tell me exactly what you saw."

"It was just a snippet in time. You were standing on a porch talking to a man." *That was it?* "That's not all," Emory said, giving me a knowing look. I blinked because Josh had jokingly called him a mind reader on more than one occasion. "It was the scowl on your face, Detective, not me peering into your brain."

"It's still creepy," I told him.

"Right?" Josh asked from where he sat on the floor.

"I feel ridiculous for practically running across the yard with an ominous threat with virtually no information to back it up. I know just how much you law enforcement officers want hard, concrete evidence."

"Juries kind of demand it, Emory," I told him dryly. "Tell me what you saw."

"I feel ridiculous now that I'm about to say it out loud." He released a long breath and said, "I saw a quick snippet of you talking to a man on a porch."

"Our front porch or back porch?" Josh asked. "Front door visits imply that the person doesn't know us well or maybe not at all. Friends and family would come to our back door."

"Neither," Emory replied. "It wasn't at this house."

"What did the house look like in your vision?" Josh asked. *Who was the detective here?*

Emory closed his eyes like he was trying to remember every detail. "It was a big, wide porch, with large white pillars and dark wicker furniture with gray and blue striped cushions." He opened his eyes and said, "It seems familiar to me, but I don't know why." A shiver of fear snaked its way down my spine.

"Like this?" Josh asked. He scooted over to Emory and showed him a picture on his phone. I knew without asking which house he was showing him. It was the one we were going to buy so we could start the next phase of our lives. We'd discussed it the day I asked Josh to marry me right before we went on his birthday trip. The house was exactly how Emory described it, minus the dark wicker furniture with striped cushions. But damn if that didn't sound like something Josh would buy to put on that big porch.

"Yes, just like that!" Emory exclaimed. "Whose house is that?"

"It's our forever home," Josh said confidently. "We just need to buy it."

"You don't know why the guy was there or what was said, and you can't tell me what he looked like. Is that right?" I asked. I wanted to give credence to his words but it was hard to do with such vague details.

Emory blushed a little, and I felt guilty for making him feel bad. "He was taller than you by a few inches, and he wasn't as muscular as you," he said. "I know this sounds ridiculous, but my visions or impressions have never been wrong. There will be a man who comes to your front door, and he will bring anger and resentment with him. He's dangerous."

"Thank you, Emory," I said, unsure what else to say. "I appreciate you looking out for me."

"I won't stay any longer," he said, rising to his feet. "I know you probably have a lot to do now that you're back from vacation." There was only one thing on my mind, and I'd pounce on it the minute he left.

"Are you coming to dinner tomorrow?" Josh asked him when he reached the top of the staircase.

"You mean I'm still invited?" he asked softly.

"Of course," Josh replied. "Don't be ridiculous."

Emory looked at me as if he felt he needed my invitation as well. "Don't be ridiculous," I said, mirroring Josh's words. I had a minimum of fifty pounds of muscle on Josh, but I knew damn well who was in charge. Besides, Emory wasn't trying to hurt either of us. He thought he was helping.

"I'll be here," Emory said, but again I noticed that he hesitated.

"*He* won't be here," Josh answered. I wasn't sure who Josh meant. "See, Emory; it's creepy when someone reads your mind."

Emory chuckled and headed down the stairs. I followed behind him to lock the back door. "See you tomorrow," I told him. My words were met with a wave as he headed down the porch steps. When I returned upstairs, Josh was in our bedroom watching Emory through the window.

"I'm worried about him," Josh said.

"Emory?" I asked. I didn't want to sound like a big baby, but wasn't *I* the one who received the dire warning? He'd been freaking out since Emory moved next door, but he was calm as a cucumber when he turned and walked to me.

"You being in danger wasn't what brought him here, Gabe. Jonathon Silver is the reason he's here. I'm not saying we ignore what he said," Josh added when my mouth dropped open in shock. "But I told you that I'm not living in fear; I meant it."

"Good, that means we march forward with our plans to buy Georgia's mansion. I'm calling her lawyer tomorrow to tell him that we're buying the place." I pulled him tight against my chest and lowered my head until my lips hovered above his. "That's not all we need to plan," I reminded him. "I can't wait for you to become mine."

"I'm already yours," Josh whispered back.

"I want it official before you change your mind," I told him, earning myself a snort in reply. "I don't want big and fancy like the weddings featured on your segments on Channel Eleven. I want it intimate and real with our closest friends and our families." Josh's hazel eyes softened at my words. "You know where would be a great place to get married in September? Our new backyard," I said before he could answer. "We could set up an arbor and chairs in that big backyard where we'll have barbecues, and our kids will play on their swing set someday."

Panic began to replace the warm mushy feelings as I threw out a specific time frame. "This September?" he asked. "As in three months?"

"Yes, that's plenty of time." He opened his mouth to argue, but I silenced him with a quick kiss. "I'm going to marry you on September sixteenth, Josh Roman. Instead of arguing with me about it, how about we just make it happen."

"Okay," he said softly. "I will marry you on the sixteenth of September, but why that specific day?"

"It happens to be my parents' wedding anniversary," I told Josh.

"The sixteenth it is then." I wanted to seal his promise with a kiss, but he jerked back and wagged his finger in front of my face.

"Oh no, you don't. If I'm going to marry you in three months, then I need to start organizing right this minute."

"It can't wait ten minutes?" I asked whiningly.

"When have you ever fucked me in ten minutes?" Josh replied. "Let me outline a plan, and then I'll rock your world."

"How about I rock your world now and then you can outline a plan while I fix us something to eat for dinner?"

Josh tipped his head to the side as if he was giving it some serious consideration. I unbuttoned the jeans he had purchased and snuck into my drawer. They weren't the fit I preferred, but I had to admit I looked damn good in the tighter jeans and Josh went wild when I wore them. Lust replaced the determination that had been in his eyes as he watched me stroke my erection.

"Okay, maybe I'll squeeze you in," he said as if he was doing me a favor.

"You've never had a problem squeezing me in before," I said, walking him toward the bed.

"Never cheesy," Josh said, repeating one of our house rules, but his lips twitched from wanting to laugh. Once we were naked, he handed me a condom then reminded me of another promise we made to one another during vacation. "Last night with condoms." We decided to get tested and give up condoms if the results came back as we expected.

There were several condoms left on the strip. It seemed like such a shame to waste them, so I didn't give Josh the chance to start on our wedding plans that night.

# TWO

## Josh Roman

I WAS WIDE AWAKE AT THE ASS CRACK OF DAWN, MY HEAD SPINNING
with so many thoughts that I feared it would explode. I eased out
from under Gabe's heavy arm and tiptoed into the bathroom to
start my day. I don't know why I bothered being quiet because there
was no way Gabe could hear me over the sound of his snoring. I was
fairly certain that I'd want to hold a pillow over his head to buffer it
someday, but we were still in our "everything is cute" phase.

Buddy followed behind me with a wagging tail and a hopeful

gleam in his eye that we were going for a run. "Yes, Buddy," I told him as if he understood me, "but can a guy get a bit of privacy here?" I gestured to my cock with the hand that wasn't holding it steady over the toilet bowl.

It didn't take me long to scrub my teeth then throw on a pair of running shorts and a tank top. Gabe didn't even twitch when I dropped a kiss on his cheek before I left. I locked the back door then set out to clear my head—or at least organize and prioritize my thoughts—with a hard run. A guy couldn't think about every-thing all at once for fuck's sake. Food and fucking were usually the top thoughts on any man's list, but I neglected both of those that morning.

The biggest thing on my mind should've been planning my fu-ture with Gabe, but if Emory was correct, the life I wanted with him could be in jeopardy. It was a completely helpless feeling, and I had to find a way to come to terms with it or risk letting fear ruin every good thing in my life. I meant what I had said to Gabe; I was through with fear running the show. So, I decided I would examine what Emory said, look for any hints of what was left unspoken, pro-cess it, then tuck it away until I had solid evidence that I should be worried. What other choice did I have?

Emory hadn't said much, and it didn't seem like he was leaving anything out, so I was tucking it away like a spent dick before I even made it out of my neighborhood. I looked down at my faithful furry friend and noticed how the sunlight caught the diamonds in the ring Gabe had slid on my finger. It was such a beautiful band and re-membering the look in Gabe's eyes when he asked me to marry him never failed to get my heart pumping. *Damn, I am one lucky man!*

Wearing the ring while on vacation made it feel like we were on our honeymoon, which made me ponder if I wanted to wear the ring during our engagement or wait until after we were married. I was surprised how much I wanted to wait, even though the thought of taking it off made my stomach hurt. Gabe wasn't going to like my idea, but I thought it was one of the times that I had to stand my ground about what felt right to *me*.

The thoughts of our engagement led to the biggest source of my hysteria—the wedding! Yes, I know how shallow that seemed considering Emory's prediction, but the wedding was something tangible I could grasp onto where Emory's words were just words—and vague ones at that. Gabe demanded a wedding in three months and hell if I didn't want to make it happen.

I easily pictured an outdoor wedding in early September because fall was my favorite season. I would've loved an October wedding with the changing leaves in the background but the weather that month in southern Ohio was too unpredictable for an outdoor wedding. It could be sunny and seventy degrees, rainy and fifty degrees, or it could even snow. It was also possible to experience all of them before noon. September was the ultimate month for an outdoor wedding and ours would be spectacular.

I pictured a beautiful arbor with flowers and greenery woven in and out of the white arches. I saw my gorgeous man standing in a sexy, charcoal suit with an aqua striped tie and matching pocket square. Behind him stood Adrian dressed in a similar suit in a lighter shade of gray. He was beaming with happiness as he watched us exchange vows. I didn't have eyes in the back of my head, but I knew who would stand with me on my big day. There was no way I'd say "I do" without Chaz and Meredith beside me.

Renting suits, chairs, and an arbor shouldn't be that hard to do. The hardest part would be finding a caterer with only a few months' notice. Luckily for Gabe, I had met an amazing caterer through the wedding series I filmed for Channel Eleven. Cliff had told me he'd be happy to cater our big event when Gabe proposed on set, but I was sure he expected more than twelve weeks to organize it. My nerves calmed considerably when I realized that I knew all the right people to make our big day go smoothly. I didn't need a big binder with a detailed plan after all; I just needed to sit down with Gabe and find out exactly what we wanted on our special day before I called my new friends and begged for their assistance.

I felt much lighter after my realization. I decided I could go home for my favorite two F's when I heard someone calling my name behind me. I stopped and let Emory catch up to me.

"Are we okay?" he asked me.

"We're fine, Emory," I assured him and meant it. What Emory did the night before was done out of concern for his new friends. It was hard to be upset with him when he was only looking out for Gabe. "We expect to see you at dinner tonight. Gabe is grilling chicken and plans to wow us with his grandmother's barbecue sauce recipe. Telling him that death is coming for him is okay, but missing out on his special sauce isn't cool." Emory paled, and I immediately regretted my brashness. "Not that kind of 'special sauce.' Only I get that," I said teasingly, trying to undo the damage I caused. *Filter, dumb ass. Use a filter.*

Emory chuckled a little, but I could tell he was doing it more for my benefit than his. "I have a feeling that I don't want to miss it," he replied.

"I see what you did there."

I liked his little play on words. Emory was guarded when he moved in next door, and my nearly-hostile attitude hadn't helped, so it was nice to see a bit of personality shine through. I'd witnessed his gut-wrenching pain the day I went to his house after he missed his hair appointment at my salon. I held him in my arms while he sobbed over the loss of his husband that occurred years before and the sorrow he felt after seeing a vision of himself with another man. I firmly believed what I told Gabe after Emory's revelation. Emory wasn't in Blissville to save Gabe, he was there to be saved by Jonathon Silver.

"Can I please bring something? Wine? Side dish? I'm not helpless in the kitchen. I can't match your skills, but few people can."

I liked Emory even more. "No wine sales on Sunday here, but

you can feel free to bring whatever you like. I'm going to make potato salad, baked beans, and corn on the cob. How about a dessert?" I asked him.

"How does strawberry shortcake sound to you? I'm talking homemade, not that spongy, Twinkie-like substance people pass off as shortcake."

"You're my kind of people, Emory. That sounds delicious."

We set off together on a jog once the decision was made. Emory was a tad taller than me, but our strides were equally paced, and it was a pleasant experience. Gabe preferred to lift weights over cardio and Chaz preferred to spin over running. Neither of us had anything to say so we ran in easy silence rather than fill it with nonsense. That's how you knew you were comfortable in someone's presence.

We parted at our driveways with a small wave. Buddy and I eagerly ran up the steps once we got a whiff of bacon after I unlocked the back door. Sure enough, Gabe was standing at the stove making breakfast.

"Did you have a good run?" Gabe asked without turning away from his task, which was good because he was cooking in his underwear. Sounds hot, right? In fantasies, it sure as hell was, but in reality, it made me shiver, but not in a good way. Bacon grease is very hot and not what you want to be splattered on your bare chest or cock and balls. His designer briefs were thin and offered no real protection from sizzling, popping grease, but they offered me one hell of a view. Oh yeah, my eyes locked on those firm, round ass cheeks and I imagined myself grabbing onto them while he pounded away inside me or even spread apart to receive my cock. "Josh, you're making my dick hard by staring at my ass."

I snapped out of my daydream long enough to respond. "Your dick is always hard." My gaze wandered up the broad expanse of his back to take in the wide shoulders where I often rested my calves while he…

"Josh!"

"I can't help myself and don't pretend like you didn't wear that to get this exact reaction from me," I said, marching over to the coffee pot to pour myself a cup. "Hey, can I have one of those Ninja coffee bar things Sofia raves about in our new house?"

"Who's Sofia?" Gabe asked.

Just because he was gay didn't excuse him from not knowing the world's most beautiful woman. "Gabe, I just don't know what to do with you sometimes." I shook my head sadly for emphasis, which he didn't see because he was still paying close attention to the bacon. And who could blame him with his magic wand and beans so close to the fiery pits of hell? "Sofia Vergara, Gabe. She's an actress and is married to Joe Man..."

"Oh, *her*." I didn't like his tone, not one bit. It was the same one I'd heard rolling off the lips of every jealous woman in my salon as they cattily tore her down when she and Joe started dating. I thought they were a beautiful couple and I was happy for them. Only people who wanted Joe for themselves sounded bitter.

"Awwww, did she steal your man from you?" I asked mockingly. "Is he your celebrity crush?" Six months ago, the thought of Gabe crushing on a big, muscular guy would've sent me into a panic. Not anymore because I was certain of two things: there was nothing wrong with the way I was, and Gabe was crazy in love with me.

"Was," Gabe confessed sheepishly.

"Awww, you dumped him because of me," I cooed as I moved closer to him, but not so close that the grease was going to get me. He was cooking his meat on too high of a temperature and endangering my favorite meat in the process.

"It was because he got married. I don't lust after married people. It just feels wrong."

I shook my head sadly; it looked like he had further to go than I realized. I had three months to whip him into perfect husband material, which I didn't think would be too difficult since he was already within striking distance of perfection. "Gabe, as much as I appreciate your honesty, there are times when it doesn't hurt you to stretch the truth just a tiny bit."

He whipped his head around to gauge if he'd screwed up. "He got married a year before I met you, Josh. Had I met you first, that would've been the reason I gave." He looked pretty damn smug about his smooth recovery.

"Nicely played," I told him as I gestured to the frying pan with my hand so that he'd pay attention.

Gabe chuckled and turned his focus back to cooking. "Are you worried I'll burn down your house or scratch the nonstick surface of your pan?" He held up the tongs that had a silicone coating on the bottom and around the edges. "Your skillet is safe."

"I was more concerned about your cock and balls getting splattered with hot grease," I told him. "Take a damn step back or something."

"You don't find this sexy?" Gabe asked, sounding a bit pouty.

"Of course, I find it sexy, but that doesn't mean I want you to risk your safety."

"I guess it's a good thing I didn't cook in the nude," Gabe grumbled.

"Now that's just gross," I told him. "Nobody wants pubes in their food, Gabriel. I adore you naked, but not around my food."

"You didn't seem to worry about pubes when you deep-throated my dick covered with whipped cream on vacation," Gabe said to me.

"That was different," I said defensively.

"How was that different? Your lips were against my pubes," he pointed out.

"It was dessert," I said like that explained it. "No one is going to eat lobster bisque soup off your crotch."

"Ouch," Gabe said.

"Yeah, multiply that times a thousand to imagine how bad hot grease would feel," I told him. The grease popped just then as if fate wanted to emphasize just how right I was about the dangers of frying bacon while scantily clad—no matter how good, or sexy, the intention.

Gabe jumped back and yelled, "Son of a bitch!" Then he looked at me accusingly as if I made it happen. He moved the skillet off the burner and turned to face me fully.

"Son of a bitch! Son of a bitch!" Savage repeated while flapping his wings.

"Just great," I said. "Savage is going to be saying that nonstop."

"As if he doesn't already say worse," Gabe replied. "I seem to remember him propositioning me for a blow job the first night I was here. You can't blame me for that one."

"Maybe he was channeling my thoughts," I confessed a little shyly. I had mentioned to Gabe once that I had noticed him around town, but I never fully admitted to him—or myself for that matter— just how much I wanted him from the moment I laid eyes on him. I looped my finger in the waistband of his undies and pulled him even closer to me. "Do you want to know who my celebrity crush *was*?"

"No," Gabe said petulantly like he couldn't stand the thought of my attention directed toward anyone but him.

"Anderson Cooper *was* my celebrity crush," I told him, making sure to stress the word was.

"The news guy?" he asked.

"Yes, him. I love a silver fox." I placed my hand over Gabe's heart and said, "I forgot all about him the moment I laid eyes on you. It's a fucking miracle I didn't shave Kyle Vaughn bald when he sat in my salon chair, and believe me when I say it crossed my mind."

"Are you saying that you crushed on me for a long time?" He didn't sound very convinced because I played my cards so well when we began interacting that I almost convinced myself I wasn't crazy about him.

"It's embarrassing how much you starred in my fantasies or how badly I wanted you to be different from any other man I had met. It's why I reacted so harshly when you were about to say I was too feminine for you. It wouldn't have bothered me so much had I not cared what you thought about me."

"We've come a long way since then, haven't we?" Gabe asked. "There's no more hiding our feelings behind snark," I knew his remark was mostly aimed at me, "or pretending that we don't want to just crawl inside one another every free second of the day."

"No more games," I replied. I raised up on my toes and pressed my lips to Gabe's for a quick kiss. "Now feed me and fuck me so we can get on with our day. We need to go to the clinic for our tests before we stop at the grocery store to prepare for Gabe's Big Barbecue Night."

Gabe tilted his head to the side and looked at me suspiciously. "You doubt my abilities."

"I do not," I said honestly. "I know it's going to be great. It's our first big barbecue with all of our friends invited, so it's an event worthy of a name."

"I'm going to show you just how good I am," he promised in a rumbling, sexy voice. "Which do you want first—food or a fuck?"

I knew I was in for a treat, regardless which of the F's came first, which would set the tone for a day that held so much promise. I smiled up into the eyes of the man I loved more than my next breath and said, "Surprise me."

# THREE

## Gabe

OH, I SURPRISED HIM ALL RIGHT. HE WAS EXPECTING ME TO THROW him over my shoulder and carry him off to have my way with him, and under normal circumstances that would've been the case, but that day was different. I couldn't stop thinking about being bare inside him once we had the sex without condoms talk. It wasn't like we practiced abstinence while we were on vacation—quite the opposite actually—but I was hours away from having not even a thin layer of latex separate us. So, I chose to feed him before we headed out to run our errands to prepare for the barbecue.

It should've been a crime that it took longer to drive to the closest clinic that offered HIV testing than it did for the rapid test results to come back. There was no excuse for making it harder for people to be responsible and get tested. As irritated as it made me, I focused on the delights that lay in wait for me that evening. I had another surprise for Josh up my sleeve, but I wouldn't be sharing it with him until after the last guest left.

Luckily for us, we got to the grocery store before church let out and back home in plenty of time to let my granny's Coca-Cola barbecue sauce simmer on the stove for a bit before I refrigerated it to thicken. I heard Josh mumbling about something thickening as he put the potato salad together, but I ignored his complaints. Some things were worth waiting for, as he should damn well know since he tortured me for the longest time.

I wasn't the only one with surprises that morning. I expected to find Josh at the dining room table hard at work planning our wedding when I woke up, but instead he was out running. I had also expected a little less calmness out of him about Emory's gloomy, albeit vague, premonition. Once I caught onto the inner workings of Josh Roman's mind, he wasn't so hard to figure out, but every once in a while, he puzzled me. I could reason that Josh had become close friends with a group of people to help him plan our wedding, which I suspected was the reason he wasn't making seating charts the second we got home from the store. It was his laid-back attitude about Emory's visit that had me stumped. I tried my hardest to sort it out on my own, but after a few hours I gave up.

"Why are you so calm about Emory's vision?" I asked him while he spread a checkered tablecloth over one of the fold-up tables he'd set up beneath the shade trees in his yard.

"You want to do this now, babe? Our guests will be arriving any second," Josh replied. "Including Emory."

"How long of a discussion were you planning?" I asked in

confusion. I heard car doors closing and realized that his supersonic hearing had picked up on their arrival.

Josh straightened up from smoothing out nonexistent wrinkles in the tablecloth and faced me. "Baby, I'm just glad that I'm getting a break from the crazy this time. I'm thinking I've had enough for a while between Oscar trying to kill me and then Billy stalking me." My mouth dropped open in shock. "Sure, Wanda knocked you upside your head that one time but you've lived a relatively charmed life recently. I mean, we want to be equals in all things, right?"

Before I could answer, Willa, Meredith, and Harley rounded the corner of the house and entered the side yard where Josh had the shindig set up. Meredith and Willa both held covered dishes in their hands while Harley held a twelve pack of beer that I thought might come in handy.

"I can tell by the look on your face that my boy hasn't lost his touch," Willa said, crooking her finger for me to bend down so she could kiss my cheek. "Just march and clap alongside him, baby." While it was true that Josh marched to his own beat, we were usually in rhythm.

"I just need a minute of Sunshine's time," I told them. I nodded my head for him to follow me. I turned to face him once we were out of sight of prying eyes. "Okay, I know damn well you didn't mean that flippant response. So, how is it that you've come to terms with what Emory said?"

"Before you have, you mean?" Josh asked.

The truth was, Emory's warning bothered me more than it should've based on what little he said. The problem was, I had plenty of people in my past who might want to cause me harm. "Maybe," I confessed.

"I decided to be practical, even in the light of the most impractical scenario," Josh said. "Emory couldn't say for sure that your life is in danger, and he sure as hell couldn't give us a hint as to the identity of the man you'll be having words with on the front porch of our future home. Hell, for all we know it could be the cable guy who was late to hook up your service at the new house, which caused you to miss out on the next best sporting event in the whole damn world. There's one nearly every single week," he added sarcastically before he smiled broadly.

"No more fear," Josh reminded me. "It robs us of the moment we're experiencing. I had enough moments without you, Gabe. I cannot allow myself to imagine my world without you again. I won't do it." His voice cracked with emotion, and I regretted pushing him.

"You're right, Sunshine," I said, folding him in my arms. "I won't mention it again."

"You two didn't get enough of that last week?" Chaz asked, walking up the driveway. "Some of us are lovelorn, so could you knock it down a notch, or ten?"

Josh pulled out of my arms and faced his friend. "Lovelorn?" he asked. "When did you start using words like that in place of horny?"

"That too," Chaz admitted sheepishly.

Josh opened his mouth to reply then closed it just as quickly. I knew he was about to suggest how Chaz could take care of his problem but then changed his mind. He learned his lesson when his matchmaking attempt at Easter created tension between the two of them. *Or maybe not,* I thought to myself as I saw Kyle park behind Chaz's car.

"I, um…" Josh said sheepishly as Chaz looked to see what—or rather who—had caught my attention.

"… Just can't help yourself," Chaz finished for him, but I noticed that his tone was lacking anger. "Don't worry about it, Jazz. It's cool." I noticed he didn't stick around for Kyle to catch up to him before he joined the party.

"Are you sure this is okay?" Kyle asked. He ran his hand over the back of his neck like he did when he was nervous. I might've been guilty of not picking up on every little nuance of Kyle's personality when we were together, but that was a familiar gesture.

"It's fine," Josh assured him. "Besides, he'd be angry at me and not you."

"Okay," Kyle said uncertainly. "If it's a problem…"

"It's not," I assured him. "What'd you bring?" I nodded at the covered bowl in his hands.

"Melon balls, you know I don't cook worth a damn," Kyle said with a self-deprecating scoff.

"Spiked?" Josh asked hopefully.

"Maybe next time." Kyle winked and headed around the corner to join the rest of our guests.

"So, are we good here?" Josh asked.

"We're amazing," I replied.

A smile spread slowly across his face. "We kinda are," he agreed before we returned to our party.

I began grilling chicken and ribs while Josh arranged the dishes everyone brought into categories: appetizers, side dish, and dessert. Adrian and an obviously pregnant Sally Ann showed up next, and Emory wasn't far behind them. Josh and the gals fussed over Sally Ann, making sure she wasn't given a "rickety-ass" folding chair since she was carrying precious cargo. Josh made Adrian go to the front of the house and get the chaise lounge chair with the thick, soft cushions for Sally Ann to sit on. She told them not to fuss, but she sighed happily once she realized how comfortable it was.

Next thing I knew, Josh had Adrian follow him into the single car garage that was packed too full with stored items to park Princess in, which said a lot because she was a small car. They came back out with rectangular wooden boards with legs that unfolded from the top that propped them up at an angle. Josh set one up and stepped off so many feet before he set up the other one to face the first board.

"Needs to be twenty-seven feet," Adrian said. "You have a tape measure or something?"

"Cornhole," Harley said, rubbing his hands together gleefully.

*What the hell was cornhole?* I'd heard of a glory hole but we weren't having that kind of party.

"I have one in my truck," Kyle offered.

"What the hell for?" Josh asked. "Who keeps a measuring tape in their vehicle besides a carpenter?"

"I don't know why it's there. I found it in the glovebox when I cleaned my truck last week. You want it or not?" Kyle fired back good-naturedly.

Josh scoffed and replied, "I have my own tools." He went to the garage and returned with a tape measure then measured the distance between the two boards. "Twenty-six and three-quarter inches," he said proudly. "Not bad." He let the tape measure snap back inside then blew on it like a cowboy blew on the end of his pistol in a bad western movie. I had something Josh could blow on later.

"I call Jazz for a partner," Meredith said quickly.

"You had him last time," Chaz said with a pout. "You brought your plus two with you to the barbecue, pick one of them."

"They wanted to play on the same team," Meredith told Chaz. "You gotta be quicker around here if you want Jazz on your team."

"I'll be on your team, Chaz," Kyle offered. "I'm pretty good."

"Really?" Chaz asked.

"Are you asking me to confirm that I want to be on your team or are you questioning how good I am?" Kyle asked. *Is it me or had Kyle's voice dropped to a sexier timbre at the last part?* The owlish way Chaz blinked convinced me I wasn't the only one who heard it.

"Let's do it," Chaz said boldly, then blushed furiously when he realized how his response could be taken a few different ways.

Kyle's smile spread slowly across his face showing the dimples that gave him his nickname. "Alrighty then," he said gleefully.

"What the hell is going on here?" I finally asked.

"Cornhole," Josh said as if that explained everything. "Oh, I forgot the bags."

"What's cornhole?" I asked him, but he was already heading

24

back to the garage.

"It's sort of like horseshoes, but you throw a square bag of corn at the hole in the board instead of a metal horseshoe around a stake in the ground. You get one point if your bag lands on the board and three if you toss it in the hole," Chaz said, then went on to explain how the scoring worked.

"So, I take it that Josh is good at this game since you two were fighting over him," I said, gesturing between Chaz and Meredith with my tongs.

"Of course, I am," Josh said when he returned to the group. It would've come across as bragging with anyone else, but not him. He was stating a fact. He was one of those annoying people that did things effortlessly and made everyone else look bad.

"I guess that means it's you and me, Emory," I told him. Hell if I was going to sit out.

"I would've brought my boards if I'd known you were playing," Kyle said. "We could've had a tournament."

"Where the hell did you store cornhole boards?" I asked him. I'd lived with the man for two years—one in Florida and one in Ohio—and I'd never seen a set.

"I didn't take them to Florida when I went to veterinary school and didn't pick them up from my mom and dad's house until after you moved out. I got away from playing and forgot how fun it could be."

"How much longer on the meat, babe?" Josh asked. "I need some serious protein for tonight's festivities."

"Now we're talking," I said, perking up, even though I suspected we were talking about two different types of festivities. "Fifteen minutes."

"Perfect," he said then went back to making sure everything was set out for our first barbecue.

I had been confident earlier when I whipped up the barbecue sauce, but that faded when people eagerly waited to taste it. I hadn't grilled for so many people before, and sweat began to pop out on my forehead. Josh came over a few minutes later and wiped my brow with a paper towel.

"I sampled your sauce earlier, and I have to tell you that it's amazing. I might've been doubtful about the ingredients, but together they are perfect. Like us."

"I'm so glad you like my sauce," I told him honestly.

"I love your sauce, Gabe." I could tell we were moving into naughty territory and there was no time for that or I'd burn our dinner.

My nerves about my grilling skills faded once the compliments started coming in. People volunteered me to grill every Sunday going forward, and Willa and Sally Ann asked for Granny's recipe. Any side dish a person could want was available to our guests. My plate was loaded down with grilled meats, macaroni and cheese, coleslaw, baked beans, corn on the cob, and Josh's potato salad. I was weighted down by so many carbs that it was a miracle I could move let alone play cornhole.

Emory had never heard of the game either, so we were given pointers and allowed to have several tosses before the games started. We decided that the winner of each game would continue until they got beat or bored. I knew we'd need to beat Meredith and Josh for them to walk away from the boards. Their first challenge was Willa and Harley, who put up a good battle but were no match for their opponent. Josh and Meredith dispatched Emory and me quickly, which set up the showdown against Kyle and Chaz.

I would never admit this to Josh, but I wanted Kyle and Chaz to win. It was cute to watch them interact, especially when they were the first team to take the lead against Mere and Josh. I stuffed my face with strawberry shortcake, so I had an excuse as to why I wasn't whooping and hollering for my man to crush his enemy. The lead changed several times, and each time Chaz and Kyle got it back, the friendlier they got with one another. Their high-fives gave way to an excited hug at the end of the game.

Josh wouldn't admit it, but I knew that he purposely overshot the board on his final throw that gave his opponents the win. He confirmed my theory when he smiled at the victory celebration the two men shared. We swapped partners and played a few more games before it got too dark to see the boards.

Willa and Sally Ann packed up leftovers for everyone to take home while the rest of us put up the tables and chairs. I could hear thunder rumbling in the distance indicating that a pop-up storm was heading our way. That prompted everyone to say goodbye and thank us for a wonderful evening, which was okay with me because I was ready for everyone to leave. I loved nothing more than listening to the sound of rain on the metal roof when I made love to Josh and later held him in my arms. It was the only thing I would miss once we moved.

The sky opened up just as we waved off our last guest. That was when I tossed Josh over my shoulder and carried him off like he had expected me to that morning.

# FOUR

## Josh

NOW WE WERE TALKING. YEAH, BABY, TOSSED OVER GABE'S BACK and carried off caveman style. Maybe it wasn't very enlightened to want Gabe to manhandle me, but damn I loved it. There was something so sexy about reducing your man to his baser needs where he could only rut and grunt because he wanted to be inside you so fucking bad.

I expected Gabe to toss me down on the bed and start tearing off our clothes, but he slowly lowered me to my feet so that I could feel how excited he was when my body slid down the length of his. I looked into his gorgeous brown eyes and realized it was going to be a slow burn kind of night with our emotions on display and not hidden behind rutting and grunting.

Gabe cupped my face in his large hands and stared into my eyes. Thunder from the approaching storm rumbled louder and longer as it neared us. I thought it fit the mood perfectly since the emotions I saw in Gabe's eyes were as stormy as the weather. I knew him well enough that I could easily name them: desire, devotion, and love—so much love. "It's just the two of us now from here on out, and it's a damn good thing because there will never be a man who loves you the way that I do."

Truer words had never been spoken, and they deserved a response that was equally honest and free of snark. I slid one hand around Gabe's neck and covered his heart with the other one. "I didn't know I was capable of loving someone the way that I love you; I didn't know my heart could feel so full. I surely never dreamed that a man like you would love me the way you do."

We started undressing slowly and treated every inch of revealed skin like a cherished gift we'd been waiting for our entire lives; flesh that was too precious not to kiss or taste. There was a slight tremble to Gabe's hand when he bumped his fingers teasingly along my spine and to his lips when he pressed them to the skin over my heart.

"Gabe," I whispered when he slid a finger along the crack of my ass to tease my pucker. There'd be no jokes about pleasure portals or anything else that night because it would cheapen what was going to happen between us.

"My Sunshine," he whispered back just as reverently.

"Always."

There was no time for talking after that because our mouths were too busy kissing and catching the sexy sighs that escaped our souls. Gabe lowered me to the bed then followed me down. I spread my legs and opened my arms to him. He fit naturally between them because it was where he was meant to be. As excited as I was to feel him inside me, I didn't want to miss a second of the buildup to the moment when he slid bare inside me for the first time.

I slid one hand into his hair and raked my fingers down his back with my other until I reached his tight, muscular ass. I gripped a cheek and pulled him tighter against me as I thrusted my hips up into him, grinding our erections together. My stomach became wet and sticky from our combined pre-cum, and my ass quivered with eagerness for Gabe to fill it.

We kissed until I couldn't take it anymore, the need to have him burned throughout my body until I thought I'd die if I didn't feel the sting of his penetration. I broke our kiss and retrieved the bottle of lubricant from the bedside table. Gabe took the bottle from me then rolled onto his back. He crooked his finger at me to follow, which I eagerly did because I was under his seductive spell. I thought Gabe wanted me to ride him, but he showed me how wrong I was when he reached down and coated my dick with the lube. I looked at him in surprise.

"I want to feel you come inside me first then I want you to ride my cock until I explode," Gabe said. I thought it was sexy as fuck when he told me exactly what he wanted, even sexier when he spread his legs wide, exposing his hole to me. I reached for the lube, but Gabe stopped me. "I want just enough to ease penetration."

I growled because that was exactly how I liked it too—enough oil to ease the way, but not so much it took away the sting of penetration. I positioned myself between Gabe's thighs but didn't push in right away like some animal. I circled his pucker with the head of my dick to tease and entice him. Gabe's eyes lost their focus, and he gyrated his hips up and down in anticipation of being filled. I pressed my lips to his when I pushed inside him, capturing Gabe's gasp as we truly became one.

I didn't expect sex to feel that much different once the thin layer of latex was gone, but I was so wrong. Gabe's heat and the tightness of his clench were a lot more intense as I moved slowly in and out of him. I broke our kiss to look into his eyes; the heat I saw there sent an electric current to my balls. I dug my knees into the mattress and changed my angle so I could peg his prostate and make it as good for him as I could while I lasted, which I didn't think would be long. I already felt the telltale signs of my approaching orgasm. My muscles tightened and my skin felt like it was a few sizes too small to fit my body.

Gabe gripped my hair in a tight fist. "Fuck me, Josh. Fill me."

I slammed into him gracelessly, rutting inside him as my body demanded. I didn't close my eyes; I wanted my gaze locked with his when I spilled inside him for the first time.

"That's it, baby. Fuck me hard. I want it all." Gabe's dirty mouth snapped what little control I had left and I came hard inside him. Gabe reached between us and slicked his cock for me while I sucked air into my lungs. "My turn," he demanded hungrily.

I saw how swollen and angry his cock looked and knew just what he needed to feel better. I eased my dick from Gabe's ass and repositioned myself to straddle him. Penetration after an orgasm wasn't usually the most comfortable experience, but I was still semi-hard and aroused when I eased down onto his erection.

I placed my hands on Gabe's pecs then raised and lowered myself slowly a few times until I was completely stretched and ready to fuck. Damn, his dick felt so good, and my nerve-laden hole sucked him in greedily as I rode him. Gabe's body shook beneath mine, and his hands gripped my hips tight while I used my inner thigh muscles to work myself up and down.

"Spread your legs wider; I want to see you," Gabe growled. "Fuck!" he yelled when I lifted my arms above my head and lost myself in the moment. "So damn sexy," Gabe said before he traced his finger over my puckered opening where it stretched around his dick.

"I want to make it so good for you, baby," I told him.

Gabe's response was to grab me by the waist and roll me over until my calves were propped up on his shoulders. "Any better and my heart would explode." Then he began to pound me as Suave Gabe turned into Caveman Gabe. He fucked me until I was fully erect and coming a second time before he released inside me. I thought I knew all of Gabe's sex sounds, but I'd never heard the raw, animalistic ones he made as my ass milked every hot drop of his seed.

He lowered my legs and collapsed on top of me when the last quake left his body. His weight pinned me to the mattress and made it hard for me to breathe, but I didn't care. The storm had descended on us at some point during lovemaking. The wind thrashed outside my bedroom window, rain danced on my metal roof, and the lightning split the darkness seconds before the world shook and rolled from the loud, roaring thunder, not unlike the way Gabe looked the moment that his climax tore through him.

Gabe eased off me and said, "Let's get cleaned up before..." The lights flickered a few times and went out just then as if mother nature wanted to prove to us that she was always in charge. "We'll improvise," he said good-naturedly before he gave me a quick kiss and rolled off the bed.

"Wait," I said before he tripped over a shoe on the way to the restroom. "I have just the thing." I reached over and pulled out a flashlight from the bottom drawer in the bedside table. "Most people keep a Fleshlight in their drawers, but that's not helpful during a power outage."

"Oh, I think it could have its uses," Gabe said jokingly.

I set the flashlight on the bathroom vanity so we could take a shower. There was plenty of hot water stored in the tank, so we didn't need to rush. I liked the dimmed light in the bathroom while I ran soapy hands all over my man's body. It wasn't as sexy as a candlelit bath, but it was still pretty hot.

After we finished, we lay together in the dark and listened to the sounds of rain on the roof. It was one of Gabe's favorite things, and I wasn't sure how many times he would get the opportunity to hear it before we moved. I noticed I didn't think *if*, because buying Georgia's mansion was a foregone conclusion in my mind. It was our dream, and it would happen.

The rain continued long after the lightning stopped and the wind died down. I figured we'd just lie there quietly until we fell asleep, but Gabe had other plans. "Close friends and family only," he said into the darkness. "Sweet and simple."

"Next week's barbecue?" I asked in mock ignorance. "Damn, I was thinking about having a block party." Gabe pinched my ass hard enough to leave a mark. "Ouch!"

"I'll kiss it later if you stop being a brat," Gabe said. "You know damn well I'm talking about our wedding."

"Yeah, I know," I told him. "I was just revving you up. What kind of wedding did you think I had in mind?"

"It's hard telling with you," Gabe said.

I raised up on my elbow and looked down at him, even though I couldn't see anything. "What's that supposed to mean?"

"I don't know," Gabe said. "I was just revving you up."

"Oh, in that case," I said, lying back down beside him. I pinched his nipple hard enough to make him hiss and arch his back.

"You little hellcat," Gabe said. I could hear him rubbing his hand over his affliction.

"I'll kiss it later if you stop being a brat," I mimicked.

"It'll have to wait until tomorrow because I probably can't get it up again until then," Gabe said.

"That's a glowing endorsement if I've ever heard one," I said. "Not even married yet and I've rendered you limp."

Gabe rolled me to my back to switch our positions and leaned over me. "Yeah, you rendered me limp because your tight, greedy ass milked every ounce of spunk I had. It's going to take some time for my splooge factory to make some more."

I laughed hard at his ridiculousness even though I felt a little pride that I wore him out; it was no easy feat. "You need to get some sleep anyway, since you're returning to work tomorrow," I said.

"I seriously want to hear what you envision for our wedding," Gabe said to me.

"I hadn't given it much thought yet," I replied honestly. "It's *our* wedding so *we* should discuss what *we* want for the big day."

"No fucking clowns," Gabe groused. "That much I know."

"Gabriel Allen Wyatt," I said in frustration. "We're having a wedding, not a circus. Why in the hell would I have clowns at our wedding?"

"Just throwing that out there," Gabe said like it made perfect sense to him that it should be part of the conversation.

"I would never do something like that to you," I told him. It was true that I wanted to send that new clown emoji a time or two, but I didn't. People should take phobias seriously. "I was thinking less circus tent and more elegant and timeless. I have thought about what we're going to wear," I confessed then told him what I had in mind.

"Perfect," Gabe said. "I'll try not to get a raging hard-on while thinking about you wearing your aqua blue undies beneath. Are you going to put an aqua streak in your hair?"

I thought about it for a few heartbeats then shook my head. "Nah, as fun as it is sometimes, I don't think I want that in our wedding pictures. It's not elegant or timeless."

"What about food?" Gabe asked, getting to the heart of his priorities. "Are we going to eat outside?"

"Hmmmmm. I think I know," I said, envisioning a large marquee with gauzy white fabric and buffet tables laden down with a variety of savory meats and delicious side dishes for our guests to choose from. I described what I saw in great detail and smiled at the happy sounds Gabe made. My man loved only one thing more than food, and that was me.

"We know what we're wearing and what we'll be eating," Gabe said. "Who do you want to officiate our wedding? Rocky?" I tried to tweak his nipple again, but he pinned my hands above my head before I could land my pinching fingers.

"I was thinking about my dad's best friend, Niles McDonnell," I told Gabe. "He's a retired county judge who fills in during vacations and illnesses. He'd still have the authority to marry us, and I always thought of him as my uncle and not just my dad's best friend."

"He sounds perfect," Gabe said. "Location, food, judge, and outfits," Gabe said, making us sound like Ken dolls. "What else is there to decide?" he asked.

"Guest list, DJ, flowers, and the song that we'll dance to as hus-bands," I told him. "That's all I can think of right now because I'm engaged to a liar." I rubbed my leg against his erection.

"I guess my spunk monkeys were working overtime," he said.

"It was the food talk," I told him.

"No," he said softly. "It was the beautiful picture you painted for me. I could see us standing at the altar and you're looking at me in the special way that you do."

"How do I look at you?" I asked him.

"Like I'm the only man you can see, the only one who you'll ever love and share a life with." Gabe's words moved me to tears. I was silent for several long moments, unsure of how to respond.

"Well, duh," I finally said, wiping away the hot tears on my face. *Come on; I could only hold the snark at bay for so long.* "You're my *everything*, Gabe," I said after he stopped chuckling. "Of course, I'm going to look at you like that. It's exactly the way you look at me too, and it's why I'm just not willing to be afraid anymore." I wrapped my hand around his dick and stroked him up and down. "We better take care of this so you can get some sleep. You gotta go back to being Bad Cop tomorrow."

"Surely, things will slow down for us now," Gabe grumbled, but

I noticed he wasn't distracted from reaching for the lube again.

What's that saying about famous last words? I still needed to tell him my thoughts on taking off our rings until our wedding day, but we were too tired after round two of sex in the raw to do anything but sleep. *I'll tell him tomorrow,* I thought to myself as I started to drift to sleep.

# FIVE

## Gabe

"Last Monday off for a while," I said to Josh the next morning. He would begin shooting his new series for Channel Eleven the following week. "Inventory and the usual stuff?" I asked him.

"Actually, no," he said, wearing a triumphant smile. "Chaz took that over for me when I began shooting the wedding series, and he did a wonderful job. In fact, he's more intuitive about the trending product sales than I am. I'm thinking about asking him to take on more of a management role at the salon and hiring someone else to book appointments and stuff, especially since I plan on expanding the salon."

I blinked at him several times in surprise because Josh was beyond hands-on with his business. It was his baby, and he wouldn't just trust it in anyone's hands. I wasn't sure Chaz wanted the extra responsibility, but I knew without a doubt that he'd be honored when Josh asked. "Sunshine, that's a great idea."

"I know," he said, brushing my hands away to take over the task of buttoning my shirt. I was used to him undressing me but not the reverse. He got to the second to the last button and paused. I saw his eyes soften as he studied the Saint Michael pendant he bought me for Christmas resting against my chest. The sentiment behind the necklace told me how much I meant to him long before he said the words. He ran his finger over the medallion reverently then leaned forward and kissed it. Regardless of his brave words the previous day, his actions told me that Emory's premonition struck him harder than he wanted me to know. "I love you, Gabe," he said tenderly.

"I love you too, Sunshine. More than anything in the world."

Josh nodded as he swallowed down a lump of emotion. "That's why I'm going to call the bank today to schedule an appointment with my loan officer so we can get the process started to buy Georgia's mansion. I'm so excited to buy that house and marry you, Gabe. I just need to find out what they'll want from my accountant to show my income. I'm going to guess the last two years of tax returns and a profit and loss statement for the current year. They'll probably just need to verify your income and…" I held my hand up to stop him. "Is it too early in the morning for this kind of talk?" he asked me.

"No, it's just not necessary," I told him. "I might've downplayed my net worth when we discussed buying the mansion." I grimaced when he narrowed his eyes suspiciously and took a step back from me.

"Downplayed how?" he asked. "Are you talking about the

amount or how you obtained the money?" Josh loved to rile me up about my past run-ins with Internal Affairs. It had become one of his favorite snarky jokes when he was trying to throw shade my way.

"Both," I said dramatically then had to bite my lip to keep from laughing when he reached between us and grabbed my balls hard enough to get my attention but not enough to hurt me.

"Quit playing around and tell me everything now," he demanded. Josh squeezed my sac a little harder when I could no longer hold back my laughter. "You think it's funny, do you?"

"I'm laughing about how easily you get riled up over IA but not about the way you're gripping my cum depots in your fist," I answered. Josh loosened his hold but didn't remove his hand altogether. "I hope you plan on kissing them to make it better."

"Can you please be serious?" Josh asked, which was a complete turn of events from our usual scenario. "What do you mean about the mortgage talk not being necessary, Gabe?"

"I might've already talked to Georgia's lawyer before I proposed marriage and mentioned buying the house to you. I wanted to have an idea of what he wanted to sell it for before we discussed it. I also didn't want him to sell it to anyone else until I was sure of your response."

"None of that answers my question," Josh responded impatiently. "You said you inherited some money from your grandparents that you wanted to use as a down payment on the house to minimize the mortgage payments. Now you sound like you don't need a mortgage on the property at all."

"Okay, this is the part that I think you won't like," I told Josh. The tilt of his head and the way he crossed his arms over his chest told me he was bracing himself for the impact of my words. *At least he didn't have a grip on my nuts any longer.* "I thought that maybe we can just buy the house outright since you already have a mortgage here and…"

"No fucking way." Josh shook his head emphatically. "We are

going to be partners in all things. I'm not going to live in a house that you bought me. Besides, we're going to need that money for the heathen children's college funds."

The talk of heathen children took the sting out of his rejection, but it was still there. "I have the means to buy the house for *us,* and you're going to refuse it?"

"I am," Josh said stubbornly. "I work for what I have, Gabe. I work very hard. I won't be a kept man, and I don't want any handouts!"

"Sunshine, this isn't a 'handout,' and you won't be a 'kept' man," I told him, trying hard not to laugh at his outrage. *Just when I thought I had my guy figured out.* "No one is going to start filming the Househusbands of Blissville. Not that you wouldn't be awesome," I assured him when it looked like my attempt to soothe him only made things worse.

"Damn straight I would," he said saucily. "Okay, let me take a step back here and try to explain this better."

I pulled Josh closer instead of letting him step back. "Tell me from here." I wrapped him up in my arms and waited patiently for him to talk about what was bugging him. He would in his own way and at his pace. I just needed to give him the time, but I wasn't willing to give him space. I liked him right where he was.

"My business and my home were the only things I was prideful about before I met you, Gabe. My parents sold the house to me for a ridiculously low amount of money, but I built this business on my own. I don't need to be better than anyone else or have more, but I demand equal. Can you understand where I'm coming from?"

I nodded because I did. "Can you also see that this is something amazing I can afford to do for *us*? Why have two mortgages when we don't need it?"

It was Josh's turn to nod and agree. "I know that we can reach a compromise that will make us both happy. Let me do some thinking about it today and put together a proposal."

"But you don't know how much money I have to invest in *our* future," I argued.

"Nor do you know how much *I* have to invest in our future." He had me there. I knew his salon was wildly successful, and even more so after his wedding special aired on the news.

"Okay, tonight we show each other our assets and decide what to do with them," I said agreeably.

"Yes, and afterward we'll talk about finances," Josh said sassily before he gave me a quick peck on the lips. "You're going to be late to work if you don't get going."

I released him because he was right. I had a meeting with the Carter County prosecutor to discuss the pretrial hearings for Rylan Broadman. I sure as hell didn't want to be late for that. "Hand me that tie," I said pointing to the burgundy silk one that he loved so much. In fact, he always got a certain gleam in his eyes whenever he held it. I was pretty sure I recognized what that glimmer meant and vowed to test my theory that evening. He sure as hell had the upper hand on me several times.

I faced the mirror to make sure I got my tie on perfectly straight. I saw Josh checking out my ass in the reflection and didn't bother hiding my pleasure that he wanted me so much. I might've preened a bit and flexed my glutes for him. Once I finished with the tie, I checked my overall appearance and noted that my hair was looking a little messy.

"Before things get too serious tonight, do you think you could give me a trim?" I asked Josh. His gaze shifted from where it had been locked on my ass to meet mine in the mirror.

"You don't trust me to cut your hair afterward?" he asked semi-playfully, tipping his head to the side to study me.

"I trust you; shall I prove it?" I challenged.

Josh shook his head slowly then closed the distance between us. He slid his arms around my waist and rested his forehead between my shoulder blades. "You never have to prove anything to me, Gabe."

The morning had taken on such a serious tone, and I wanted to change it so that we both started our day on a positive note and had something to look forward to that night that didn't involve a haircut or serious talks about mortgages and finances.

I turned in the circle of his arms and looked down at his up-turned face. "Here's how I see this evening playing out," I told Josh. "Dinner, haircut, mapping out our plan to buy the mansion *together*, and we'll end the night in our bedroom. I'm going to tie your talented, wicked hands to the bed with this tie," I ran my finger over the silk for emphasis, "and then I'm going to make you come with just one finger."

"Braggart," Josh whispered shakily.

"It's not bragging when it's true," I reminded him, using a similar phrase he'd used with me in the past. Josh wasn't the only one impacted by my words. Once spoken aloud, my dick was ready to play again even though he'd had his workout that morning in the shower with Josh. "There's probably going to be a lot of tongue action too." Okay, that didn't help my situation any.

Josh stepped back from me suddenly. "Go, go now and don't look back or else you're really going to be late."

I stopped long enough to grab a quick kiss before I left the bedroom. Savage let out a sharp whistle. "Big Daddy! Big Daddy!"

I stopped at his cage and said, "Love my Dirty Bird. Be a good boy today."

"Suck me!" he squawked in response.

I laughed the entire way down the steps and out the door to my car. I never considered owning a bird before, but I could honestly say I had never loved an animal more than that one.

I noticed that Adrian looked a little anxious when I arrived at the police department and I felt bad for him. The closer they got to Sally Ann's due date, the more haggard he looked. "How's she feeling?" I asked him.

"She's fine," he replied. He ran his hands through his hair until it was standing up all over his head. "I'm the one who's a fucking mess. Damn, Gabe, I hate the thought of her being in pain, even if it's to bring our daughter into the world."

"I'm sorry, partner. I'm sure that all expectant dads feel the same way. I wish I had some words of wisdom that made you feel better." I wasn't sure what else to say because I knew nothing about childbirth or any method the doctors might have to make her more comfortable. It wasn't something I planned to know either since I wanted to adopt kids rather than find a surrogate. Of course, Josh and I hadn't determined how we were getting our kids, just that we would have some.

"I appreciate it, man," Adrian said. "I'm not sure I can do this again."

"Do what? Work with Whitworth?" Dorchester asked when he arrived at the end of our conversation. "You get used to it and sort of live to find ways to twist the stick he has shoved up his ass." He demonstrated with a hand gesture that looked like he was giving the imaginary stick a good twist.

I nearly spit my coffee out all over Adrian. As happy as I was to be working with Adrian again, I missed hanging out with Dorchester. He could give Josh a run for his money when it came to shock value.

Once Adrian stopped laughing, he said, "Nah, man. My wife is due to have our first baby next week. I'm just worried about them both. I can't wait to meet my daughter, but I'm not looking forward to seeing my wife in pain."

"Don't wimp out," Dorchester told him firmly. "It'll be the most beautiful moment of your life. Women are warriors—always have been and always will be—so you need to be equally as strong for her when she needs you most. When you hear your daughter's first cry and see her in your wife's arms, you're going to be glad you weren't sitting out in the waiting room like our grandfathers were. Can I give you a little bit of advice?"

"I'd love it," Adrian said earnestly.

"Fix yourself, man. You look like hell!" Dorchester waved his hands up and down Adrian's torso. "You're unshaven, your hair is a mess, and did you sleep in those damn clothes? Is this how you want to look in the pictures with your wife and infant daughter? Are you trying to scare your baby girl?"

Adrian stood taller and puffed out his chest a little. "No."

"Then shave and clean yourself up when you get home. Pull yourself together for your wife. You think she doesn't see how nervous you are?" Dorchester crooked his finger for Adrian to come a little closer. He lowered his voice and said, "Maybe you try to have some sexy time with your wife before the little bundle of cockblocking joy arrives."

Adrian blushed an interesting shade of red I'd never seen before in all the years I'd known him. "Uh, yeah, I'll see what I can do."

"Good man," Dorchester said, slapping him hard on the shoulder before he turned to me. "Ready to meet with the prosecutor?"

"You're something else, Dorchester," I told him.

"Yeah, but have you figured out what yet?" he asked me as I followed him outside to my vehicle.

"No, but you'll be the first to know when I do," I answered. "Dorchester, do you and your family have plans on Sunday afternoon?"

"Not that I'm aware of, but I'd have to check with the boss before I can commit to anything. Why? Are you wanting to catch a game like we talked about this spring?" Dorchester had mentioned Josh and me attending a game with his family. I thought I had a better idea in mind.

"We have a weekly dinner with our friends, and I thought

maybe your family would like to come over and barbecue and play cornhole with us," I told him.

"That sounds awesome. Count us in," Dorchester said.

"I thought you said you had to check with the boss?" I asked.

"Just did." I could see him wiggling his cell phone out of the corner of my eye. "She said that sounded much better than brunch at her sister's house."

"I don't want to cause any problems," I told him.

"You didn't. You asked if we were free and we decided we were. I've heard you go on and on about Josh's cooking, so I'm looking forward to sampling it."

"Actually, I'm the grill master," I said proudly. "If you're a really good boy, I'll invite you over for one of the Sunday meals where my man cooks a feast. We'll try you out now to see if you're deserving of such a treat."

"Fine," Dorchester said with a pout. "Just for that, I'm not asking my wife to bake her apple pie."

"Fine with me," I shot back. "No way her pie is better than Josh's anyway."

"You want to bet?" Dorchester asked.

"Yeah, I actually do," I replied.

"Well, I insist on impartial judges," he said haughtily. "It's clear that Josh has home field advantage."

I snorted in derision. "Like he needs that," I said arrogantly. "We'll do a blind taste test. Only the contestants will know who is pie A or pie B. People can vote for their favorite via secret ballot."

"Fine!" Dorchester exclaimed as he texted furiously on his phone.

"Deal," I said, going for my phone as soon as I parked outside the courthouse. I sent Josh a quick text.

*Sunshine, I just talked up your apple pie to Dorchester. He thinks Deanna can bake a better apple pie than you. Apple pie bake-off on Sunday. I need you to annihilate her, and I don't care if her kids are watching. Don't let me down. Love you!*

I probably should've talked to Josh before I invited the couple over, but what was five more people to feed? I also probably should've considered Josh's time before I volunteered him to enter a bake-off against Dorchester's wife. I might've sounded a little crazy, and I wondered what kind of reaction I would get from Josh. My phone vibrated with an incoming text just as I entered the courthouse. I glanced at my phone and smiled when I saw the message.

*I will show her no mercy!*

Damn, I fucking loved that man!

# SIX

## Josh

"What have you gotten me into, Gabe?" I asked out loud before I pocketed my phone. I couldn't imagine what prompted the debate between him and John, but I was glad that I would finally get to meet the man. I didn't know why it hadn't occurred to either of us to invite the Dorchesters sooner. I acknowledged that their first visit to our home might be the last since I was going to humiliate Deanna when she entered her pie in the contest.

Before Gabe texted me, I had called Chaz and asked him to

come over for brunch. I felt like we hadn't spent any quality alone time together in ages and I missed him. At first, he sounded suspicious of my call, and then he acted like he was too busy to come over for an hour. I won't lie, it hurt my feelings to the point that I almost told him to forget it. There were other ways I could spend my time that didn't involve me forcing myself onto my so-called best friend. *Yeah, I totally pouted until he got there.*

When he arrived, he was all smiles and happiness to see me; it was the tale of two Chaz Hamiltons. "I have to admit I was suspicious when you called me," Chaz said.

"I could tell," I replied. "Have a seat and let's eat while this is hot."

Chaz began shoveling frittata in his mouth like he hadn't eaten in days, which I knew wasn't true since we fed him the night before at the barbecue. Maybe he was in a hurry to leave or perhaps he worked himself into a big appetite, but he wasn't known for a lot of exercise, unless…

"Oh my God! You're bumping uglies with Dr. Dimples!"

Chaz spat his orange juice all over my dining room table, earning a death glare from me. It wasn't just any table; it was my great grandmother's that I lovingly restored and maintained. You couldn't find quality furniture like it anymore.

"I'm so sorry," Chaz sputtered as he began mopping up the OJ with a paper towel. "You just shocked the hell out of me."

I rose from my chair and got a damp towel to wipe away the sticky residue left behind. I smiled inwardly when I recalled the time Gabe fucked me to within an inch of my life on that same table, and I nagged at him to make sure he cleaned every drop of jizz.

"I guess that's a resounding no then?" I asked.

"Yes," Chaz said absently while he checked his phone.

"Yes, I was right that *you're not* having sex with Dr. Dimples, or yes, *you are* having sex with Dr. Dimples?" I asked. "Which is it?"

Chaz released a frustrated sigh and set his phone down. "Josh."

Chaz said my name in a serious tone I hadn't heard since he told me he was gay, like the fact I had caught him a month prior beating off to a picture of Ricky Martin hadn't been a big enough clue. "I honestly appreciate that you think Kyle is interested in me, but it's simply not true. Yeah, he thinks I'm cute and given a chance I'm pretty sure he'd tap my ass." *Crude much?* "I don't want that."

"You don't want him to 'tap your ass' even a little?" I asked in disbelief.

"I want what you have... what you and Gabe have," Chaz amended. "I realize that I don't want to be someone's hookup anymore. I want to be 'the one.'"

"I didn't know that Gabe was 'the one' until after we'd hooked up," I told him. In actuality, it took a while for me to stop running scared from Gabe. "I took a chance, and for once it didn't blow up in my face."

"You found your lobster," Chaz said. I smiled at his *Friends* reference and thought to myself that it was apropos he used it since he and Dr. Dimples shared a love for the sitcom.

They shared a love of video games, had the same favorite television show, and they had mutual friends in common. Relationships were formed and lasted with fewer things in common than that, but I didn't bring him over to lecture him on his love life.

"Believe it or not, I didn't invite you over to talk about Dr. Dimples. I just noticed the aggressive way you attacked your food and thought maybe you worked up a good appetite doing something sexy. It was wishful thinking for you on my part, and I apologize."

"Why did you invite me over?" Chaz's tone turned suspicious again. "Did something go wrong with the salon while you were on vacation? I wasn't aware of any issues."

"The opposite, actually," I told him. "Everything went right with the salon while I was gone and I realized that maybe I'm not employing you to your fullest potential."

Chaz squinted as he thought about what I said. "You're not?" he asked.

"I'm not," I confirmed. "I'll need to relinquish some control as the salon grows and my attention is diverted to filming segments for Channel Eleven, or risk burning my candle at both ends. There are things Gabe likes to do to both my ends and hot wax isn't one of them. Yet."

"Wow." Chaz's shocked expression at hearing me talk about giving up some of my ironclad control of the salon was comical.

"Yeah, I know." I smiled broadly at him. "How would you like to become the salon manager?"

"Me?"

"Yes, you!" I rolled my eyes at his response. "Once I move the spa area upstairs, I'll be able to open more stations and…"

"Move the spa area?" Chaz asked.

"Oh, that's the best part," I said excitedly. "Gabe and I decided to buy a house and live away from the salon. I'll free up some space for expansion, and we get to make a home together that neither of us lived in prior to meeting each other." My eyes lost focus as I thought about remodeling parts of the mansion, the wedding in the yard, and future little Gabriels running all over the house with Buddy close on their heels and Savage… My fantasy came to a screeching halt. Oh man, Gabe and I had serious work to do with that bird before we brought kids into our lives.

"Jazz, that's awesome!" Chaz leaned forward and hugged me as best he could with the corner of the table in the way. He grabbed my hand and ran a finger over the sparkling diamonds in my ring. "You deserve every bit of happiness you've found with Gabe and all the moments you haven't lived yet." Chaz dropped my hand and sat back.

"Nice," I said, smiling at him. "You sounded a little poetic there." Chaz's face blushed a pretty shade of pink that would make a lovely nail polish. "What's with the blushing? I was paying you a compliment, you know."

"I do," he said with a slight nod. "Just like your offer to promote me to salon manager is a big compliment."

"I'm sensing a 'but' here," I said.

"There might be a 'but' here," he confirmed then nibbled on his bottom lip while he turned something over in his brain. "I think I better tell you what's really been going on in my life because it does impact you more than I ever thought it would."

I sat up straight, both excited to get to the truth out of him and a little worried about the visible anxiety on his face and in the way he bounced his knee. "You want me to call Meredith and ask her to come over so you can get this all over with at once?" I sounded like I was doing him a favor when in reality I wanted her there to support me too because whatever he had to say was big. I was dialing her number before Chaz even finished nodding. "Girl, we need you here," I said dramatically into the phone. "Chaz is ready to confess."

"Confess?" Chaz and Meredith both asked at the same time.

"Yes," I said to them both. "Chaz is about to tell us what's really been keeping him up late at night."

"I'm on my way."

"I'm here, sugar!" Meredith said five minutes later as she ran up the stairs. "Whatever it is, we'll get through it together. Remember that one time Josh was convinced he had an STD and it turned out to be a bladder infection? Of course, a person needed to engage in a sexual activity of some sort and not just think about it to pick up an STD," she added with a snort. "Anyway, we're here for you just like that."

"Wait a minute," I said throwing up my hand. "I *had* been engaging in sexual activity."

Chaz quirked a brow humorously and said, "Jerking off next

to someone and not getting any of their spunk on you—hell, not even their hands or mouth—isn't the kind of sexual activity she was talking about, Jazz."

"Okay, you made your point," I said with a hint of defensiveness. I had been jerking off too much and not washing my hands enough. The films we'd watched in school about safe sex had me convinced the burning sensation when I urinated was from an STD and not from bacteria caused by bad hygiene. My two besties cackled like hyenas. "There's nothing funny about STDs," I said firmly. Or my naivety when I was younger.

"Of course not," Mere said after she had a good laugh. "I'm just lightening the mood, honey." She covered Chaz's hands with hers, and I laid mine over the top of both. "Tell us what's been going on, love."

"Please, please don't be mad at me for not telling you about this sooner. I never thought my late-night activities would develop into something worth discussing," Chaz said.

"Oh my God! You're dating Dr. Do Me," Mere said giddily. "I knew it!"

"No, but that's what I thought too," I told her.

"Damn," Meredith said. "You have me stumped then."

Chaz took a deep breath, held it, and released it slowly. "Okay, um, I don't know how to say this except to blurt it out there." He paused for dramatic effect then said, "I wrote a book," in a rush so it sounded like one word. "And Kyle is also part of my confession."

"You wrote a book?" I asked.

"What kind of book?" Meredith wanted to know. "And how does it involve the good doctor?"

Chaz pulled his hands from beneath the pile and rose from his chair. "I *am* the guy he was gaming with," he said while he paced my polished floors. "I'm the guy he's been wanting to meet."

"I have so many questions that I don't know where to start," I said to Chaz.

"Ditto," Mere said softly beside me.

"Okay, we'll save the book talk for last because it's the best part. I joined the online gaming community for research purposes for my book," Chaz said. "I never expected in a million years that one of the guys I played on a team with was Kyle. Anyway, I, um, got what I needed from the late-night games and chats then shut down my account and focused on writing my book."

"Chats?" Mere asked. "Like phone calls or text messages?"

"More like a private messenger program for gamers. You can chat in groups or individually and I spent more than a usual amount of time chatting up Kyle. It's how I knew who I was talking to, not that he tried to hide anything."

"What was his username?" I asked out of curiosity.

"Doc Paws," Chaz whispered. "Cute, right? Anyway," he said before I could respond, "he talked about moving back to his small hometown to take over a veterinary practice and a few other things that gave him away to me."

"Like what?" Mere asked. "There are a lot of small town vets out there."

"Not many of them have a detective for an ex-boyfriend who's moved on with his life with a salon owner," Chaz said.

"Oh," I said. "Is Kyle truly okay with Gabe and me or is he pretending?"

"He's honestly fine with it. He mentioned that he and his ex just weren't meant to be, but he hoped to find a love like his ex-boyfriend found someday. See, you and Gabe have become our relationship goals," Chaz said. I scoffed at him, but Meredith nodded that he was right.

"Okay, so you were playing games and chatting up Dr. Dimples. Why then were you saying that the guy he was looking for wasn't you? Why pretend you weren't the one he was spending time with?" I asked.

"Yeah, what he asked," Mere said with a nod. "You outright lied to us. Why?"

"I created a fake account and pretended to be someone I wasn't for research purposes so in essence he wasn't chatting and falling for *me*. He fell for fake me," Chaz said. "Damn, it hurts too." He rubbed his hand over his heart as if that could ease the pain he felt. "To entertain the thought that someone like him could fall for someone like me was… Let's just say it was cruel."

"Honey, I think you're being unjustly hard on yourself here. What parts about you did you make up?" she asked.

"Age and career," Chaz answered. "Hobbies too."

"Okay, but we've seen Kyle interact with the real you. He doesn't have any problem with your career—well, the one he knows about anyway—or your age. You both clearly have the same taste in television shows and video games," I told Chaz.

"Yeah," Chaz said softly. "I just don't see it working out for us long term. I wish I had the confidence that the two of you have, but I don't." He looked down at his feet for several long moments so he didn't see Mere and I exchange scheming glances. "Anyway, who wants to hear about my book?"

"Me!" Mere and I both chimed in, our matchmaking thoughts put temporarily on hold.

"When can we read it?" I asked.

"How long did it take you to write it?" Mere questioned.

We peppered him with several more questions before he could even answer the first ones. Finally, he stopped trying. He just stood in my kitchen and shook with laughter over our excitement for him. Once we'd run out of breath, he said, "It was something I've always wanted to do. I wrote fan fiction short stories about a boy band we all loved in junior high but never shared them with anyone. One night last year, I just decided to write a damn book. I never expected to finish it, let alone publish it."

"Publish it?" Meredith and I asked at the same time.

"You mean it's already done and published?" Mere questioned.

"And you're just now telling us about it? Why wouldn't you let us read it first?" I asked Chaz.

"I thought I was going to be laughed at when I released the book and I didn't want you to know my humiliation," Chaz told us.

"Honey, we're best friends. Your humiliation is our humiliation," Mere said tenderly. "Wait, that didn't sound right, did it?" Chaz and I shook our heads. "You know what I mean. We're here for you for the long haul, not just for the giggles and good times. So what happened when you published your book?"

"It became a best seller," Chaz said giddily. "I still can't believe it. Now people are emailing me and asking when the next book will be and how many there will be in the series. Can you believe that people want to read something that *I* wrote?"

I crossed my arms over my chest, still peeved that I hadn't had inside information on this. Hell, I was besties with a best-selling author and didn't even know it! "Well, it's hard to say since I haven't read anything you've written," I said.

"Oh, but you have," Chaz said with a wicked smile.

"What? I haven't read a book since…" Then it hit me! Sally Ann had come into the salon for a trim and told us all about the hot new gay romance book she was reading. Chaz had choked and coughed, but I thought he had just swallowed his drink down wrong or something.

"You're C.B. Hesterson," I said. Chaz smiled when it sounded like an accusation. "C.B. stands for Charles Bailey and Hesterson is your mother's maiden name."

"Yep, that's me," he said proudly.

"Chaz, that's so amazing. All Josh talked about for days was that book," Meredith said. "I meant to buy it, but I've been busy."

"I just bet," Chaz said with a lecherous wink. "You don't have time to be reading romance when you're making your own."

"That's what you think, doll face," Meredith said, as she whipped out her phone and started typing. "I'm going to start this baby, tonight."

"Thank you," Chaz said to Meredith then looked at me. "Back to your business proposal, Jazz. I will gladly help you manage the salon for now while you expand your business, but there could come a time where I want to work part time or maybe even focus on writing full time if things work out for me the way I hope they do."

"Sweetie, that would be amazing," I said, going to him for a hug. "I'll take whatever you can give me, and I promise to be supportive when you need to focus on your writing or even if you leave me altogether. Just promise me that you'll never miss a Sunday dinner."

"That's a promise I can easily keep," he told me.

"Good thing too. Gabe decided I was having an apple pie bake-off against Dorchester's wife on Sunday. I need all the votes I can get." It was then that I realized that Meredith had gone completely silent. The smile slid from my face when I turned to her and saw the hurt expression in her eyes. "What's wrong, Mere?"

"You've decided to expand your business?" she asked with a raised brow and a tone that said she wasn't amused. "When were you going to mention this to me?"

"I was going to call you later because there's more to the story. I needed to talk to Chaz first because his answer was the deciding factor on how quickly I could pull it off," I explained.

"He and Gabe are buying a house together and are going to re-vamp this space to meet the spa needs so he can use the entire first floor for salon services. More stations and stylists. He wants me to manage the business so he can focus on filming his segments for the news channel and remodeling the business."

"Is that right," Meredith asked Chaz. "Where is he moving to?"

"He didn't say," Chaz responded. "Care to tell us where you and the detective are moving?"

"Georgia's mansion," I told them. They just blinked at me, and I knew they were wondering just how in the hell we were going to af-ford it. I wasn't comfortable talking about mine and Gabe's financial situation, and even if I had been, I didn't have anything to share since I was still kind of in the dark. "We're still working out the details."

"Bet you're getting a good price since Georgia…" Chaz let his words trail off when he realized what he was about to say.

"Probably haunted, which is what you deserve for not telling me about your plans," Meredith said snarkily. She didn't back down or use kid gloves when handling anyone.

"You guys want to hear about how I plan to decorate or not?" I asked.

"Duh!" they both said. And just like that, everything was back to normal.

# SEVEN

## Gabe

MY FIRST IMPRESSION OF COUNTY PROSECUTOR PAMELA BUXTON was that she was a woman who worked her ass off to reach the office she'd been elected to serve. She walked proudly into the conference room and projected confidence in every gesture, reminding me of a certain someone that I loved madly.

"Detective Wyatt," she said, shaking my hand firmly. "It's good to meet you finally."

"And you, ma'am," I replied with a nod.

"It's good to see you again, John," she said to Dorchester. It was obvious by her casual greeting that they were familiar with one another. I glanced over at him briefly then did a double take because he blushed slightly. Dorchester was brash and bold, not a blusher. There was a story there, and I'd be damn sure to find out what it was. Lord knew he didn't hesitate to harass me at every turn about Silver and Paul hitting on me. *Turnabout is fair play, buddy.*

"You too, Pam," Dorchester said softly. "How are your folks?"

"Same as ever. Mom's struggling with my dad being home all the time now that he's retired. He messes up her routine, and she doesn't like it." She sighed and shook her head in humor. "How about your folks?"

"They're doing well. They had the same adjustment problems when they both retired a few years back. Now they split their time between their second home in Arizona and here. They're never gone more than two months at a time because Mom misses the grandkids too bad," Dorchester answered.

Pam's expression softened at the mention of his children. "You have a lovely family, John. I'm happy for you."

"Thank you, Pam. I'm happy for you also. You've kicked some ass to get the life you wanted," Dorchester said, looking proud of her.

"Yes, well it hasn't been easy, and I had to make a lot of sacrifices along the way. Some hurt more than others, but I think things worked out the way they were intended," Prosecutor Buxton said.

"I couldn't agree more," Dorchester replied.

I looked back and forth between them, feeling like I was stuck on the set of some television drama. My excitement to tell Josh all about it was a close second to ribbing Dorchester about the exchange.

"Let's get started," Buxton said. "I'm sure you both have a lot to do today." I sure as hell hoped not. The last few months had been pure chaos with a dead body turning up every time I turned around—or so it seemed at least. "I need to make you aware of the drama surrounding Broadman's trial."

"Already?" I asked. "He's only been arraigned for his plea. You've not even had your first pretrial hearing yet, and there's already drama?"

"Well, these crimes were committed in two different counties, and the prosecutors have different ideas on how to proceed," she explained to me. "It's not unlike two different law enforcement agencies fighting over an investigation."

"Yeah, I understand that," Dorchester said, "but the investigation that led to Broadman's arrest was conducted by a multi-agency task force. We're living proof of how well it works when people come together for a mutual goal."

"I agree with you, Detective," Buxton replied, "and I've tried very hard to be a team player." She'd returned to the professional she was in both her tone and the way she addressed Dorchester. She was no longer his past friend, or whatever else; she was a woman who wanted to convict the man accused of committing crimes in her county. "I'm not the problem in the situation, but I've decided that I'll be the solution."

"What does that mean?" I asked.

"We initially talked about moving the Broadman trial to Cincinnati so that we could try him once for all four crimes. I had planned to file the motion for the change, but Prosecutor Willison and I couldn't agree on terms. So," she said then paused for effect, "we're going to hammer down and go to court before he does and fucks up our case against Broadman."

"Now we're talking," I said as if we were discussing the outcome of a sporting event and not justice. To tell the truth, I was very competitive in all aspects of my life, and I liked her attitude.

"We're going to try him for Turner and Robertson since those crimes were committed here. We have the how and when figured out, but we don't know why. Juries have a hard time convicting a person if they can't figure out what motivated them to commit the crime. I need you guys to make finding a motive your top priority. I'll even be nice and share the information with Willison when the time is right so he can prosecute the man for crimes committed in his county. I'll never impede justice, but that doesn't mean I don't want it for us first."

"We'll get right on that, Prosecutor Buxton," I assured her.

"That's not all," she said when Dorchester and I started to rise out of our seats. "Depending on the outcome of your investigation, we could be looking at first-degree murder with capital punishment as a possible sentencing outcome. We've never had a capital punishment case in Carter County, so the state Attorney General's focus will be on us. We cannot afford any screw-ups, Detectives."

"There won't be, ma'am," I promised her.

"We won't let you down, Pam," John assured her.

There was so much more at stake here for her than for us. The first female prosecutor and the first capital punishment trial in the county amounted to a lot of pressure on her shoulders, but I was confident in her skills to get the job done.

"My ultimate goal is to use the possibility of the death penalty to get a confession out of Broadman for two life sentences to save the taxpayers a lot of money," she told us. "It's a long shot, but I'm going to give it a try. I need your help to make that happen."

"We'll see what we can dig up for you," I told her, but I wasn't confident that we'd find the concrete evidence she'd need to get a confession out of Broadman unless we found a witness or co-conspirator.

Buxton's assistant came into the conference room to let her boss know the phone call she'd been waiting for had come through and the caller was on hold. That facilitated a brief goodbye and request for updates as we investigated before she left the room.

"How the hell are we going to make this happen?" Dorchester asked when we exited the courthouse.

"One step at a time like every other investigation. Let's head back to my office and formulate a plan." Once we were back in my car, I turned to look at him instead of starting the car. "So, John," I said in a feminine, breathy voice to imitate the prosecutor's use of his first name, "what's the story here?"

"No story," he said, but wouldn't look at me.

"Oh, there's always a story," I said. "Obviously, you two used to date or something. Were you high school sweethearts?"

"You could say that," he mumbled. "Pam was my first girlfriend. We dated all through high school and our first year of college even though we'd chosen different universities. We simply grew apart, and realized we wanted different things in life. She was right when she said things worked out how they were intended because I can't imagine a life without Deanna and my kids."

*Man, I almost felt bad that Josh was going to put the pie smackdown on his wife.* Then I recalled the hard times he gave me and got over it. "So, how's the missus going to feel about you working with your first love?" I asked him.

John turned his face slowly to look at me, narrowed his eyes, and said, "Don't you breathe a single word about this on Sunday."

"I would never say a word," I said, jerking in my seat like I was shocked by the thought. I rubbed my hand over my heart like Dorchester had just stabbed me there. "Ouch."

"Okay, so maybe I had fun at your expense with Turner, Silver, and Paul but that's different," he said.

"How do you figure?" I asked him.

"Your interaction with them was limited where my wife had Pam thrown in her face during the entire campaign. She had to hear all about how smart Pam is, how beautiful and confident she is, and how close I was to marrying her, which couldn't be further from the truth. Deanna doesn't do makeup and glam; she hauls our kids all over God's creation to get them to their activities. Hearing nonstop about Pam's attributes is making her feel like she's somehow less, that her role as a wife and mother is somehow not enough. I hate that for Deanna almost as much as hearing her ask me if I regretted the choices I made when I was younger. It's a very sore subject."

"Oh," I said, feeling like shit. Sure, Josh had his moments of insecurity, but his unwavering knowledge that I was completely in love with him strengthened his confidence.

"I'm just kidding, man," John said then burst into laughter. "Deanna could care less about everyone else's opinion, and she's very confident about her place in my life. She's my queen and knows it."

"Well played, Dorchester. Well played."

"Come on, partner," Adrian whined when we got back to the police station. "You have to talk to Captain about letting me help you. I mean, it sounds like Buxton needs answers quick and three people can cover more ground than two."

"Four is even better," Captain Reardon said walking up behind us. The man had serious ninja skills. "I just got off the phone with Prosecutor Buxton. The BPD and CCSD will be working together to get her the information she needs as quickly as we can. I've just placed a call to Sheriff Tucker; he's sending Detective Whitworth over to work with you. You can set up in the conference room, and I'll have lunch delivered for you guys."

Adrian might've let out a tiny whimper at hearing he'd have to work with Whitworth again, but he swallowed down most of it when the captain narrowed his eyes at him. "We'll make you proud, sir," Adrian said.

"See that you do," Captain Reardon said then returned to his office.

We got to work setting up the conference room while we waited for Whitworth to arrive. He showed up with a tense smile, looking uncertain about the kind of reception he was going to receive. The bag of pastries he dangled in his hands appeared to be a peace offering.

"As long as you left your stick outside we'll be fine," I told Whitworth.

"Stick? As in I flew over on a broomstick?" he asked.

"Hey, that's funny, but I was referring to the one you've had lodged in your ass every time I've been around you. Just relax, and everything will be just fine," I assured him.

"Yeah, okay," he agreed. "I can do that."

"Good man," I said before I snatched the pastry bag from his hand as a test. He laughed instead of bitched, so I thought we made a big leap in progress right off the bat. "First, we need to comprise a list of people who knew, or suspected, what Broadman was up to, but I'm willing to bet that it's a short list and they might all be dead already."

"That's a cheerful thought," Adrian said. "Let's put the events in chronological order and see if the motive stands out."

I went to the whiteboard and started writing down the events as they occurred—starting with the threatening emails Nate received.

"The only common denominator is Robertson's land," Whitworth said in between sucking the glaze off the tips of his fingers. "He's a proud fifth generation farmer and Robertson's land getting turned over to the consortium might've put him over the edge."

"Why would he agree to represent Robertson the first time around then?" I asked Whitworth.

Whitworth knocked the crumbs off his tie before he responded. "He probably knew there was no way in hell the elected commissioners at that time would approve the construction of the casino. He lucked out that the statewide vote was against the measure and wasn't willing to take the risk a second time. My guess is that Spizer mentioned it to Nate after what's his nuts from McCarren decided not to pursue it."

"Michael Larkin," Dorchester said, supplying the name of the guy at McCarren who'd resumed the casino talk. "He did say that he talked it over with Rick Spizer. Let's say Rick brought it up to Nate after Robertson ignored the letter from McCarren we found in the safe deposit box, then what?"

"Spizer contacted his old buddy Rylan Broadman who just happened to represent Robertson. I bet they hadn't seen each other in years before they negotiated that land deal together," Adrian suggested.

"I agree," I told the group. "Spizer phoned Broadman and asked him to intervene on Nate's behalf with Robertson about selling the land. I bet Spizer even offered to sweeten the deal somehow so that Broadman could get a kickback for helping close the deal. Broadman probably went along with it so that he could keep an eye on the situation. Maybe he told Spizer that Robertson wasn't interested and thought that would be the end of it."

"Nate probably didn't want to let the idea go once it took root. He saw the potential for income and wanted to take a crack at talking to Robertson, possibly through Broadman at first," Dorchester supplied.

"Now we need to figure out how Owen Smithson got pulled into this. We know that his dad used to play baseball with Spizer and Broadman when they were kids," Adrian said.

"I bet the kid had some legal trouble," Whitworth suggested. "The parents called one of these attorneys, who in turn put Owen's computer skills to work for them. Broadman eliminated him when he became a liability."

"Damn, that's cold," I said. "Then again, what do we expect from someone who kills in cold blood?"

"So, he threatened Nate, but not with anything specific that we could trace back to him. Broadman thought that Nate would put two and two together and back away from the casino deal. The threats escalated when Nate went to the police, but we don't know how because Nate didn't specify in the email to me. How did he know that Nate went to the police?" I asked the team.

"They could've bugged his phones or maybe they attached a tracking virus to the first email Owen sent Nate, allowing them to monitor his electronic activity," Dorchester said. *Or someone inside the CPD alerted Broadman.* I hated that the thought even popped in my brain, but I couldn't help myself.

"Maybe that virus was the reason why Nate's email to you got flagged by the BPD servers and not keywords in the content," Whitworth added.

"Good point," Adrian told him, earning surprised stares from all of us. "What? He brought us pastries."

"Continuing with that theory," Dorchester said, pulling us back on track, "Broadman arranged to meet with Nate then ambushed him? That was awfully late at night for a meeting."

"Maybe the meeting took place at a decent time but the pop-up snowstorm that came through delayed him heading back to Cincinnati until later," Adrian suggested. "We always assumed Nate was coming to town because of where his car went into the ditch and struck a tree. From that vantage point, it looked like he was coming into the county, not exiting. The snow storm could've covered the tracks on the road that showed he lost control and ended in the ditch on the opposite side of the road."

"Then he killed Owen to make sure the kid didn't talk to the police once Nate's death was made public," I said. "Why kill Robertson though?"

"Robertson must've found out about it somehow, and Broadman silenced him too. Or he was on a damn killing spree and decided why not? That was one way to make sure the land didn't get sold," Whitworth said.

"Spizer either knew it was going on and kept quiet because he was scared or he started to figure things out and Broadman killed him," Dorchester added.

I stood back from the board where I'd been writing notes and thought that the theory was pretty damn plausible. "Now we just have to prove it," I said. I looked up as Sergeant O'Malley walked in with several carryout bags from the diner. "But not until after lunch," I told the team. After all, a man needed to have his priorities set.

The captain treated us to the diner's best dishes for our first day as a newly formed task force. After our trip to Carb City, we comprised a list of witnesses that we wanted to interview then divided them up. It was hard for me to choose which man should ride shotgun with me when it came time to track down our witnesses. Adrian was my original partner and my best friend, but Dorchester was my partner on *that* particular case, and it felt wrong not having him with me. So, I made the decision that made the most sense to me.

"Adrian, you're going to team up with Dorchester and Whitworth is riding with me," I announced.

"I am?" Whitworth asked.

"He is?" Dorchester and Adrian questioned at the same time. They both sounded perturbed, which was what I had hoped to avoid in the first place.

"Yes, he is," I told them. "Dorchester and I have the most knowledge about this case, so it only makes sense for us to split up to work with the newest members of the team. Switching partners keeps things interesting."

"I wouldn't know," Dorchester said with a sarcastic sneer. "Some of us don't get propositioned with such things."

"Huh?" Whitworth asked.

"Long story," I told my newest temporary partner, slapping him on the shoulder on our way out of the conference room. "Say, did you know that Dorchester used to date Prosecutor Buxton?" I made sure to say it loud enough for Dorchester to hear.

"Gabe," he said in a warning tone, but I didn't stop to

acknowledge him.

"Really?" Whitworth asked.

"Yep. You should've seen Dorchester blushing at our meeting this morning," I added.

"Blush? Dorchester doesn't blush," Whitworth remarked.

"Oh, but he does."

By that time, I was far enough away from Dorchester that I couldn't quite make out what he was saying, but Adrian's laughter over the situation rang loudly down the hall. The four of us working together sounded like a bad idea at first, but I realized it might actually be an enjoyable experience.

"Can I play the bad cop today?" Whitworth asked.

"Sure, what the hell," I responded. New day, new team, so why not try to be the good cop for once.

# EIGHT

## Josh

MERE, CHAZ, AND I SPENT HOURS CHATTING AND GOSSIPING LIKE we hadn't done in ages and it felt amazing. The hard truth was that our lives were changing and evolving; finding time for just the three amigos had become difficult, which meant we had to enjoy it while we could. I told them all about my vacation because there hadn't been much of an opportunity during the Sunday barbecue. Our primary focus had been on eating then later it was all about winning cornhole. Meredith gave us an update on how things were going with Harley. I could tell my best girl was as in love with her man as I was with mine and it made my heart soar. Chaz talked about his writing a lot, such as what his process was like and where he found inspiration. I was fascinated that he could just sit down and create a fictional world from his imagination. I was happy for him and excited that he'd found his passion.

I was trying to figure out what to make for dinner when Gabe called me. "Come to the hospital! Right now!"

"What? Why? Are you hurt?" It seemed like a rational question to ask at the time, but once my heart stopped racing, I realized that he couldn't be injured too seriously if he was the one dialing me.

"Sally Ann's water broke! Adrian's a hot-fucking-mess right now. We're having a baby!" Gabe said excitedly like we were the ones bringing baby Adrianna home. It hit me right in the feels, and I realized what an amazing dad he was going to make someday. First, we were going to be the best damn uncles to a precious little girl.

"I'm on my way!"

I checked to make sure the pets were good on food and water before I hopped in Princess and zoomed towards the hospital. I might've done some rolling stops at intersections and drove a little over the speed limit in my haste to get there, which resulted in me getting pulled over. The incident occurred outside of town on a county road about the midpoint between my home and the hospital.

I knew the sheriff's deputy busted me when I zoomed by the church parking lot where he sat running a radar gun. Sure enough, he pulled onto the road behind me and flipped on his lights. "Fuck!" I pulled over and sat with my hands on the steering wheel as my mother had taught me.

"*Never reach for anything because they don't know if you're going for your insurance card or a gun. Flip on your interior lights if it's dark out, roll down your window, and wait until the officer approaches your car and can see what you're doing before you move again.*" My mom never missed an episode of *20/20*, *60 Minutes*, or *Dateline*. My favorite was her advice on what to do if someone tried to pull me into a car. *"If they point a gun at you, run in a zig-zag pattern to make it harder for them to shoot you. Even if they do shoot you, it would be better than getting in the car and having them do God knows what to you."* I hoped like hell that advice never came in handy.

"License and registration, please," the deputy said when he approached my car. "Where are you headed to so fast, Mr. Roman?" he asked once I handed the items to him.

"I'm sorry I was driving so fast, Deputy. My friend is in the hospital having a baby, and I want to be with her," I told him.

"How happy would your friend be if you ended up in the morgue because of your carelessness, or worse, what if you hurt someone else with your selfishness?" he demanded hotly.

*Stay calm, Josh. Stay calm.* "Deputy, I accept full responsibility for driving twelve miles over the speed limit, but I'd hardly classify it as careless or selfish. I wasn't driving under the influence of alcohol or drugs. Now, can you please write my ticket so I can get back on my way to the hospital?"

"I don't think I like your attitude," he said snidely before he walked away.

"Yeah, you're not the first, and I promise that you won't be the last," I said to myself. "I know I don't like yours."

He was back with my driver's license and insurance card faster than I expected. I noticed he didn't include a ticket or a written warning when he handed them back to me. "I'm sorry about that, Mr. Roman. You're free to go now. Slow it down; okay?"

"Wait a minute," I said when he started to walk away. "You were all gloom and doom five minutes ago with your morgue talk. Where's your fire and brimstone now?" I asked although I suspected I knew the answer. Did Gabe have some alert placed on my license so I wouldn't get a ticket?

"I didn't realize that you were…"

"Oh no," I said, stopping him before he could continue. "I did the crime; now I'll pay the fine. I want the ticket, Deputy."

"Excuse me?" he asked, clearly not expecting my response to his kind gesture. "Are you saying you want me to write a ticket even though I was prepared to let you go with a verbal warning?"

"That's precisely what I'm saying. I do not want special treatment because of my relationship with Detective Wyatt." The deputy started laughing then.

"You think I'm not giving you a ticket because of your boyfriend?" he asked.

"Fiancé," I corrected.

"It had nothing to do with your fiancé, but I would've offered him the same courtesy had I known," the deputy said with a smile. "My wife just drove by and saw that I had you pulled over and threatened to cut me off if I gave you a ticket. Her opinion—or threat in this case—far outweighs that of Detective Wyatt's. Seriously, just slow it down so that you don't become a sad statistic."

"Thank you, Deputy," I looked at the embroidered name across his chest for the first time, "Jasper. I'll be sure to let Linda know how nice you were." I leaned a little closer and asked, "Do you want me to stretch it a bit, so you get extra play time?"

He laughed hard at my question. "My wife knows I'm an asshole so she would know you were lying and we concocted this scheme together." He rapped his knuckles on my car door, but not hard enough to draw my ire. "Drive safe, Mr. Roman."

"You be safe too, Deputy," I told him before he walked away.

It wasn't often that someone called me Mr. Roman; most people called me Josh or Jazz. The deputy had me thinking about what my last name would be once I married Gabe. My Gemini twins went to war in my brain over what they wanted. One twin wanted me to be traditional and take Gabe's name, and the other wanted me to keep my name as it was. I decided a compromise was the best bet and I planned to hyphenate my names, but I wondered what Gabe's thoughts were on the subject?

Once I got to the hospital, all my attention shifted to Sally Ann, Adrian, and baby Adrianna. I entered Sally Ann's room and found her lounging peacefully on her bed doing her Lamaze breathing while Adrian huffed and puffed like a dragon in the chair beside her. Gabe walked over to the side of the bed where Adrian sat holding Sally Ann's hand. He patted Adrian's shoulder comfortingly and grinned like a goober at the same time.

"How's it going?" I asked softly when I approached the hospital bed.

"It's great!" Adrian said with false cheer. "Everything is going to be great."

"Yes, it is so please try to calm down, darling," Sally Ann said soothingly. "My body was made to do this, and I'm going to be just fine. A little pain isn't going to… Holy Fuck!" I jumped back because I'd never heard Sally Ann use foul language. "Son of a bitch, that fucking hurts!" I tried my hardest not to smile because there was nothing funny about seeing my friend in pain. "How much fucking longer is this going to take?" Sally Ann asked. Okay, maybe it was funny when she changed from a sweet Disney Princess to a cursing sailor.

"I'm so sorry, baby," Adrian said, looking heartbroken that he played a role in her pain. "Dorchester said it will all be worth it when we hold our baby girl for the first time."

"Dorchester, huh? How many kids did he squeeze out of his body? Last time I checked, a vagina was required to deliver a baby into this world. A uterus, at least. Not like you're going to pack an eight-pound baby in your prostate gland for forty weeks then squeeze it out your ass."

The dam on my laughter broke, and it rolled out of me loud and long. I wasn't the only one either. It seemed to be what Adrian needed to get over his freak-out, and Gabe finally gave into the temptation to have a laugh at his best friend's expense. None of us laughed harder than Sally Ann.

"Oh, Sally Ann. I love you so much," I told her. "I'm taking this memory to the grave, but not before I bring it up at every single one of Adrianna's birthday parties. My Lord, girl. That's just priceless."

"And painful," Gabe muttered. I could tell he was squeezing his pucker tight in reaction to her vivid comparison.

"I'm sorry," Sally Ann said tearfully. "You're only trying to help, and I didn't mean to turn on you."

"Honey, you can call me every name in the book; I won't care," Adrian assured softly, as he ran his hand over the top of her head. "I'd take this pain for you if I could." Sally Ann sniffled as she nodded her head. Adrian leaned forward and kissed her forehead tenderly. I was a sucker for forehead kisses, and I felt my eyes tearing up.

I caught Gabe's eyes and tipped my head toward the door so he'd follow me out into the hallway. "I think they could use some private time," I said once he joined me.

"I agree with you. Want to grab a snack or something?" Gabe asked me.

"Want to find a supply closet and make out?" I counteroffered.

"Oh, you're my favorite kind of snack." Gabe hooked his arm around my neck and pulled me close so he could growl and nibble on the flesh there.

"Gross," a man said hotly, reminding me that we were in public.

Gabe turned loose of me and looked in the direction of the person who was offended by our PDA. There were several people who had passed us in the hallway, so it was impossible to know who had run their mouths.

"Who gives a damn what they think?" I asked, slipping my fingers between Gabe's and giving him a little tug so that we could continue with our day and forget the loser.

"Frankly, not me, Scarlett," Gabe replied in his best Rhett Butler voice.

"That movie you know," I said, tossing my hands up in the air.

"It's my mother and grandmother's favorite movie. I probably know every word by heart," he confessed.

"Did you crush on Rhett?" I asked him. I mean, who didn't? Ashley was a horrible weasel.

"I sure as hell didn't crush on that loser Ashley," he scoffed.

"That's my man," I said approvingly, giving his hand a squeeze. "How'd your meeting go with Prosecutor Buxton?" Gabe's laughter at my question caught me by surprise. "What's funny about Pamela Buxton? She seems kind of kick-ass."

"There's nothing funny about Prosecutor Buxton," Gabe said. He leaned closer and lowered his voice. "She and Dorchester used to date. He got all flustered and pink-cheeked around her this morning. It was hilarious." Then Gabe told me about how his teasing backfired when he fell for a bullshit story that Dorchester made up. "He didn't like it when I razzed him at the station later in front of Adrian and Whitworth."

We had arrived at the hospital cafeteria by the time Gabe finished his story. "You're not the only one with gossip to share. In fact, mine is juicier than yours," I boasted proudly.

"Are we still talking about gossip or have you moved onto how juicy your…" I covered his mouth with my hand. No one around us wanted to know about my load of joy juice chilling out in my sac just waiting to be sprayed all over my man. I felt Gabe's lips curve into a smile beneath my hand.

"Behave now, and I'll tell you all about it. You're not going to believe it," I said, using our familiar phrase.

"Try me," Gabe said, using the familiar response.

"It *was* Chaz that *was* playing *World of Warcraft* with Kyle," I told him.

"What? That's great!" A deep V formed in his brow as his happiness gave way to confusion. "Why are we acting like this is a secret. They have *Friends* and *WoW*. I've seen people with less in common give it a go."

*Like us*, I thought. "I know, Gabe, but Chaz feels pretty inadequate compared to Dr. Delicious."

"Will you quit calling Kyle those names?" he asked with a hint of aggravation. "I'd like to pretend that you don't notice things about other men and I'm the only one you see. Let me have my delusions for a little while, okay?"

I narrowed my eyes at Gabe but decided not to address his absurd remark right then. "Anyway, Chaz created a false identity to go undercover for the book that he wrote and he happened to run into Dr. Dreadfully Ugly in the process. They struck up a friendship then Chaz bolted when he got the impression that Kyle wanted to take things further."

"Kyle was ready for that step," Gabe said. "Wait a minute," he said after a brief pause. "What book?"

"Oh! That's the best part. Remember that book I read Easter weekend about the guy who fell in love with another gamer he met online."

"The one where the love interest turned out to be a serial killer?" Gabe asked.

"Yes!" I told him. "That's Chaz's book. He's C.B. Hesterson!" I said excitedly.

"Really? Wow!" Gabe tilted his head to the side, and I could tell he was rolling the discovery around in his brain. "That book was really hot. Do you think he based any of it on real activities between him and Dimples?"

"Art imitating life kind of thing?" I asked.

"I think the saying is 'life imitating art,' but I guess what you said applies more in this instance," Gabe said. He pulled me to him and smiled down at me. "Just what are we going to do about this new development?"

"*We're* not going to do anything about it," I told Gabe. "They're both adults who are capable of making decisions on what's best for them."

"What you're saying is that you haven't formulated a plan yet," Gabe replied.

"Yeah, pretty much," I agreed. "How about you buy me some of that fancy chocolate cake and a cup of coffee so I can start my plotting and planning."

"Or, why don't we use this time to pick up where we left off this morning. I want to make an offer on that house before it gets away from us," Gabe said.

I doubted that anyone would wrestle us over the mansion, but it probably was best not to take that for granted. For all I knew, Rocky was trying to find a way to get that house back for himself. Georgia would love for kids to live in her home, but probably not the ones that came from his loins. *Little rat bastard.* "I haven't given it too much thought yet, but I ..."

"*Josh?*"

I turned to see who interrupted me and found myself face to face with a man I hadn't seen in a very long time. "Trent! Wow, I didn't expect to run into you here. I'd heard you'd gone to Ohio State University to medical school."

His eyes moved appraisingly up and down my body before he answered me. "I did, and now I'm doing my residency here." Trent's eyes flickered to Gabe as if he just realized he was standing there. "Hi, I'm Dr. Adamson," he said, extending his hand to Gabe. Trent winced slightly when Gabe gripped his hand.

"Josh's fiancé," Gabe said sharply.

"Ahhhh," Trent said, and wisely took a step back. "Well, it was good seeing you again, Josh. Nice to meet you, Josh's fiancé." He chuckled then walked away.

"About that chocolate cake," I said, nudging Gabe.

"I don't like him," Gabe said, still watching the doctor walk away.

"Me either," I agreed. I tugged on Gabe's burgundy silk tie until he looked at me. "We'll probably never see him again."

Famous last words because guess who was doing his obstetrics and gynecology rotation with Sally Ann's doctor? Yep, Doctor Dildo. The look on Gabe's face when he walked in the door was priceless. I'll give Trent credit, he remained professional and avoided looking in Gabe's direction whenever they were in the same room.

Gabe and I hung out with the expectant couple when it looked like they needed company and gave them privacy when they didn't. Adrian's parents showed up after dinner to spend time with them, and Sally Ann learned that her parents were boarding the first flight they could get from Maine. It was a long night, but one that I'd never forget as long as I lived when I got to hold Adrianna Marie Goode in my arms for the first time around eleven o'clock that night.

"She's so tiny," I told Gabe. "I'm not sure I ever want a little person this small."

"She sure is perfect." Gabe ran his finger over her tiny fists. "You did great, Sally Ann."

"What about me?" Adrian asked.

"What about you?" Sally Ann countered. "I did all the hard work, and she doesn't even look a thing like me. She's definitely your girl."

"I'll share her with you," Adrian promised, grinning from ear to ear.

We didn't stay much later because the new parents were exhausted and we were looking a bit droopy ourselves. Neither Gabe nor I said much on the way home, but I loved our comfortable silences. We had our individual space while being together at the same time. We got ready for bed after we paid attention to our pets. Gabe got in bed and curled around me big-spoon fashion like he was holding me close and protecting me from the world at the same time.

"I can't wait to start a family with you, Sunshine," Gabe said softly in my ear.

"Not even married and you're already plotting out the little

Gabes," I teased. Hell, we hadn't even hammered out the details of buying the mansion yet, and we were already filling it with kids. "I can't wait either, babe."

"Tomorrow we'll have our talk about the house," Gabe said. "No more putting it off."

"Deal," I said after I yawned big enough to crack my jaws. "Tomorrow."

# NINE

## Gabe

LIFE HAS A WAY OF INSERTING ITSELF AT THE MOST INCONVENIENT times and reminding you that you're not really in charge. Discussing a mortgage versus buying our home outright seemed like a quick conversation two men who were devoted to making a future together would have as soon as possible. As I'd come to learn, nothing with Josh happened quick and it sure as hell wasn't easy.

My man was very complicated, and I could see that he was working through his thoughts on the subject. I knew Josh; he wanted to be fair to me, but he wanted to make a decision that made him comfortable too. Accepting a house outright wasn't going to be one of them. I also suspected that something else was weighing on his mind, but I couldn't figure it out for the life of me.

As much as it bothered me that he wouldn't let me buy the house for us, I respected the struggle he was waging inside. The only thing I could do was let the attorney representing Georgia's estate know that Josh and I would be buying the home. He was relieved to hear it and promised that he had no issue with waiting for us to make arrangements to buy it. With that assurance in hand, I was fine to sit back and wait for him.

It wasn't until the following Saturday, the eve of his apple pie bake-off with Deanna, that he brought it up again. "I think I've found a solution to our problem," he said while peeling apples.

"What problem?" I asked as if I didn't know what he meant. To me, it was more of a compromise than a problem.

Josh gave me the look I expected to receive for the rest of my life when I was acting deliberately obtuse. He raised one brow high over a wide eye and narrowed the other into a one-eyed squint. He gave new meaning to the term two-faced; half surprised and half annoyed. I'd never seen anyone wear two expressions simultaneously and look adorable while doing it. I bit down on my bottom lip so I wouldn't laugh because I could tell he was serious, plus he held a sharp knife in his hand.

Josh let out a resigned sigh then turned back to slicing his apples. "Gabriel," he said in a tone I expected him to use on our future children someday when they were working his last nerve. "You know damn well what I'm talking about so don't be cute."

"I was born this way. My mama said so," I said smugly. Josh released a cute snort but he didn't stop his work to argue with me. Secretly, I think he agreed which was why he wasn't fussing with me over my choice of words.

"I'm not comfortable with you buying the house outright with no financial contribution from me at all," he said. I started to open my mouth to argue, but Josh raised his hand holding the knife in the air to stop me. He resumed talking and slicing at the same time. How he didn't cut off a finger was beyond me. "*I* needed to find a compromise and work my way through this to see how much of it was pride and how much was practicality. I think I've figured it out."

"I think I'm ready to listen," I said.

"As I said, I'm not comfortable with you buying the house out-right, but you have a valid point that we don't need two mortgages. What you don't know is that my parents sold this house to me for what they paid for it in the '70s, which wasn't much at all. The value of the house was four times what I owed on it before I made renovations to modernize it. I've had greater success than I ever imagined and have been able to save a substantial amount of money in a relatively short time." Josh put his knife down and turned to face me. "I want to be your equal, your partner in every way. I can afford to pay for half of the house myself and then we won't need a mortgage for the property."

"We are making progress, but I think you're failing to see that we wouldn't be equal partners in the true sense of the word." I looped my hand around his waist and pulled him closer. "How is it fair for you to keep the mortgage on this property and deplete a huge portion of your savings to pay for half of the new house?"

"I can't let you buy the house all by yourself. That's not right," Josh argued. "Then I'll use my money to pay off this mortgage, and we can finance the new house together."

"I don't want you depleting your savings account to make this happen, Josh." It was rare that I called him anything other than Sunshine, but I needed him to see how serious I was.

"It's okay to deplete your savings but not mine?" he asked irritably.

"The funds I'd use to buy the house isn't money that I earned or saved. It's an inheritance left to me by my grandparents to do something that will make me happy. That was seriously the only instructions they left me. 'Be happy.' *You* make me happy. Building a life with you makes me happier. I'll still have the money I've been saving since I was old enough to work. That won't be the same for you so how is that equal?"

Josh nodded his head slightly to the right, and I knew what I said was sinking in. "Okay, then I'll make you part owner of the salon." *Then again, maybe not.* "I see that look," he said, rolling his eyes. "You want me just to let you buy a house and slap my name on it without paying a cent out of pocket, yet you aren't willing to be listed as an owner of this property and business. Why? Is my business too girly for you?"

"Don't you even go there. I can't believe you'd say that to me, Josh. I thought we got past my mistake." He paled at the anger he heard in my voice.

"We did," he said so softly I could barely hear him.

"Apparently, we didn't if you think that I'm embarrassed by what you do or that I think it's somehow less significant than my career. I have never implied that to you, Josh. I'm extremely proud of the business you've built on your own."

"Uh oh, still using my first name," he muttered.

"Damn right I am," I said fiercely. It was our first real fight since the time Josh threw me out of his salon before Thanksgiving the previous year and ended the *something* we'd just started. Damn, I was angry. Too angry to stand there in the kitchen with him right then. I needed space, fresh air, and time to myself to get over the knife he figuratively stabbed through my heart. I grabbed Buddy's leash off the hook and said, "I'm going out for a bit. I'll be back."

"You better," Josh said firmly, but I still heard the fear in his voice. So that he had no doubt about my intention, I slid my hand around to cup the back of his neck and pulled him to me for a hard but brief kiss.

I let out a short whistle for Buddy to come to me. "Dirty Dog!"

Savage squawked jealously from his cage, making me smile.

"I love you, Dirty Bird," I told him as I walked by him. Savage lived in a large cage and we let him out of it frequently, but I felt it wasn't enough. Hell, that mansion was so damned big he could have his own bird paradise inside.

The thoughts of creating a space for Savage brought me back around to the reason I was taking Buddy for an evening stroll. I knew Josh well enough to realize that he hadn't meant to hurt me by striking out the way he did. He was scared about the changes in his life and falling back into old habits of projecting his fear into anger—even when it wasn't warranted.

Instead of me telling him he had nothing to fear, I needed to find an argument that would make sense to him and not feel like I manipulated him to bend to my will. There was one part of Josh's life where his pride never wavered, and that was his salon. His business was his first love and the fact that he offered me half of his business was a huge deal. One that I didn't fully appreciate when he mentioned it because it surprised me so much.

To him, my perceived rejection was the same as someone calling his baby ugly. It was an insult to him. That was never my intention. What I meant was that I didn't want ownership of something that I didn't earn and… *Oh, that's how he felt about me buying the mansion outright.* Okay, so I got it, but how did I fix it?

I continued my walk, trying to figure out the perfect answer to the puzzle that would make us both happy. I didn't want two mortgages, and I finally acknowledged that me buying the house alone wasn't right either. I determined that the best answer would be to talk to a banker to find a solution that would make us both happy, which meant that we would own both properties equally but only carry one mortgage.

The night was beautiful with the sunset casting shades of pink and gold over the small town. Buddy seemed to be enjoying the walk so I didn't turn back around right away after I concluded that

Josh and I would need professional recommendations to make us both happy. I let Buddy take the lead and smiled when I realized he was taking me on the same path that he and Josh took for their morning runs. The gazebo in the little park was the midway point, and I noticed that it was currently occupied.

Although he'd had his hair cut short a few months before, it still took me a second to recognize him. Emory's body language was that of a broken man. I didn't know what brought him out to the gazebo that night, but perhaps it was a little bit of divine intervention. Even though his vibes screamed that he needed to be alone, the anguished look on his face said he needed to be with someone who cared. It was funny that Jonathon Silver's image popped up in my head just then because that was the last person Emory would want to see.

Buddy went to him and rested his head on Emory's knee. I sat down beside the grieving man. I wasn't exactly sure what to say, so I said nothing for a few minutes. I couldn't begin to imagine the pain that he still carried in his heart from losing his husband or the toll that his visions had on him. There was nothing I could say that would make him feel better or lessen his burden, but saying nothing at all seemed wrong. "I'm truly sorry, Emory. Josh and I are here for you anytime you want to talk."

He nodded then wiped furiously at the tears that spilled over his eyelids. "Today is the anniversary of our first date, first kiss, and the first time I knew it was okay to be gay. I looked into River's eyes and knew he would be worth any flack I got from my family or anyone else. To not love him would've been the travesty, not me falling in love with another man. We were inseparable from that day forward until the accident when I lost everything. I woke up from my coma a week after the accident to find out that, not only had River died, but his family had his funeral without me. I had to get a lawyer involved for them to even tell me where they buried him, Gabe. Can you imagine?"

"No," I said honestly. "I probably would've lost my mind."

"I think I have," he said almost frantically.

"No, you haven't, Emory." I knew my words wouldn't bring him any comfort that night, but I could tell him how strong I thought he was and hope that it would at least reach through the grief. "What you do might seem unorthodox, but it's a selfless act to make the world a better place. You set your sadness aside to help others, and that's amazing. My brother died twenty years ago, and my family still doesn't know who killed him. You bring closure to people so that they can start to heal, Emory."

"It's not enough," he said brokenly.

"You act when you get information, and that's all you can do," I assured him.

"Yeah, I was so helpful to you," he replied sarcastically.

"I know to make Josh answer the door when we move," I said, attempting to lighten the mood with a bad joke. It worked because Emory snorted a bit. "You told me what you knew when you knew it. What else could I ask for?"

"A description of the man for starters," he said dryly.

"That would be a good start, but I do know that someone is looking for me who might spell trouble. I know to be on the alert thanks to you," I replied.

"Yeah, I guess," he said then rose to his feet. "It's starting to get dark, so maybe I should head home."

"We'll walk with you," I said, "unless you're afraid you'll get shot by mistake or something."

"That's not even funny, Gabe," Emory said, but I noticed the hitch of laughter. "Come on."

"Is everything else okay? Are you having any problems in town?" I asked.

"You mean besides Mrs. Haskerville trying to set me up with her daughter?" Emory let out a soft sigh. "I broke the news to her gently."

"How'd she take it?" I asked with a smile

"Pretty well. Mrs. Haskerville said she should've known by how well-decorated and clean my house was when she brought over cookies to welcome me to the neighborhood. I never get tired of hearing that people think all gay men know how to decorate or keep things tidy. River couldn't match a pillow to a sofa if he was paid and never had I seen a bigger slob." He let out a broken sigh before he said, "I'd give anything to trip over one of his shoes again."

"I wish you could have that too, Emory," I told him.

"Thanks, Gabe." We were almost home before he cleared his throat and spoke again. "Have you heard from Jonathon Silver lately?"

His question shocked me because I knew that Jonathon was the one person he didn't want to discuss. He'd had a vision of the two of them, and although he didn't go into great detail, I was sure it was intimate. Since then, he cut his hair and made certain that Silver wouldn't be at our house before he accepted an invitation. Silver had only been there the one time they'd met, and I didn't expect him to turn up again. "No, why do you ask?"

"I feel like there's something wrong," Emory answered.

"Like he's in danger?" I probed.

"No, that's not the vibe I get. It's more like loneliness," Emory told me. "I think he could use a friend."

I thought back to what Josh said about Emory's purpose for moving to Blissville; he said it was because of Silver, not me. Between the vision Emory had of Silver and the connection they shared, I was starting to agree with him. I wasn't about to play matchmaker like my guy though. "I'll give him a call and check on him."

"Thanks," Emory said before he turned up the sidewalk to his front porch.

"See you tomorrow," I said, making sure he knew we expected his attendance at the barbecue.

"Yeah, okay," he said with a sigh that made me smile.

Buddy and I headed home to find that our apartment above the salon was empty. The music coming from the attic let me know where I could find my man. I gave Buddy a treat then filled his water bowl before I went upstairs.

Josh was lost in the music and didn't know I was there. I happily watched him spin around to Pink's "Try" so naturally that it seemed like the pole was an extension of him. I was always caught up in his spell no matter what he was doing, and I'd never choose for it to be any other way. When the song ended, I clapped softly.

"I didn't hear you come back," he said breathlessly. "You boys have a good walk?"

I rose from the chair and went to him. Later, I'd tell him about my run-in with Emory but not until after I got my most pressing thoughts out in the open. "You were right," I said.

"No, I wasn't," Josh replied. "I acted like you're trying to be *the man* and own me and that's not what you were trying to do."

"You tried to share with me your most treasured possession, and I resisted. I was wrong, Sunshine. Let's talk to your banker next week and figure out a way to make this work so that we only have one mortgage and we jointly own both properties. It's not yours and mine; it's ours. All of it."

"Yes, that's what I meant, but I should've worded it better," Josh said softly as the tension faded from him. He wrapped his arms around me and pressed his forehead into my shoulder. "I'm sorry that I upset you so much that you needed to leave. Thank you for coming back."

I tipped his chin up so that he was looking in my eyes. "Never doubt it," I told him. "Especially when you're about to bake pies." His laughter warmed my heart and was happy that our argument was over.

"There's something else I want to talk about, but I don't want to ruin this happy vibe we have working right now." Josh bit his lips nervously while he looked down at his hand that sported the ring I gave him.

"You can tell me anything," I replied, even though I knew for a fact I was going to hate the words that came out of his mouth next. I listened patiently as he explained that he wanted us to remove our rings until our wedding day. I bit down my frustrated response because I didn't want to undo the progress we made that night.

"That pulsing vein on your forehead tells me how much you hate the idea," Josh said. "Can I ask exactly why it bothers you?"

"Because I want the world to know that you're mine," I told him, sounding like a jealous knuckle dragger.

"I'm already yours and nothing will change that," Josh said patiently. "I just want our rings to be a symbol of that special day."

I blew out a frustrated sigh and nodded my head. I thought he had a valid point, even though I hated the thought of him taking off his ring. "Fine, but I'll slap a collar on your neck if I start seeing the dudes sniffing around outside our door." My remark eased the tension and I was rewarded with a sweet kiss.

"It better be shiny and pretty," Josh replied.

"Black leather with metal spikes," I countered.

"Oh, I saw one of those at Brook's Pets! That's much more cost effective than the one from Tiffany & Co. that I was picturing," Josh told me. "Maybe I'll just ink your name on my forehead or something." From there it went downhill with one ridiculous suggestion after another.

"Why don't I smell baking pies?" I asked suspiciously after we were done laughing at ourselves.

"They're soaking in my secret sauce," Josh told me, waggling his eyebrows.

"What's your secret sauce?" I asked.

"Follow me, and I'll show you something that I've never shared with anyone else," he said mysteriously. There was no way that I could resist an offer like that! Downstairs in the kitchen,

Josh pulled out a large bowl covered in plastic wrap from the refrigerator. I knew exactly what was in his secret sauce the second he peeled back the plastic wrap. The apples were soaking in bourbon.

"Deanna doesn't stand a chance," I said smugly.

# TEN

## Josh

WE SURVIVED OUR FIRST LITTLE TIFF AS A COUPLE AND CAME OUT stronger on the other side. It couldn't get any better than that. Thinking that Gabe and I would never argue was stupid because we both had strong opinions on just about everything and we were both stubborn. I also learned that I fell back into old habits and was quick to strike out when Gabe hurt my feelings. Striking and counterstriking was not an effective way to resolve issues and would never lead to a happy union.

Gabe, as usual, was onto me and knew my insecurities had once again reared their ugly heads and was leading the assault when he didn't immediately jump all over the offer to co-own my salon. Besides my heart, Curl Up and Dye was the most precious thing that I could share with him. *Note the growth here! I want it on record that I didn't say a damn thing about my pleasure portal.* When he rejected my suggestion outright without a discussion, I took it the absolute wrong way and snapped at him.

Watching him walk out the door with Buddy nearly killed me. The kiss he gave me before he left expressed his intentions of coming back to me, but how many times had life fucked over someone's plans to return home? I was sure the evil bastard had lost track of the number of lives he had ruined. I couldn't dwell on that—or Emory's prediction—and retain my sanity, so I went upstairs after soaking my apples in bourbon and cinnamon.

I got lost in the music and found comfort in the way it rolled through me, blocking my thoughts and worries, which was good unless I wanted to risk a nasty injury. I didn't mind so much if Gabe caused me to pull a muscle during an enthusiastic sexual performance, but I wasn't too excited about the potential of a broken bone—or worse, a broken neck—from falling off my pole. I couldn't imagine explaining that one to the hospital and doubted they'd believe it, which could mean another IA investigation for Gabe. Luckily, none of that happened.

My intense focus on the routine also meant that I didn't know Gabe was in the room with me until he clapped. The heartfelt discussion that occurred afterward was adorable, the secret sauce reveal was fun, and the make-up sex was phenomenal. There were not enough adjectives in the English language to do it justice but toe-curling and life-affirming were the first two that came to mind. The only rough spot came when it was time to put our rings in the drawer until our wedding day. I had only worn the ring for a short time, but my finger felt naked without it. Still, I meant what I had told him and stood by my decision.

The next afternoon, Gabe hovered while I made the crust for the pies. "Just seeing what other magic you have up your sleeve."

"Baby, you've been up my sleeve plenty of times to know what magic it holds inside for you. It's the Magic Cumdom," I said. *Yeah, I hadn't grown that damn much.* Gabe's response was to pinch my ass hard enough to make me yelp.

"You know damn well I'm talking about secret sauces," he told me. "Don't even," he said when I opened my mouth for rebuttal. *Come on! How can I resist when he leaves himself wide open for such remarks?* "Do you add alcohol to the crust or is it just the filling in a boozy apple pie?"

"Drunken apple pie," I corrected him. "No booze in the crust and the alcohol bakes out in the oven and just leaves behind a rich flavor that takes the pie to a whole new level."

"I'll say," Gabe replied. "Um, are you making an extra pie just for me?" The hopeful look in his eye and the way he bit his lip was so damn adorable. My man loved his apple pie almost as much as he loved me.

I divided the dough into four pieces so I could make two pies. "Of course, I am." I pointed to the empty saucepan on the stove and the ingredients he set out. "Don't you think you should start whipping together the new barbecue recipe you found?"

"Yeah, okay," he said like he hated to look away from the pie. "Don't get too distracted by my awesomeness at the stove and fuck up the pie. I'm sure Deanna is a nice woman, but she married a mouthy man who needs a set down. He thinks he's going to bring his wife over here and beat my guy at pie baking. Does he think because you have a pair of balls that you can't bake?"

*God, I have created a monster.* "Babe, has John ever talked about either of us in a demeaning way?"

"No, but he's a smug punk just the same. I invited him to our home, and he wants to throw down with a bake-off. I'm going to wow him with my special sauce too so that he knows not to challenge my grilling abilities."

I had a feeling that a barbecue battle the likes that *Pitmaster* had never seen would soon occur. I stood ready with my bottle of liquor to help Gabe achieve master grilling status for all to fawn over. "What kind of sauce did you decide to make today?" I asked as he poured a can of crushed pineapple into the pot with soy sauce, liquid smoke, and tomato paste before he added brown sugar and some more liquids.

"It's a Hawaiian barbecue sauce," Gabe told me. "I was thinking that Hawaii would be an awesome place to go on our honeymoon and it got me looking for sauces I could make today for the chicken."

"Sounds perfect," I replied.

Gabe looked up from stirring the sauce and captured my gaze with his charming, boyish grin. "The sauce or the honeymoon destination?"

"Both," I replied. "How long would you like our honeymoon to be?"

"Hmm," Gabe said, rolling it around in his brain. "I'd like to hop from island to island, so I was thinking between ten and fourteen days."

"Wow, that's a long honeymoon." I loved the idea of just the two of us for two whole weeks. Our week in the Bahamas for my birthday was amazing but ended too soon. "I love it."

"We should probably make travel arrangements right away," Gabe said, turning back to his sauce. "How about tonight after everyone leaves?"

"After I get my victory rim job," I told him.

Gabe snorted. "Like I need a special occasion to munch on your ass." He tapped the spoon on the edge of the pan then pointed it at me. "Remember that one time you licked your own ass?" he asked, reminding me of the time I called him Detective Butt

Munch and he pointed out that I kissed him afterward so it was like I licked my own hole.

"I did not," I said after my fit of laughter. "It was diluted by your saliva."

"Keep telling yourself that," Gabe said smugly, "but I know how much you liked it."

"Keep thinking it," I replied just as sassily.

"You always need to have the last word, don't you?" Gabe asked.

"Do not," I fired back.

"Do too," he responded just as quickly. I saw the challenge in his eyes, and it nearly killed me not to take the bait. Instead, I blew him an air kiss and went back to assembling the pies.

"See!" he said.

"What? That was an air kiss, not a word!" I argued.

"It made a noise and was more than a cutesy gesture. It was just a sweeter way of flipping me off," Gabe contested.

"You are out of your mind, Gabriel," I said, but my mock anger wasn't convincing when I couldn't keep the smile off my face or humor from my voice. He was also right so I couldn't protest too much.

"Mmmmmm hmmm," he replied.

*I would not take the bait. I would not take the bait. I would not...* "You sure didn't mind my mouth opened this morning when I wrapped it around your dick."

Gabe laughed so hard that he had to step away from the stove. He reached for me, but I evaded him by stepping back until there was nowhere for me to go with the kitchen counter behind me. "Gotcha," he said dramatically.

"Yeah, you do." I smiled up into his face.

"Don't ever change, Sunshine," he said, mirroring words I'd spoken to him another time. There were no more words after that because the tender kiss that followed rendered me speechless.

I was so glad when Adrian, Sally Ann, and Adrianna arrived before everyone else so I could fuss over the little sleeping princess. I couldn't resist taking off her little hat so I could see all the dark hair she'd inherited from her daddy. I was forced to give her up once Meredith and Willa arrived because they hadn't met the little angel yet.

Gabe smiled crookedly when I interrogated the ladies to make sure they had washed their hands before I passed her over. I knew he was thinking about what a nitpicky dad I was going to be and he was right. My little Gabriels and Gabriellas wouldn't be held with rough, germy hands.

Emory arrived with a peach cobbler that looked and smelled good enough to rival my apple pie. Gabe told me about the conversation he'd had with the man the night before, and I tried my best to hide the sadness I felt over his heartbreak. I refused to believe that happiness was out of Emory's reach and his comment to Gabe about Jonathon Silver made me smile. Whether Emory knew it or not, he connected with Jonathon on a level beyond the physical one he'd envisioned, but that was something he'd have to come to terms with in his own way and on his time frame, not that of an annoyingly happy friend.

John, Deanna, and their three kids were the last to arrive. I was happy to meet the man that Gabe talked about so much. He was every bit of the jokester that Gabe said he was and their kids were too freaking cute for words. Buddy barked and bounced happily at having children to play with, and it was obvious he was good with them.

Deanna Dorchester was one of the sweetest persons I had ever met. She set her covered pie on the picnic table and threw her arms around my neck for a hug before she did the same with Gabe. "I'm so happy to meet you both. Thank you so much for inviting us to your home," she said. You'd think it was an invite to the White House or something by how happy she seemed. "Where can I put my pie?" she asked. I could tell by the way she rolled her eyes that she wasn't pleased with her husband.

See, I had puffed out my chest and strutted about like Foghorn Leghorn from my Saturday morning cartoons when Gabe entered me into the bake-off. Deanna looked mortified that John would do something like that to her. I felt a little shitty and a whole lot shallow when she followed me upstairs to put her pie in the kitchen.

"We don't have to do this, you know," I said once she set her carrier down. "We can tell the guys we refuse to play along with their silly games."

"I wouldn't dream of it," Deanna said. "Your pie is going to trounce mine and John will learn to never do this to me again. In a marriage, one spouse's humiliation is also worn by the other."

"How do you know that my pie is going to win?" I lifted the lid off her dessert carrier then said, "Oh."

"Oh, is right," she said then began laughing. "Only a serious baker would recognize a frozen pie that's been passed off as homemade."

"There's nothing wrong with frozen pies," I told Deanna. In fact, I'd been known to use them in a hurry.

She tipped her head to the side and narrowed her eyes at me. "Oh, I would agree in most cases, but I have a feeling your pie will humiliate mine."

"My pie isn't *that* great," I lied.

"Show it to me," she demanded.

"Deanna, we've just met," I said in mock horror. "I don't show 'it' on the first date."

She laughed and slapped me playfully on the arm then walked over to where I had my pies sitting on the counter. She released a shaky breath as if she was about to uncover a rare, ancient artifact before she removed the foil off one of the pies. "Oh man," she said when she revealed the perfect, golden lattice crust. She breathed deeply, inhaling the spice of the cinnamon and the bourbon. "It's what I get for deceiving my husband all these years."

It's not what she deserved at all. So, after we feasted on Gabe's delicious grilled chicken and enough side dishes to feed a battalion, I did the only thing that felt right. I told the group that I had dropped my pie on the kitchen floor before I could slice it into slivers for the contest. I saw the disbelief in Gabe's eyes, but he wisely didn't point out that there was a second pie. I knew my lie would go unchallenged because he wanted that pie all to himself. I apologized profusely, and we all fussed over Deanna's pie and Emory's cobbler before we started the cornhole tournaments.

That time, Mere and I were split up and put on different teams. We decided to pair up with our guys since they showed real promise when we beat them the previous week. I did notice that Kyle and Chaz remained a team and looked even cozier than the last time they teamed up. Like the week before, Mr. Best Seller and Dr. Dimples were my final opponents.

Gabe pulled me close and lowered his mouth until it was pressed to my ear. "Do not throw the game like you did last week and the pie bake-off today. I'm onto you, Sunshine." Fine, so he busted me both times, but I had good reasons. I wanted to see Chaz and Kyle hug since it looked like they'd been working up to it as the game progressed. I had been right, and I hoped the connection would spark something amazing between them, but that decision was up to them. I couldn't throw Deanna to the wolves like Gabe wanted me to, and I'd give him my reasons later—after I annihilated the budding lovebirds at cornhole.

Halfway through the tournament, a surprise visitor arrived. "Hey, everybody. Sorry I'm late," Jonathon Silver said, waving awkwardly.

It was hard to say who was surprised the most between Emory, Gabe, and me. It was easy to see who Emory held responsible for his discomfort when he looked at Gabe suspiciously. He wasn't the only one either. Gabe mentioned that he would check in with Jonathon but not until after the party because he knew how uncomfortable Emory was in his company. Yet, there he was as if someone conjured him out of thin air or sneakily called him. Gabe shook his head to say it wasn't him. It sure as hell wasn't me, and I could tell by the shocked expression on Emory's face that he didn't call Jonathon either.

"Maybe I shouldn't have dropped in on you guys," Jonathon said, sounding embarrassed and very uncomfortable. His eyes searched the gathering like he was looking for someone and I knew who when his eyes locked on Emory. "What the hell did you do to your beautiful hair?" Jonathon asked as if he had the right.

Emory narrowed his eyes, sat straighter in his chair, and lifted his chin proudly. "Josh cut it for me." Jonathon looked at me like I'd given top secret information to a hostile government rather than finish a service I'd been hired to provide.

"Hey, I do what my clients ask. Emory wanted the Bieber special, and that's what he got," I said defensively.

"Not that it's your business," Emory said icily. Jonathon made a beeline for Emory, ignoring his standoffish tone and demeanor. He sat in the vacant seat beside the man and kept looking at him until Emory couldn't ignore him any longer. "What?"

"It makes your eyes look even bigger and greener," Jonathon answered.

"I don't have to sit here and listen to this," Emory replied as if he'd just been insulted instead of complimented. He rose to his feet and practically stomped across the yard in the direction of his house. Unfortunately for him, Jonathon was right on his heels.

"What's your problem?" I heard Jonathon ask, but couldn't hear the rest he said to Emory. It was clear by his body language that he was as confused as hell.

"Gabe, maybe we should…"

"No," Gabe said, wrapping his hand gently around my bicep to prevent me from following them. "Let them handle it."

I looked into Gabe's warm gaze and melted a little. "Okay." He would've been the first person to intervene had he thought trouble was brewing, so I went with his lead. "Ready to finish kicking some cornhole ass?"

"Yes, so we can get these people out of here, and I can go upstairs and eat both pies." He rubbed his nose behind my ear. "Did you buy that vanilla ice cream I love so much?"

"Does your dick get hard when I spin on my pole?" To me, his question was just as absurd. Of course, I bought him the ice cream he liked.

Gabe's eyes darkened with a desire for more than pastry, apples, and ice cream. "Let's get this show on the road then."

We beat Kyle and Chaz so bad that they couldn't believe it. They wanted a rematch, but Gabe rudely told them to go home instead. He wanted pie, ice cream, and sex. No one else seemed to find his behavior odd when they said goodbye, so perhaps I was the only one who noticed.

The look on his face was priceless when he ran up the stairs and didn't find his beloved pie waiting for him on the counter. "Someone took the pies home with them by mistake," he said. "Who takes home two whole pies?" He was disturbed by their selfishness.

"Gabe," I said his name calmly to stop the tirade I saw brewing. I opened the oven door to reveal the two pies I'd hidden inside. "I couldn't leave the pies out in the open for our guests to see after I announced I had dropped and ruined them."

The relief on Gabe's face was sweet and comical. You know what was better than eating pie and ice cream? Eating it buck-ass naked while straddling Gabe with our hard cocks pinned together between our abdomens. It was hard to tell if the groaning and moaning was due to the delicious dessert or the sensations we were building inside one another. Either way, we got sticky in all the right places and for all the right reasons.

# ELEVEN

## Gabe

JOSH PROVED TO ME ON MORE THAN ONE OCCASION THAT HE WAS A better man than I was, even though people might argue that point. Sure, he was bristly and abrupt at times, but there was always a good reason for it. I never had a good explanation for the stupid shit I did, like entering Josh into a bake-off without his permission. Hey, at least I wasn't as clueless as Dorchester, who'd been eating frozen pie for over a decade and didn't know it. What did Josh do when he found out? He faked dropping the pie to prevent Deanna's feelings from getting hurt. I'd like to think I would've been as kind.

I had no intentions of breaking the news to Dorchester either, no matter how annoying he was the next day. Not even when he said, "Could you have been anymore obvious that you wanted to have a go at your guy last night? Jesus, you were packing us up and sending us home before the final bag cleared the cornhole. Wow, man, I was embarrassed for you."

"Whatever, Dorchester," I said, rolling my eyes. I had hoped that I wasn't as obvious as Josh said I was, but apparently my motives were transparent. See, I could've let loose with Apple Pie Gate right then, but I kept my mouth shut.

"Or was it Josh's apple pie you were after?" Dorchester asked.

"I don't know what you're talking about?" I said, grateful I was driving and not looking him in the eye.

"It's okay, Gabe. Deanna told me the truth last night. I think Josh is sweet for what he did. I guess it's also kind of nice how you didn't just throw it in my face right now," he added.

"It was harder than you might expect," I confessed. "So, how do you think it will go with Lucy Williams today?" I asked Dorchester, switching our conversation to the interview we were about to conduct. Rylan's receptionist had been on vacation when we first went to her home to talk to her.

"I don't know, man. You shot Broadman in front of her so she might not be too friendly," Dorchester replied with his usual sarcasm. "Good jobs are scarce, and I'm not sure a person can claim unemployment in this type of circumstance."

"Maybe I should've let him shoot your smart ass with your gun after he knocked you out and took it off you," I replied good-naturedly. We both knew there was no way in hell I would've let that happen. "Save you from a life of frozen apple pies." I made it sound like a fate worse than death. To be honest, it was really good frozen pie; it just wasn't in the same stratosphere as Josh's, so a comparison just wasn't fair.

"You wound me," Dorchester said while covering his heart. "I probably should show you a bit more gratitude when we work together since you made it possible for me to go home to my family that night. Mostly I'm mortified that Broadman got the jump on me," he added humbly. Dorchester had been plenty thankful, and nothing more was needed, wanted, or required.

"Nah," I replied waving him off. "At least it wasn't a seventy-year-old woman who took you down."

"Very true," he said, sitting straighter in his seat. "Thanks for always making me feel better about myself, Gabe. You have a real talent."

"Anything to please," I said dryly, pulling up in front of the light gray bungalow house on Bay Street. "I hope this goes better than talking to Rylan's parents did the second time."

"Whitworth said they didn't like you much," Dorchester said, resuming his smartass demeanor.

"Not at all," I replied with a wry smile. "I didn't care for Broadman's parents either, so it was okay. Whitworth seemed to enjoy the interview since he'd never seen me in full dickhead mode." I discovered Whitworth wasn't as bad as I thought once he let down his guard and I got to know him better.

"He liked being out in the field doing this kind of work. We spend the majority of our days enforcing warrants and investigating drug-related crimes, so it's been a different experience for him. Not that I want there to be more homicides and arsons in the county," he amended. "I'm ready for things to slow down and serve warrants again." He acted like there wasn't any danger knocking on the doors of people who didn't want to be found.

With Adrian on paternity leave, Whitworth returned to the sheriff's department instead of us forming a three-man team. He was only a phone call away if we needed him, but I hoped that we wouldn't. Like Dorchester, I was ready for things to return to the peaceful, small town life I'd come to love.

"Here we go," I said, opening my door. Lucy had been pretty hysterical the first time we interviewed her after Broadman's arrest in the office. It was true that I shot him in the shoulder in front of her, which shocked the woman, but I think the hardest blow was finding the money Broadman stole from Robertson in the office safe. She had seemed very genuine in her denial that she knew anything about Broadman's activities. The second time around, I wanted to focus more on the motive since we found the connection between Broadman and his victims.

Lucy at least attempted a smile when she answered the door of her parents' home. "Hello, Detectives." She stood back for us to enter her home.

"Did you have a nice vacation, Lucy?" I asked, hoping that small talk would relax her nerves a bit.

"Yeah, it was what I needed," she answered. "Would either of you like something to drink? Coffee or something?"

"We're fine, but thank you for asking," I told her. "We appreciate you agreeing to meet with us this morning."

"I'm not sure how helpful I'll be since I already told you everything I know," she replied. She might've known more than she realized so it was worth interviewing her again. "I'll try my best."

"That's all we can ask for, Lucy," Dorchester said, spreading his better-than-good cop routine on extra thick that morning. His charm caused the young lady to blush profusely.

"Do you recognize the name Nate Turner?" I asked.

"Besides what I read in the papers and saw online?" she responded.

"Yes," I answered. "Do you recognize that name as someone who called the office in the past?"

"Not that I remember, but none of the people that Mr. Broadman allegedly killed ever phoned the office. They called him directly on his cell phone," she told us. "I know for a fact that he took a call from Rick Spizer the week that Rick died. I heard him talking on his cell phone through his closed office door. Well, at least he referred to the caller as Spizer."

"Lucy, we got copies of Broadman's cell phone, home, and office records and there were no calls between Broadman and any of his alleged victims." It was a key piece of evidence any half-decent defense attorney would use in court. Unless... Damn it; I should've picked up on it sooner. "He must have used a different cell phone for these calls, and we missed it when we searched his home, office, and truck."

"I guess that's possible, but I had never seen him with two phones, but then again I had never seen him act the way he did when you came to arrest him. See, I'm not very helpful," she said dejectedly.

"But you were," I told her, convinced we overlooked a key piece of evidence. "You've seen the faces of the men he's accused of killing on the news, correct?" Lucy nodded her head. "Had any of them visited the office that you can remember?"

"Not recently. Mr. Spizer had been to our office during the first land contract negotiations between Mr. Robertson and McCarren Consortium, of course," she replied. "But not since then and none of the others ever came to the office."

"Is there any possibility that they called using fictitious names?" Dorchester asked.

"Fictitious?" she questioned.

"You know, clients who called repeatedly but there was no record of them in your system," he explained.

"Not that I can recall," she answered after thinking about it for several moments. "Honestly, there was never a single occurrence where Mr. Broadman acted in any way other than a kind man who loved his farm and his community."

"Thank you for your time, Lucy," I said, rising to my feet. "Hopefully, we won't have to bug you again."

"It's no bother, Detectives." I bit back a laugh when she batted her eyelashes a little extra in Dorchester's direction.

"Not a word," he said to me once we were outside her house.

"Oh, I see how you are," I remarked. "You can dog me all you want but turn super sensitive when the shoe is on the other foot."

"Jackass," Dorchester said, opening the door.

"Cry baby," I said, rounding the front of my car. "All jokes aside, you know what we need to do now, don't you?"

"Go back to your house and eat some of Josh's apple pie?" he asked.

"You think I'm going to share my pie with you after the 'jackass' remark?" I countered.

"Okay, probably not," Dorchester concluded. "Well, it sounds like we're going to ask a judge for a new search warrant so we can look for the extra phone."

"Yes," I confirmed, "and while we're waiting for that to come through we're going to do an internet search to see how many stores there are in a thirty-mile radius that sells disposable cell phones and prepaid wireless minutes." I thought that was a reasonable radius to begin our quest.

Dorchester groaned unhappily. "Do you know how many places that will be? Every grocery store, department store, pharmacy, dollar store, and convenience store. There will be dozens of them."

I scoffed at him, but he got the final laugh when it turned out there were over a hundred places in the radius that sold disposable phones and prepaid minute cards. "Call Whitworth and have him meet us at the station. We'll split the list in thirds to get them all done. We'll show Broadman's photo around to see if anyone recognizes him."

Dorchester called Whitworth and asked him to meet us at the station. By the time we arrived, he'd already printed off the list of stores and was sorting them by area. I sent him toward Columbus, Dorchester toward Dayton, and I took off toward the Cincinnati area. On my way out, I stopped by the desk of Sergeant Sonia

Dawkins, who acted as our IT department. I asked her to run the call lists for all victims, besides Robertson since he didn't have a phone, to see if we could flag any commonly dialed numbers between them. Once we identified the numbers, we could match them up to their owners and see if we could at least pinpoint the phone number Broadman might've been using. We would nail his ass if he fucked up one time and paid with a credit card.

"I have the software to do it, but it might not happen as quickly as you'd like. It just depends on the volume of phone calls on their logs. It could take a few days," Sonia said.

"I know you'll do your best," I told her before I headed out.

I decided to start at the furthest point and work my way back. I figured Broadman was smart enough not to buy the damn phone and prepaid minute cards close to home, but I wasn't sure how far he'd go out of his way to cover his tracks. The other concern was hitting the right store at the right time, or I could end up at the same store he used but not know it because I talked to people working during the wrong shift.

A few hours later, I hadn't learned anything about Broadman's cell phone purchasing habits, but I learned some other interesting things. Carver's gas station on Old State Route 349 served the best hot dogs, Jackson's out on Highway 92 had chocolate chip cookies that *almost* rivaled Josh's, the Walmart on Higgins Road sold a larger variety of lube than I expected to see and nifty little vibrating finger sex toys. Most importantly I discovered that McCaskells on Route 548 sold heartburn tablets pretty cheap for when the things I ate earlier didn't digest so well.

I popped a few in my mouth and chased them down with a long drink from a bottle of water while I waited for Dorchester to answer his phone. "Any luck?" I asked when he answered.

"Nope. You?" he inquired. I told him all about my findings, minus the sex toys and lube. "I can do you one better," he said smugly. "The walking tacos at D'Angelos in Burtontown are the bomb. I ate three."

"What the hell is a walking taco?" I asked. My Hispanic mother never fed me anything of the sort, and I wanted to know if I missed out on something.

"It's a small bag of Doritos or Fritos mixed with taco meat, cheese, lettuce, tomatoes, and sour cream. They're delicious," he said. It did sound rather interesting, but I was confident that anything my mother made was far superior. Nonetheless, I thought it might be fun to eat walking tacos on a night where Josh worked late, and neither of us wanted a big meal.

"Well, I know where you can get heartburn meds dirt cheap if you need them later," I offered.

"Iron stomach," Dorchester replied. "I'm about to lose cell phone range in about a quarter of a mile. I'll check in with you in a bit."

"Sounds good."

I hit the button on my steering wheel to disconnect the call just as a familiar teal convertible with silver racing stripes zoomed past the parking lot. *Well, what do we have here?* I put my car in drive and hit the switches to turn on my lights and siren as I pulled onto the road. The convertible top was down, so I easily saw Josh's reflection in the rearview mirror when he looked into it in surprise. His sunglasses hid his eyes from me, but I saw his smile bloom across his face.

He was laughing by the time he pulled over. I had a hard time keeping a serious expression on my face as I approached his vehicle. Hell, it had been years since I'd pulled someone over for a routine violation. I figured it was like riding a bike and was prepared to go through the normal routine until Josh lowered his sunglasses and I could see the orneriness shining in his hazel eyes.

"Did I do something bad, Detective?" he asked breathily. "Are you going to break out your cuffs and dickstick?" He batted his eyes and licked his luscious lips.

"Well, I hadn't fucking planned on it, but I have to say I'm mightily tempted, young man," I replied. "I think maybe you were driving a little fast on these back country roads. I'd like to see you slow it down a bit since you're precious cargo."

"Awww, isn't that sweet?" he replied. "What's the likelihood I can talk you into coming home early and playing naughty cop with me?"

"I'd say your chances look damn good," I replied honestly. I had worked through all but my last ten stores. "I should be home in about an hour unless something breaks in this case."

"Great, I'll get dinner started in about forty-five minutes then," Josh replied.

I braced my hands on the side of his car and leaned in for a quick kiss, not giving a shit what any onlookers might think when they drove past. "I got a surprise for you," I said, thinking about the little vibrating fingers and lube.

"I love surprises," he said.

"No you don't," I reminded him. Josh liked to be in control and absolutely hated surprises.

"I do when they come from you," he amended.

"This one will bring us both pleasure," I promised him.

"Detective Dirty Talker, did you stop at a sex toy store?" he asked hopefully.

"No, Walmart," I responded.

"*Walmart?*" Josh asked in disbelief.

"Trust me; I found things there I never expected to find." I waggled my eyebrows at him. "Slow it down, Sunshine." I bumped my fist on his car door and took a step back. "I love you."

"Love you too."

He zoomed off before I even made it back to my car. Knowing the fun time I had ahead of me at home helped me get through the last stores on my list. I came up empty at all my stops, but hoped that either Whitworth or Dorchester had better luck. I had just turned onto my street when a call came through my stereo system. I could tell by the number on the display that it was the police station.

I hit the answer button and said, "Detective Wyatt."

"Detective Wyatt, I found something you need to see," Sergeant Dawkins said. "It really can't wait until the morning. I called Captain Reardon first, and he requested that you report to the station immediately."

"I'm on my way," I said without hesitation. I decided to wait and call Josh once I knew how late I'd be home. Could be a long meeting or a short one; I wouldn't know until I got there. Either way, I knew whatever Sonia discovered was huge if she called the captain back to the station.

# TWELVE

## Josh

I HAD BEEN NERVOUS ABOUT RETURNING TO THE NEWS STATION. I was embarking on a solo career and, although my anxiety wasn't at panic-inducing levels, I was a bit of a wreck. It didn't help when the producer, Cindy Rollins, pulled me into her office the moment I arrived.

"How was your vacation?" she asked.

"Are you just making small talk before you lower the boom on me?" I asked suspiciously.

"No, I'm asking how your vacation was after such a sweet and romantic proposal," Cindy said patiently then added a reassuring smile.

"Oh, okay then," I said in relief. "We had an amazing trip, and I returned home to some very exciting news. I learned that my best friend is also a best-selling author." I smiled when I thought about his budding relationship with Kyle and Meredith falling in love with Harley. "I can't remember a time when all the people I love were so happy."

"Best-selling author, huh?" Cindy said, her brilliant dark eyes came alive as she thought of an idea. "You think he'd like to do an interview to promote his book?"

"I doubt it, but I'll ask him." I was done making decisions for my friends. I'd overstepped with Chaz when I attempted to set him up with Dr. Delicious, and I wasn't doing it again, even if I had only love and good intentions in my heart.

Cindy nodded and said, "Let me know if he's interested." She placed her arms on top of her desk and smiled professionally. I could tell that our niceties were over and it was time to get to work. Cindy proceeded to outline what she wanted to accomplish with my weekly segments that would air throughout the week. The goal was to film three segments every Monday that would air on Monday, Wednesday, and Friday of each week. Monday would be about health and fitness regimens for hair, skin, and nails. Wednesday would be about testing new products that were out on the market, and Friday would be fun stuff like makeovers. "As structured as it all sounds, I want you to run with it and be yourself. I want your honest thoughts on items you're testing and have fun with the Friday makeovers. In fact, I want to be your first Friday makeover."

"Uhhhhh," I said, not sure it was a good idea.

"Stop, you're going to be fine, and we'll have fun. I'm not always so uptight," Cindy said with an exaggerated eye roll.

"I don't think you're uptight at all," I assured her. "It's just that you already know how to perfectly balance glam and business. You don't need my help." I wasn't kissing ass either, Cindy knew her shit.

"Okay, fine. You can do my hair and makeup as if I was about to get my groove on at the club. We'll film it last, and you can paint my face like I'm about to paint the town. And who knows, maybe I will," Cindy said.

"Yeah, okay," I agreed, getting excited about the prospect. "That will be fun. Are there any color schemes you don't like?" I asked, making sure we didn't waste the crew's time later.

"Yellow," she replied.

"Got it," I responded, although I thought the color would look beautiful against her dark skin. "I'll see you in a few hours then."

I left Cindy's office feeling a little better than when I first arrived. I wasn't sure about the source of my anxiety because everyone on the crew had been very welcoming to me—well, except the hair and makeup gal who got offended when I said I'd do my own for the show. *I mean, hello, what is it that I do for a living?* There was one other person, a very popular news anchor who gave off vibes that she didn't like me very much.

Her disdain for me brought out my inner bitch, and I acted extra campy when she was around in case her dislike was due to my sexuality. I thought that someone with that hair color should be a little less judgmental of everyone else. The orangey-red dye her stylist used made her skin look sallow. That color might work on someone else, or a restaurant clown, whose face wasn't constantly screwed into insta-bitch the minute the camera panned away, but it didn't work for her.

Of course, it didn't help my cause when I said her constant scowling would cause wrinkles and recommended a good rejuvenating cream. Imagine my surprise when the same woman threw open her arms to welcome me like a long lost relative she loved and hadn't seen in decades. "Josh, honey, you're back."

"Like a bad case of herpes, Joyce," I told her.

"Oh, you're so damn funny." She gripped my biceps when she pulled back from the hug and looked into my eyes. "We missed you while you were away. I didn't know how dull it was around here until you came along. You're so sparkly and vibrant in a room filled with boring gray people."

"Just call me Sparkles," I said, then narrowed my eyes as a thought hit me. "You've been using the cream I told you about."

"Yeah," Joyce said nodding happily. "It's like a miracle cream!"

"I'm glad you like it, Joyce." I bit my tongue, wondering if I could press my luck a little further and tell her how wretched that hair color was for her complexion. "Can I be frank about something else?" I asked her.

"You hate my hair," she replied.

"Well…"

"I know, it's terrible, but I'm not sure what to do," Joyce said. "I go to the same hairstylist as my mother, and she uses the same color on both of us. I end up looking just like my mother, and although I love the woman dearly, that's not a compliment. This hair color is awful on me," she said, stating the obvious.

"Do you want to be my makeover for next week? I have one scheduled for today already. We'd film it on Monday, and it would air on Friday. What do you think?" I asked her.

"I think you're a lifesaver and I was a horrible uptight bitch to you when you first arrived," she replied. "Forgive me?"

"Of course," I said naturally. I saw the camera guy waving to get my attention and knew he was ready to film my first segment. "Can we talk about it later? Pete is ready to film."

"Sure, sweetie," Joyce said then went on her merry way.

We've all had days where we felt like Alice tumbling down the rabbit hole. Sometimes what you found at the bottom was a wonderful thing and other times not. Luckily, my conversation with Joyce fell into the first category. The first segment wasn't that exciting. I talked about vitamins, minerals, and the way our eating habits affected our skin, hair, and nails. I tried to jazz it up with my humor and sass to keep it from being a drab segment. It must've worked because Pete laughed at my antics behind the camera.

We took a quick break, and I changed clothes. I didn't want people to think I wore the same adorable ensemble three days a week. I chose a more relaxed, hip outfit for the second segment to review the products sent to the station.

"What do we have here?" I asked excitedly. "I love this soft pink and black color scheme for the packaging and the font used for the lettering. It's both elegant and edgy. Let's take a look at what's inside." I pulled out a large contouring palette that offered four different highlighters and shades. "At first sight, this is a gorgeous palette with a great variety to use for all skin tones, which I think is important. Let's check out the pigment for each color."

I got a few different brushes out of my kit and put a sample of each color on the back of one hand. "Gorgeous," I said. Then on the back of the other hand. I used two complimentary shades and showed how well they blended. "They blend beautifully too. How much is this kit?" I picked up the box and saw the price. "Fifty dollars, folks. I know it sounds like a lot, but you can expect to pay double for bigger name brands and not get nearly as pigmented colors that blend this well. Besides, you get eight colors, so that's a great bargain."

I tested a few other products for my segment—some were okay, but none wowed me as much as the contouring palette. In between filming the second and final segment, I had lunch and ordered a few of the palettes online to use in the salon because we received a lot of requests to do full makeup for weddings and other special events. In fact, since it was June we were already in full swing with weddings. Cindy told me I could keep the test palette and I planned to put it to use immediately.

Cindy was a hell of a good sport, and we shared a lot of laughs while we changed her makeup from a day at the office to a night on the town. She literally let her hair down, and let me tell you; she was a show stopper!

"Girl, you need to call your friends and go out tonight," I said. "Don't waste this hair and makeup."

"I agree," Cindy replied, looping her arm around my neck. "I can see why Gabe calls you Sunshine, you know." Her remark caught me off guard because even though she was always friendly, Cindy was the epitome of professionalism. She rarely remarked on anything too personal. "You light the world up around you."

"That's what Gabe says," I replied, then nibbled on my bottom lip like I did when I got nervous or emotional.

"It's true." She gave me an extra squeeze then dropped her arm. "We'll see you next week."

I put the top down on the way home and had my music blaring. I loved the feel of the wind whipping through my hair and the happiness of a great day humming through my body. The damn police siren going on behind me startled the shit out of me, but then I saw it was my man.

Damn him for talking dirty to me and then not following me home right away to do the wicked things his eyes promised me. I wasn't angry with him because I knew if he was saying "later" to sex that something serious was going on. Still, I expected him home in the time frame he gave me. As often as I told myself not to borrow trouble, I found myself worrying when he wasn't home on time or called to say he'd be late. Before Emory's prediction, I would've handled the situation better.

I couldn't do a damn thing but wait unless I wanted to call and look like a nagging husband. Animals sense when their human is stressed, and that crazy-ass bird that I loved so much was no exception.

"Sugartits! Sugartits!" he squawked while I was trying to do yoga to calm my frigging nerves. "Little Daddy! Sugartits!"

"Dirty Bird!"

"Sugartits!"

I laughed so hard that I nearly fell out of my downward dog position. "Are you saying I'm getting man boobs?" I asked Savage.

"Talking to the bird is one thing, but expecting him to answer back is another," Gabe said, startling me.

"Oh! I didn't know you were home yet. I, um…"

"Was laughing so hard at your ridiculous bird that you didn't hear me come in," he finished for me with a faint smile. It was then that I saw the stress lines surrounding his eyes and lips.

"What happened, babe?" I rose to my feet and went to him. "You were supposed to be home a few hours ago. I was worried but didn't want to look like a nag so I didn't call you. What happened after Detective Dirty Talker walked away from me on the side of the road?"

"I shouldn't talk about it," Gabe said, but I could tell that's what he wanted to do.

"You listen to me, Gabriel. I know I seem flighty at times and my salon is a hot den of gossip, but I would never betray your trust. Sit down, let me grab you a cold beer, and you can tell me what the hell happened. You always call me when you're going to be late," I said on my way to the refrigerator. "This must be a big deal."

"Thanks, Sunshine," he said softly when I sat beside him. He accepted the beer and took a long drink. "Fuck, what a day."

"You were in such a good mood," I said, running my fingers through his silky, dark hair that still needed a trim.

"Sometimes, you fucking hate the answers when you find them, Sunshine. Fucking hate them. You start to question everything you know and everything you ever believed." I'd never heard Gabe sound so distraught and it worried me. I knew he'd tell me when he was ready so I continued to massage his scalp and wait while he drank his beer. "Prosecutor Buxton needed us to find a motive for Broadman. She wanted hardcore evidence and not supposition so that she could get a confession out of Broadman rather than go to trial."

"You guys already tried to get a confession, right?" I asked, a little confused.

"Yeah, but a prosecuting attorney has a lot more clout than a cop," Gabe said. "She wanted enough evidence to threaten him with the death penalty. We had a meeting about it last week and came up with a reasonable motive for the crimes that Broadman committed. Proving it wasn't going to be easy. We needed a miracle."

"And you got it," I said, "but sort of wish you hadn't."

"We were right, it was all about the land," Gabe told me. "He knew the casino wasn't going to happen the first time around but worried that it would the second time, especially with a new player."

"Nate?" I asked.

"Yeah," he agreed. "Broadman hired the son of his childhood friend to try and scare Nate away from buying the land. He couldn't be too specific about his threats for fear that Spizer, who had introduced the two men during a conference call, might get suspicious. This kid was busted for hacking into his college computers to change his grades, and his family hired Broadman—an old friend—to get him out of trouble. That bastard put a bullet in the kid's head once he was no longer useful, Josh. He was only twenty years old."

"I'm so sorry, Gabe." He didn't acknowledge me, so I wasn't sure he even heard me. Then he squeezed my thigh, and I knew he was just processing what to say next.

"He killed Robertson because he figured it was just a matter of time before he sold the land to someone else. First, it was going to be a subdivision until Broadman convinced the older man that his nephews were going to get paid bonuses from the deal. Robertson backed out. He figured that was the end of it, but no, the casino deal was next. He decided not to take a chance and killed that elderly man then burned his house down in hopes that we didn't find the letter from that Larkin guy from McCarren Consortium."

"What about Spizer?" I asked.

"He wasn't willing to risk Spizer piecing the puzzle together and sending him to prison once the farmer's death was ruled a homicide. He went to his old friend's house and killed him, but dressed it up to look like a suicide. I know why Broadman wanted Spizer to write the confession, but I don't know why Spizer agreed to do it. He had to know he was going to die anyway so why hurt his wife even more?"

"Maybe he was hoping to buy time and prayed for a miracle," I offered.

"Maybe," Gabe said, but I could tell he wasn't convinced. "I think it was more like he truly felt responsible since he was the one who introduced Broadman and Nate. His note said he was responsible for their deaths, not that he killed them. Broadman probably assured him that no one else would get hurt. Maybe he even threatened to harm Spizer's wife if he didn't go along with it. Either way, Broadman talked him into writing that note then killed him."

"Sounds like you got your confession, Gabe."

"Yeah, I did, but not until after I had the rug ripped out from beneath my feet." Gabe shook his head as if he still didn't comprehend it all. "No matter how many times I connected the dots, there was always one part that didn't make sense to me. Nate said that his harassment increased once he went to the police about the threats. Why? How'd the person harassing him know that he went to the police? Was he followed? Did the hacker also implant a virus that let him track Nate's email communications? Or worse?"

"Worse?" I asked because what could be… "Oh."

"I didn't want to believe it, Sunshine. I asked Sergeant Dawkins to cross-reference phone numbers on the victim's call logs to see if I could prove that Broadman was contacting them on a burner phone. He wasn't calling them from his home, office, or known cell phone, so we suspected that he found an alternative method to contact them. Dorchester, Whitworth, and I all went to stores that sold phones and prepaid minutes to try and find a witness that could confirm our theory. None of us found the right store or the right clerk, so we thought we struck out," Gabe said dazedly.

"But Sonia didn't strike out, did she?" I asked. She'd always been a girl with a sharp brain and IT skills to match.

"She isolated the burner number and obtained a warrant for the records while we were out in the field. She ran all the phone numbers, and one came back as the cell phone for a Cincinnati police officer." Gabe was staring sightlessly across the room, his eyes not focusing on anything as his brain struggled to comprehend. He'd once told me there was nothing worse than a dirty cop. I could tell his disappointment was on a personal level.

"Paul?" I asked. His only answer was a brief nod.

Gabe blinked a few times then turned his head to look at me. "Captain Reardon contacted Internal Affairs, and he was brought in for questioning. Paul said he had no knowledge of Broadman's intentions when he passed along the information confirming that Nate had filed harassment charges with the police department. Broadman and Paul met and hooked up a few times at Nate's club and had gotten chummy after Nate and Broadman first met regarding the casino. He said he knew nothing else about the situation, but I'm not sure I believe him."

"Wow," I said, not believing it either.

"In light of the evidence against him, Broadman accepted a plea deal to avoid death row," Gabe told me. "It's finally over and Nate Turner, Owen Smithson, Lawrence Robertson, and Rick Spizer will have justice."

"I'm so sorry about Paul, Gabe." There was a part of me that was glad he was out of the picture, but it was teeny. "Thank you for trusting me with the story before it was released to the public."

"Um," he said softly. "You haven't had the television on, have you?"

"No, why?"

"It already broke an hour ago on the news. I figured you

would've seen it while you were watching your segment on the news," Gabe said with a crooked smile. I pinched him hard enough to make him yelp. "I realized my mistake once I got home," he said, rubbing his aching skin.

"I don't watch my segments," I scoffed. "How much of a diva do you think I am?" Gabe smiled for the first time that night. I was so relieved to see it that I almost let him off the hook. "I can't believe you acted like I was getting some advance scoop with your 'I shouldn't talk about it' speech."

"I said that I shouldn't, not that I couldn't," Gabe clarified.

"Oh God!" I exclaimed dramatically. "You know what this means?" I asked. "Another Internal Affairs interrogation if they find out about your fling with Paul! How will I go out in public?"

"It was one time," Gabe groused, "not a fling."

Later, I'd fuss over him and do my damnedest to make it all better, but right then he needed to be jerked back to reality. Our reality, where everything was fair game. My IA remark was exactly the wisecrack he needed because, in spite of all the heartache and disappointment he felt, Gabe looked at me like I was the brightest spot in his world, reminding me that I was his sunshine.

# THIRTEEN

## Gabe

It was amazing how quickly things moved when you had some money and a bit of notoriety—well, Josh had both; I just had some money. He disagreed, of course, and pointed out that several newspapers ran articles about the case and had used my image in the photos. "Above the fold is big shit in the newspaper world," Josh told me, reminding me of his years working for the local paper while in high school. In addition to print articles, there had been several news broadcasts and even some interviews with me. "I'm not the only one with a face the camera loves," Josh had said.

I scoffed at him, but I was grateful we got our finances situated to accomplish owning both properties as painlessly as possible. It happened in a matter of weeks. On July 4th, we sat on the balcony of our second-story bedroom and watched the fireworks explode in the night sky. For such a small community, they set off an impressive number of fireworks in a field behind the high school at the edge of town.

The only thing more beautiful than seeing the fireworks burst in the sky was the orgasm face Josh made after I pulled him into our bedroom, pushed him against the wall, and fucked him hard until we had explosions of our own. Afterward, I lowered us to the floor and held him tight, loving the feeling of still being inside of him with his arms and legs still clinging to me like he couldn't stand to let me go.

We kissed long and tenderly, and I touched him everywhere my hands could reach until my dick hardened again. Josh pushed me to my back and loved me slow and gentle. He never took his eyes from mine, not even when his climax hit him, which was solid proof of how far he'd come in less than a year. He didn't want to hide his emotions and thoughts from me anymore; he opened his heart, body, and soul to me. I was the luckiest man on the planet to have found him.

During our financial planning meetings, we made sure certain funds would be available to renovate the home and make it truly ours, as well as remodel our former living space into a tranquil spa area for the salon. Within the next month, Josh was hardcore renovating the mansion. In reality, it wasn't a mansion; it was just a really large house built on three or four plots so that it occupied a large corner of the block.

"We need to call our new home something besides 'the mansion' or 'Georgia's mansion,'" Josh said one day when we were looking at fabric swatches for curtains. I wasn't even surprised when he spoke my private thoughts out loud since it happened so frequently. To be clear, Josh was looking at fabric swatches, and I was trying to check my phone for updates on the baseball game discreetly. "Gabe," Josh said in resignation, "just play the game on the MLB at-bat app so Marty and the Cowboy can keep you posted on what's going on with the game. I know that you don't want to look at these curtain swatches, baby. I just want you to feel like this is *our* home, which means I don't want fabrics or furniture that you think are fussy."

"Can I be honest with you, Sunshine?" I asked. The mildly annoyed look he threw me was comical. "None of that stuff matters to me. Guys have been saying this since the first cavewoman—or caveman," I added so he knew that I didn't apply gender roles to decorating, "rearranged rocks to sit on to better see the landscape or dragged in sticks to make their cave more festive. Some guys care *a lot* and others couldn't care less what they sit on or where. There's only one thing I want to see in this home every single day, and that's you." I leaned down and dotted his forehead with a kiss. "I know this is important to you, so I'm making the effort like when we went to the Reds game last week." Of course, Josh spent most of the time staring at the first baseman's ass the entire game. It wasn't much of a sacrifice for him.

"And you want to be rewarded handsomely later," Josh added.

"You wound me, Sunshine. Truly." I could tell he wasn't buying it. "Since when do I have to perform parlor tricks to get laid anyway? Whatever happened to 'you just need to keep breathing, Gabe'? I seem to recall you saying those words to me not that long ago."

"It's still very true," Josh said, but a bit absently as he returned his focus to the swatches. The doorbell rang, and I got up to answer it. "Don't get shot," Josh called out from behind me.

"Funny man," I muttered under my breath before I opened the front door.

"Mr. Roman?" the delivery man asked.

"Not yet, but he's here too." I looked over my shoulder and hollered, "Sunshine, you have a furniture delivery."

"It's the porch furniture," he yelled back. "Just have them unwrap it out there, and I'll set it up when I get done."

"Okay." I looked at the sweaty delivery man who looked a little confused that two men were buying furniture together. "You heard the man," I said, nudging him. "Put it on the porch, unwrap it, and we'll take it from there."

The man nodded silently and returned to where his partner was waiting for him at the back of the truck to help unload. They talked amongst themselves for a minute, and I could tell by the other guy's wide-eyed expression that the guy who came to the door was telling his coworker that they were delivering furniture to a gay couple, although the term used to describe us was probably more colorful, derogatory, or both. In my head, I started thinking of them as Dumb and Dumber because our situation seemed to be more than their simple minds could comprehend. I gave them a cutesy finger wave when they both turned and looked at me once Dumb finished telling Dumber about the situation.

They at least had the decency to at least look embarrassed at being caught. I turned and went back to Josh so the idiots could unload the furniture and get the fuck off my property. "Not Mr. Roman, yet?" Josh asked when I reached him.

"You heard that?" I asked.

"I'm fine-tuning my hearing in preparation to become a father to your heathen kids," he said, never looking away from his task. "I can't wait to see what the furniture looks like once it's set up." Remodeling progressed at a fast pace once they handed us the keys. There were only a few minor things that needed to be fixed before we moved in. Josh wanted the space completed and ready to go so that we had one place in our lives free of chaos. "I can tell you what it won't look like; there will be no dark wicker furniture with blue and gray striped cushions," he said, referencing the furniture Emory described in his premonition.

"That's for sure," I agreed. We bought white wicker furniture with solid teal cushions, and watercolor printed accent pillows. I didn't think that I was in any real danger, but why borrow trouble? "Let's talk about names while we figure out what curtains you–*we*–want to hang up in our new home. The house needs a new name, and so do we."

"You don't want us to keep the names given at birth?" Josh asked. He seemed surprised. "It's the name printed on your diploma, your employee records, and the thick file IA has on you. I'm kind of surprised you want to go through all the hassle to change your name."

I ignored his IA jab and went straight to the heart of the issue. "You don't want to change your name?" I asked, and yes, I sounded a little disappointed. I couldn't disguise the fact that I wanted my name attached to Josh, I wanted it all.

Josh shrugged. "It's one of many things that I never gave much thought to before you came along. I never saw myself getting married or having children, so I didn't waste time or energy thinking about those two things," he said casually.

"And now?" I asked

Josh put down the fabric swatch he was looking at and gave me his full attention. "And now I want to share every part of my life with you and want the same in return. I think we should hyphenate our names like all the cool kids do these days."

"Like I add your last name onto mine and you do the same with yours?" I asked.

"Mr. Roman-Wyatt and Mr. Wyatt-Roman," Josh said, then tipped his head and pursed his lip as he considered it. "Too busy," he said. "It's like someone going crazy with stripes and florals in their design." He acted like his statement should clarify things for me. Josh could tell that I wasn't getting it, so he explained further. "You can have a mix of florals and stripes, but one needs to act as

126

the primary, and one needs to act as the complementary accent. Otherwise your poor eyes don't know where to focus. Our names need to be the same, so we're either both Roman-Wyatt or Wyatt-Roman. You decide, Gabe."

"Me? Why do I have to be the one to decide?" I asked.

"Because I have a million other decisions to make on the house design then the salon remodel, and let's not forget that little thing called a wedding that is taking place in six weeks!" His pitch rose an octave higher with each word spoken.

I threw my hands up in surrender. "Roman-Wyatt it is," I announced. Then I smiled because it was truly going to happen. I looked back down at the swatches on the work table set in the middle of the living room. "I don't like this busy number right here," I said, hoping that he found it helpful if I told him the things that I didn't like.

"Yeah, that wasn't a contender and was in the pile of 'no way' swatches. These," he gestured to the five other stacks of fabric, "are the contenders. Would you please go through them and tell me which ones offend you as much as that paisley print did?"

I tried, I honestly did, but after a while, they all started looking alike. Oh my God! How many shades of brown, gray, and blue are there? I ruled several out that I wouldn't line the bottom of Diva's cat litter box with let alone hang from a wall or use on a pillow.

"Why don't you go check to make sure they delivered all the furniture I ordered. I think I'd like to have dinner out there tonight before we go back to the salon." We'd already started to refer to the other house as the salon and our new one as home. "Think up a name for our house while you're at it since it's not a mansion and Georgia isn't living with us, or at least I don't think she is," Josh added. I snapped my fingers and held one up as the name occurred to me. "Something besides Charlotte," he called after me.

I walked out on the porch with a smile on my face because he was on to me. That smile slid off my face as I stared in shock at the furniture they delivered. "Fuck!" I knew Josh was going to see that dark wicker furniture with the blue and gray striped cushions and freak the fuck out. "Fuck! Fuck! Fuck!"

"You sound like Savage," Josh said, stepping onto the porch. "Fuck!" he exclaimed too when he saw the delivered furniture wasn't what we ordered, but it was exactly what Emory had described in his premonition. Josh covered his mouth with both hands and tears filled his eyes.

"Don't," I told him, knowing where his mind had taken him. "I'll call the furniture store and have them come back and remove it." I pulled Josh tight against my chest. "It doesn't mean that something bad is going to happen to me, Sunshine. I promise you that I'm not going anywhere."

"I was stupid to think that I could thwart fate by simply picking the different furniture for our porch. Just like Emory thought he could prevent the vision with Jonathon from coming true by cutting his hair." Josh laughed dryly. "This furniture wasn't even an available option, Gabe. I thought that Emory's vision might've been far into the future and that I'd have more time…"

"I. Am. Not. Going. Anywhere. I am going to marry you in the flower garden in the backyard of this house while staring into your beautiful eyes. We're going to build a life here filled with kids, pets, arguments, make-up kisses, and so much love it makes people gag to look at us." I tilted his head back so he could look into my eyes and see how serious I was. "No one is taking me away from you. We're going to have a wonderful life together. Just you wait and…"

My words were cut off by the sound of a car door closing. I stepped out of Josh's embrace and turned to see who had arrived. I didn't recognize the dark sedan parked in our driveway or the man in the suit walking toward us. Josh tried to evade my grip so he could step in front of me. "It's okay, Sunshine." Although I didn't know the guy, he carried himself like a lawman.

"Gabriel Wyatt?" the man asked as he approached the porch.

"That's me," I said, still wrestling to keep Josh beside me instead of in front of me. I loved his passion, but no way in hell I'd ever let him take a bullet destined for me. "What can I do for you?"

"My name is Ryder Pinelli and I'm a private investigator from Cincinnati." He held out his hand, and I shook it.

"Can I see some identification?" I asked, unwilling to take his word for it.

"Absolutely," he replied, reaching into his jacket pocket. "Here you go." He flipped open a rectangular wallet that had his picture ID on one side and his PI license on the other. "I've been hired by your birth mother to find you, sir." Honestly, I think I would've been less surprised had he pulled out a gun and aimed it at me.

"Her family used to be good friends with mine," I told the man. "Why not call them instead of hiring a PI?"

"Mrs. Gutierrez worried that they wouldn't approve of her requesting to meet you after all this time, so she hired me. She asked me to give you this letter and let you know the decision is all up to you and she'll not force herself into your life or try to contact you again." Pinelli held out an envelope toward me, but I could only stare at it.

"Thank you, Mr. Pinelli," Josh said, easing the envelope from the man's fingers. "I'll make sure he reads it when he's ready."

"Very well," Pinelli said formally. "Have a nice evening."

I said nothing as the man returned to his car and drove away. Hell, I don't think I even moved until Josh slid his fingers between mine and tugged me over to the wicker furniture we didn't even want. "Wow," I finally said after several minutes of quiet.

"This feels like an episode of *The Twilight Zone*," Josh said. "Hey, maybe that was the man in Emory's vision. He wasn't from your past, but he brought news *from* your past. Maybe the colors and auras that Emory saw were more about what the man carried inside him, not what he directed at you."

I could tell how much he wanted that to be true. Hell, I wanted it to be true too. I wanted to get on with living and loving without the added worry that someone was out to get me. "Maybe," I said, but I didn't sound too convincing. I leaned back on the sofa, wrapped my arm around Josh's shoulders and pulled him against my chest.

"Are you going to open that letter?" Josh asked me softly.

"One day," I said honestly. "This was something I never dreamed about or ever expected. I have a family that loves me, and I never wanted to belong to a different family. My life changes the minute I open the envelope and how can I know it'll be for the better?"

"No one could know that," Josh said, then snorted. "Maybe Emory, but he's all hit and miss with his visions. How frustrating that must be for him."

"I'll give this the regard it deserves, but not until I'm ready. I want to talk to my parents first and find out how they feel about it. I don't want them to worry about losing me, Sunshine. They lost one son, and they don't need to worry about losing another."

"That's very thoughtful of you, but Martina and Al would never want to hold back your happiness. They know damn well that you're *their* boy."

"You always know the right thing to say," I told Josh softly.

"It's a gift," he boasted then laughed a little. "I'm not going to call the furniture company and complain, Gabe."

"You're not?" I asked. Josh was terrified when he saw it sitting on our porch.

"Nope, this set is much prettier, and it seems like it's fated to be ours," he told me.

"Yeah, let's not tempt fate," I agreed.

We sat there quietly for a while, neither of us saying much. Even though my mind was a million miles away, my heart was right where I left it—tucked safely in the hands of the man nestled up beside me.

# FOURTEEN

## Josh

TWO WEEKS LATER THE ENVELOPE FROM GABE'S BIRTH MOTHER still sat on top of our dresser. Every morning I would watch Gabe stare at it while he dressed and every night I'd catch him doing the same thing when he got ready for bed. Every morning and every night during those two weeks I just wanted to cry for the anguish he felt but never revealed. It killed me to keep silent, but Gabe had shown me nothing but patience while I came to terms with my past and my feelings for him. I'd do the same for him or die trying, which was a possibility because I felt like I was going to implode from the buildup of pressure inside me.

He spent a lot of time in his head, and I wondered what the hell was going on in his beautiful brain. Why was he so afraid to open the letter? Did he think it would be disloyal to Al and Martina? Didn't he want to know if he had brothers or sisters? Was that what upset him? Was he torn up inside because he was curious about potential siblings and thought it was disloyal to Dylan? Did he worry that he wouldn't like his birth mother?

Outwardly, it appeared that he was taking things in stride, but I knew better. He was a man who didn't stress over little things but suddenly they got under his skin. We went over to our new, unnamed home one night after work to check on the progress since we were supposed to move in the following week. I noticed that the light fixtures hung in the master bathroom weren't the ones that I ordered and Gabe's response when I mentioned it stunned me.

"I'll take care of this right now," he had said angrily, pulling his cell phone out of his pocket. "Andy needs to pay closer attention to these details. You were very specific on the fixtures you wanted. Fuck! You printed a picture of them from the internet and circled the item number for him. How much easier does he need it?"

"Gabe," I said patiently.

"These aren't the fixtures you asked for, and you shouldn't have to live with them, Sunshine."

It was all I could do not to laugh over his outrage. I mean, hearing my cutesy pet name said in a snarly voice was hilarious. It would be like angrily shouting "I love you" at a person. The irritated, scowling expression on his face was just too much, and the dam broke. My laughter echoed loudly in the bathroom, but instead of breaking him out of his funk as I had hoped, it seemed to frustrate him further.

"I fail to see what's so funny about shitty craftsmanship and poor professionalism," he said haughtily, which only made me laugh harder until tears ran down my face and I clutched my stom-ach. "Well, I'm waiting." Fuck me; Gabe was hilarious when he was in a snit!

I dug deep and found my composure after several minutes. "Darling," I said, earning a scornful, raised brow at the endearment that never slid from my lips unless I was describing something I wanted to buy. "What was the only thing you asked for when we discussed renovating this bathroom?" I asked him. I placed my hands on my hips and pinned him with a look that said I meant business. "The *only* thing," I stressed.

"Enough built-in shelves in the fancy tiled shower to hold all your grooming products *and* lube," he said somewhat defensive-ly. "Body wash burns when used as lube," Gabe said as if I hadn't learned this fact already long before I met him.

"What do we have in the custom-built shower?" I asked him.

"Jets to massage your body all over," he said defiantly.

"And?" I prompted

He blew out a frustrated breath and said, "Plenty of shelves for lube. I fail to see the point."

"The point is that the only thing you cared about was a place for the lube and you got it. You had no idea that the fixtures were wrong until I said something and I didn't even say it angrily. It was more of a 'huh; those aren't the light fixtures I ordered' kind of thing. To tell the truth, I like these fixtures better than the ones I picked out. So, put down the cell phone over there on the counter and let's test out the jets in our new shower."

"Now? The bathroom isn't finished," Gabe said, but he was al-ready pulling his shirt over his head. "How are we going to dry off?"

"It's ninety-nine point nine percent finished." I went over to the linen closet and opened it to reveal two folded towels and a bottle of our favorite lubricant. I stashed it there the day before in prepa-ration for the big reveal.

"You think of everything." A wicked smile spread across his

face as he shimmied out of his jeans.

Our shouts of pleasure echoed all over the bathroom and probably the entire second floor of that area of the home, since there wasn't any furniture or area rugs to act as a buffer. He rode me hard enough against the glass wall that we knew that the craftsmanship had indeed not been shitty. It was constructed to withstand a furious fuck. Gabe was loose as hell after that and I had hoped it was the break in tension he needed, but the next morning it had returned.

I knew we couldn't go on pretending there wasn't a giant elephant in the room but I wasn't sure what the hell to say or do. I wanted so badly to talk to someone and get their advice on how to help Gabe, but it felt wrong to talk about his struggle to anyone. I decided to just be patient and understanding while he decided what to do.

My salvation came in the form of a phone call the very next day. Brook said that she'd received a call from a friend who ran a bird rescue organization who was in possession of a bird who needed a forever home. Birds like Savage were rare and were often illegally brought into our country and sold. The owners often didn't want the expense or hassle of taking care of them properly, and many died. Savage had been well-loved, if not brainwashed with filth, but was left alone after his owner died. The bird that Brook was calling me about wasn't as fortunate as Savage.

"She's beautiful, Josh. Her name is Sassy, and she's a scarlet macaw. I think she'll get along with our boy just fine," Brook said. "Would you like me to text you some pictures?"

"Nope, I just need the address," I said into the phone. I knew Sassy was our girl the minute that Brook said her name.

The next day I drove ninety minutes north to pick up a surprise for two of my guys. Gabe had found his Sassy, and it was time that Savage found his too. It was my early night at the salon, so I headed out before Gabe got home from work. I left him a note that said I was on a secret mission for a surprise and would call him when I was on my way back. True to my word, I called when I was about thirty minutes away.

"Where'd you go for this surprise? Is it a sexy surprise?" Gabe asked hopefully, his deep voice rumbling out my speakers caused a shiver to work its way down my spine.

"I'm standing at the dildo section at Kinky Kim's," I told him. "Trying to decide if you'd like the Tonsil Tickler model."

"Tonsil Tickler?" he asked in fear.

"You know, it's so long that you can feel it tickling your tonsils when it's…"

"… Yeah, I figured that out, Sunshine."

"'Cause you're a badass detective," I replied.

"Sometimes you don't have to be real bright to figure things out," Gabe replied with a laugh. "So, when can I expect you and your new dildo home?"

"It's your dildo and about twenty-five minutes," I said, adjusting for the time we spent on the phone.

"Dildo! Dildo!" Sassy said from the seat beside me. Here's the deal, she was more articulate with her words. She sounded more human than Savage, and there's very little difference between a female and male bird voice—for lack of a better word. It sounded like I had a dude in the car with me.

"Josh, who's that?" Gabe asked slowly.

"It's your surprise, baby!" I said.

"Take him back because I only want you and I thought you only wanted me. What the hell is going on?" Gabe asked angrily.

"Just trust me, Gabe. I'll see you in less than twenty minutes."

I bet you'll never guess who was waiting for me in the driveway when I pulled in. Gabe stood there with his arms crossed over his broad chest wearing a thunderous expression. A huge smile bloomed across his face when he spied the cage in my passenger seat and the majestic bird inside it. Sassy was a little taller than Savage and mostly a vibrant red with blue and yellow feathers on her wings and tail. She was fucking magnificent, and I fell in love with her the second she blew kisses at me.

"Surprise!" I said, opening the door.

"How? Where?" Gabe just shook his head. Then Sassy made kissy sounds at him, and I swear he melted into a puddle of goo in the driveway. "What's his name?"

"*Her* name is Sassy, and she's a scarlet macaw," I told him.

"She sounds like a boy," Gabe said, clearly confused.

"You're confusing cartoon birds with reality. Sassy's tone is a little different than Savage's, but she articulates her words better and sounds more human. It's odd because usually, the male birds are better talkers than female birds."

"Well, Savage only knows gutter talk, so I'm not sure anyone spent a lot of time teaching him things," Gabe said, reaching in to pull Sassy's cage out of the car. "Hi, Sassy," Gabe said to his new pet because I could tell that she was already bonding with him. She was dancing in her cage and flapping her wings. I couldn't blame her; he made me want to do those things too. "You sure are a pretty girl."

Sassy whistled and blew kisses to him again. "Pretty girl," she repeated. I wondered how long it would be before she called him Big Daddy like Savage did.

"I'm worried how Savage is going to react to her," I said. I'd done some research, and I planned to keep them separated for a while and would let them take their time getting to know one another. Gabe wasn't joking when he said he wanted him to have a warm, tropical-looking room to live. Besides room for his lube, it was his only request. Some people had large aquariums in their living rooms, but we would have a large solarium complete with rainforest sounds. A perfect home for Savage and his new lady friend.

"Savage and Sassy," Gabe said out loud as he led the way up the steps to the back door. "Sounds like some punk rock band or something."

"Suits us perfectly," I said.

"Ready for this?" Gabe asked, pausing at the top of the steps of our apartment.

I nodded but then said, "Wait. We're going to want this on film." I pulled out my phone and walked around Gabe to go first so I could be in a position to film Savage's reaction to seeing Sassy for the first time. I was glad that I had.

Savage raised his head high then swooped it down low and to the left before he swooped back up and then back down to the right. He walked sideways on his perch as if he was trying to get a better look at her. He raised his wings high in the air and pranced on his perch some more. I thought it might be the equivalent to a bird hard-on, but I wasn't sure. Meanwhile, Sassy countered Savage's every move but opposite. When he went high, she went low, but synchronized by the time they were doing the wing dance.

"Look what Big Daddy has," Gabe said, hogging all the fucking credit. I cleared my throat. "Little Daddy went out and got you a friend, so it's his fault if you don't like her."

"Is this what I can expect when we have children?" I asked. "I'll have to be the bad dad, and you get to be the good dad?"

"Probably," Gabe said nonchalantly. "I'll be tired of bad-copping all day, so I will want to be the good dad when I get home." He gave me the boyish grin I loved so much. It had been missing since the private investigator showed up with the envelope. He turned back to his boy, Savage, and said, "Can you say hi to Sassy?"

"Blow me!" Savage squawked.

"That's no way to talk to a lady, Dirty Bird!" Gabe shook his head, admonishing Savage. "Be nice to Sassy."

"Dirty Bird!" Sassy squawked, getting Savage's attention. He did some more head rolling and wing walking back and forth on his perch. "Dirty Bird!" Sassy repeated.

"Sugartits!" Savage fired back.

"Oh man," Gabe said after laughing his ass off. "I'm so glad you're recording this."

"Big Daddy!" Sassy said, and that riled Savage up even more. He didn't want anyone calling Gabe that but him.

"Cumguzzler!" Savage practically screeched.

"Big Daddy!" Sassy repeated.

The confrontation went on for another half hour, which turned out to be one of the funniest times in my life. Gabe smiled and laughed so much that I knew I'd made the right decision to bring Sassy home without discussing it with him. After the birds calmed down and seemed happy to stare at one another through their cages, Gabe pulled me into a tight hug.

"What made you decide to get another bird?" he asked.

I told him the story and added, "I just wanted to do something to put a smile on your face. Besides, Savage is about to spend a lot of time alone, and I worried that he'd get anxious again. Now he has company."

"Makes sense," Gabe replied, nodding his head. "I'm sorry if I've been a bear to live with the last few weeks." He nuzzled his nose against the outer shell of my ear and made me shiver.

"You don't have enough body hair to be called a bear," I told him, earning a sharp slap on my ass. "Besides, you've had a valid reason for being withdrawn."

Gabe pulled back and looked down at me. "You feel like I've withdrawn from you?" he asked somberly.

"I think you've had a lot on your mind, and it's clamoring for your attention, but I'm not implying that you've neglected me, Gabe. You're trying to work through something huge, and I'm trying to give you space and the support you need while you do it."

"Withdrawing from you isn't the answer," Gabe said. I was surprised by how shaken he looked.

"Withdrawn is probably not the right word," I told him. "Distracted might be a better choice." The glower on his face said that it wasn't. "Babe, I'm not upset with you. I didn't mean to make you feel bad. I was trying to make you feel better." I wasn't getting the reaction that I wanted, so I was forced to take desperate measures.

I raised my head high on my neck then swooped it down low to the left, raised it high again then dropped it down low to the right. Still, Gabe didn't crack a smile. I had no choice but to lift my arms up like wings and shuffle back and forth. That finally got him. I added some swear words and continued to do my Savage dance.

"What the fuck are you doing?" Gabe asked breathlessly once he finally stopped laughing.

"It's Savage's mating dance," I told him. "I'm thinking about using it from now on."

"Not if you want me to take you seriously," Gabe said, then chuckled. "Just start pulling off your clothes, and I'll get the hint." He hooked my belt loop and pulled me close "Seriously, I am so sorry that I've not been here a hundred percent. I'm going to fix it right now."

"Yeah?" I asked, thinking I was getting sexy time.

"Yeah." Instead of us both going into our room, Gabe went alone and returned with the envelope that had been weighing down his thoughts. "I'm ready."

"I'll grab beers," I said. "Do we need snacks too?"

"I just need you."

I stopped in my tracks and returned to him. "I'm right here, Gabe."

# FIFTEEN

## Gabe

I BLEW OUT A SHAKY BREATH AS JOSH SAT BESIDE ME ON THE couch. I had no reason to be so nervous; nothing in the letter would change who I was, who I loved, or who loved me. I would still be Al and Martina's son, Josh's fiancé, and a detective for the Blissville Police Department. My parents would still be thrilled that I was marrying the love of my life, Josh would still look at me as if I was the one who created the sun, moon, and stars, and Adrian would be there to razz me over every little thing. Opening the letter shouldn't change anything, yet, it could change everything.

What if my biological father was a bad person? My parents had told me on more than one occasion that my birth mother had been a lively, sweet young lady. They had known her family well, but they knew nothing of the birth father. What if I had been the result of the worst thing that ever happened to her? Were the sins of the father passed onto the son? In my mind, I knew that was total bullshit. I had lived a good life and was proud of the person I was; I had no legitimate reason to be worried about the secrets the envelope held. But I was.

"You sure we don't need a snack or something?" Josh asked after I sat staring at the envelope. "I'm home later than normal, and I know how you get when your blood sugar gets too low." He made a growling noise in his throat. It was the humorous jerk back to reality that I needed.

"That's all you, Sunshine. Would you like me to get you a snack or did you grab a bite to eat on the way home?" It was well past our normal dinner hour, but nothing had been normal for us once we started renovations on the new place.

"I had a late lunch," he explained then nodded to the envelope. "I'll make you a croque monsieur after you finish reading the letter." *Oh man, he was playing dirty.* He knew I couldn't resist that fancy French toasted ham and cheese sandwich.

"Two of them," I bartered. The letter was serious shit, and although I might be damning my cholesterol level to hell, I could use some comfort food. Funny how plain-ass grilled cheese used to be enough. Not once Josh got ahold of me.

"Deal," he said happily. Then the expression in his hazel eyes turned serious. "Nothing in that letter changes who you are to me or anyone else who loves you. You're still going to become the most amazing husband to me and father to our children. Now," he nodded to the envelope again, "let's do this."

I nodded because my throat was clogged with too much

emotion to speak right then. I blew out one last shaky breath then opened the envelope. I pulled the folded letter out and looked at it for a few heartbeats before I opened it. *Here we go,* I had thought to myself before I let my eyes focus on the words handwritten on the page.

*Gabriel,*

*I have written similar letters to the one you're holding hundreds of times over the last thirty-six years. I always weighed my need to know who you've become against your need to live a life that was unburdened by my guilt for giving you up. I wrote you a letter every holiday, birthday, and whenever the pain of failure got to be too much. Once I finished, I tucked the unsent letters away in a box because I couldn't bring myself to throw them out.*

*It has taken me many years, and quite a bit of therapy, to get to the point where I can acknowledge that I had no reason to feel guilty. I was a seventeen-year-old girl who knew nothing about raising a child, but I knew that Al and Martina Wyatt would give you an amazing life filled with love.*

*Now my only regret is that I never held you at least once. The nurses and my parents worried that it would've been too hard for me and so you were whisked away before I even saw you. I heard your first cry though. You sounded healthy, strong, and a little angry at being removed from your warm, dark cocoon. There was only one stipulation I had with your adoption, and your parents readily agreed—your first name.*

*Gabriel was the name of my grandfather and the best man I had ever known. I was sure that having his name would give you strength, courage, and the discipline to do what was right when life tested you. Even though I don't know anything about you, I'm positive it worked. I feel it in my heart.*

*I also wanted to assure you that you were conceived in love, even if it was the misguided youthful kind. Gabriel, giving you up for adoption was an act of love, not regret. My relationship with your father didn't last very long, but I can assure you he was a good guy. I thought it was important for you to know that.*

*My family relocated not long after you were born. At the time, it felt like they were ashamed of me but I later realized they thought it was best for me to have a fresh start. To them, we moved to a new state, new home, new school and that closed the door on our old life in Miami, but that isn't how the heart or brain works.*

*I thought they were ashamed of me, so I was ashamed of myself and told no one about you. I kept my letters to you hidden from my parents first, then my college roommates, and later, the man I married. Last year, my husband found the stash of letters addressed to you when we moved to our new house. He was shocked I had kept your existence a secret from him but understood why. He urged me to talk to a therapist and to find you when I was ready.*

*I am ready. My name is Bonita Gutierrez and I'm a teacher, wife, and a mother. Part of my therapy was coming clean to my children that they had an older brother walking this earth. They were shocked and then thrilled. I am not saying this to put any pressure on you at all, but you have three sisters who would love to meet you if that is something that you want. I thwarted their attempts to put pictures of themselves with this letter because you didn't need the added pressure. They completely understand, as do I, if you'd rather just keep living life as you know it. There's no wrong answer here, Gabriel. My contact number is included in the envelope if you ever want to reach out to me.*

*All my regards,*

*Bonita*

I folded the letter and found a small piece of paper enclosed in the envelope. I smiled at the thought of my half-sisters trying to slip pictures of themselves inside. Josh cleared his throat, and I looked at him. It was so cute how hard he was struggling not to ask me a thousand questions. I handed the letter to him then went into the kitchen to get two beers.

"Wow," Josh said once he was through reading it. "What are you going to do?"

The letter was touching, and it nearly moved me to tears, but I wasn't sure what to do next. On the one hand, I was curious as hell to know about my sisters, but I didn't know what all that curiosity entailed. I did know that it was cruel to make Bonita wait another day. I couldn't imagine writing a heartfelt letter like she did then just sit and wait for a call that might not ever come. I was sure the PI she hired informed her that he delivered the letter to me as soon as he completed his task.

Guilt burned inside me like I had a stomach full of gasoline and had just swallowed a match. I figured the guilt I felt from making Bonita wait two weeks was a fraction of what she felt for more than three decades. So, even though I didn't know what, if anything, I wanted from her, I knew what I wouldn't do, which was make her suffer another day of waiting.

"Well, I'm going to call and thank her for the letter while you make my fancy grilled cheese sandwiches with extra cheese." The smile I gave him was as cheesy as I liked my sandwiches. "I don't know what I'm going to say yet, but I know I need to say something."

"I love you, Gabe." Josh laid the letter on the coffee table and rose to his feet. "You birds be quiet while Big Daddy talks on the phone."

"Big Daddy!" both birds repeated before they went back to staring each other down. Savage was still doing his "mating dance" as Josh called it.

I took a swig of liquid courage from the bottle and dialed the number on the piece of paper inside the envelope. My knees bounced nervously while I waited for Bonita to answer or her voicemail message to play. I was so used to people not answering their phone that it surprised me when she answered hers on the fourth ring.

"Hello," she said shakily into the phone. She must've known it was me from her caller ID screen.

"It's Gabe, uh Gabriel," I corrected. "I just wanted to call and let you know that I read your letter and I'm sorry that it took me two weeks to do it. That was horrible of me to make you wait." I heard my voice break with emotion and cleared my throat while I got control of myself. The sounds of Josh moving around in our kitchen grounded me.

"You don't owe me any apologies, Gabe," she said. "I had no expectations when I sent the letter, but I hoped that maybe you'd give me a call. Hope can sometimes be your best friend or your worst enemy."

"That's the damned truth," I said. "Oh, sorry for cussing."

"Things aren't looking good if you feel the need to lead most sentences off with an apology," Bonita said good-naturedly. "I can promise you that I've said much worse."

"Okay," I said, unsure how else to respond, although I needed to say more because the awkward silence was uncomfortable. "I'm not sure where I want this to go yet, but I just needed you to know that I have never harbored any ill will toward you. Grateful is too lame of a word to use to describe how I feel about my adoption. My mom and dad are amazing people, and I had the most wonderful big brother. You have nothing to be ashamed about or feel guilty because I've had an incredible life."

"I remember Dylan," she said. "My heart broke for all of you when the private investigator discovered that he died. I am so sorry for your loss, Gabe."

"Thank you," I said, once again at a loss for how to respond.

"I'm the thankful one," she said. "I would love to get to know the man you've become if that is something you want someday. I'm going to let you decide what you want with no pressure from me."

"Yeah, I think I'd like to get to know you too," I said honestly.

"We'll take this at your pace," she said tearfully. "I'll never pressure you for more than what you're willing to share." Her voice broke, and I heard her sniffling through the phone.

"I'll be in touch soon," I promised her.

"Okay," she replied. "I look forward to it. Goodbye, Gabe."

"Goodbye."

I disconnected the call and stared down at my phone for several minutes. I felt lighter for having made a decision and pleased that it was the right one. I blew out a relieved breath and smiled up at Josh when he brought our sandwiches into the living room.

"I smell butter, cheese, and bread," I said, rubbing my hands together in glee. "Thank you."

"You're welcome. I know how much you love these things," Josh said, sitting beside me.

I hooked my arm around his neck and pulled him to me. "Not for the food, although it's my second favorite thing about you," I said, nuzzling my nose behind his ear.

"My pleasure portal being number one," Josh said, waggling his brows.

"No, that's actually in the third position behind your cooking skills." I cupped his chin with my hand. "Your heart is my favorite thing about you. No one has ever loved me the way that you do. And do you know what else?"

"What?" he asked.

"I might outweigh you by a good fifty pounds, but you're stronger than I am where it counts," I told him. I saw the disbelief in his eyes. "People look at us and think that I'm the strong one, but you are. Look how you've carried me for the past two weeks while I sorted things out. I consider myself a tough guy, but you are," I paused while I searched for the right word, "badass."

Josh snorted then sobered when he saw that I was serious. "Gabe, I love that you think that but..." I covered his lips with my finger to silence him.

"You are a total badass in everything that you do, whether it's dance, cook, paint, make your clients feel wonderful, your loyalty to your friends, and in the way that you love me."

"Even my mating dance?" he asked once I removed my finger.

"Especially your mating dance," I confirmed. I leaned over and kissed him briefly. "I'm going to eat my sandwiches and drink another beer then I'm going to show you my very own mating dance."

"This, I got to see," Josh said then reached for his plate. He began cutting into his sandwich with a knife and fork because the melted cheese on top of the buttery, toasted bread made it too messy to eat with our hands. Josh pointed to my plate and said, "Get to eating and drinking so we can get to the dancing and the mating."

"Blow me," Savage squawked.

"Bite me," Sassy replied.

Damn, I loved my life.

# SIXTEEN

## Josh

MOVING DAY CAME ON US FAST. I WAS SHOCKED AT HOW MUCH *stuff* I had acquired. We had spent every spare minute we had boxing up our possessions and labeling them for easy sorting and unpacking at our new home, which had yet to be named. Gabe wasn't quite as organized as me and thought the labeling of the boxes was a bit fussy until the movers arrived and assured us how much quicker it would go. I didn't say "I told you so," but I might've given him a look that implied the same thing.

The movers didn't say or act weird about mine and Gabe's situation, but they did a double take when it came time to put the pole inside the van. Mover Guy One scratched his head and Mover Guy Two blushed a little while he grinned. I had already dismantled it by unscrewing the base from the floor, but it was quite obvious what the hell it was.

MG2 turned to me and asked, "Are these expensive?"

"You assume it's my pole?" I asked him, causing him to blush even more.

"Uh… um."

"I'm just teasing you," I said. "The setup isn't expensive, but pole dancing classes can be. However, it's amazing exercise and worth every penny. Honestly, I recommend people take a class for at least a year before they install one at home. Yes, it's great exercise and leads to amazing sex, but it's also dangerous if you don't know what you're doing." MG2 nodded as I spoke, but I could tell he was busy picturing a specific someone swinging around the shiny pole.

"Let's get going, Mark," MG1 said. "We're not going to get done anytime soon if you keep staring at that weird thing with a dazed look in your eyes."

"It's not weird," Gabe said, entering the room. "Different doesn't mean weird." *Dear Lord, how I loved that man.*

MG1 just shrugged then they both grabbed an end and hauled it down the stairs to the truck. Originally, I had planned to donate my furniture and buy new stuff for our new home, but the house was so damn big that I couldn't justify spending that kind of money to replace perfectly good furniture. I bought new stuff for our formal living space and put my old stuff in the library, which was my favorite room in the entire house.

It was used as an office or a study, but I had it converted to a library. I had new shelves built to match the original ones, and sealed the entrances to the hidden room—both the one that Gabe had used and the one behind the kitchen pantry shelves that Wanda used to get the jump on him. I didn't utter a single joke about the doors or what happened below. I simply hired someone to collect the old clothing for a museum since no one knew who they belonged to and had our contractor seal the entrances.

I liked owning a house that was rumored to have helped thwart oppression and slavery. I found myself thinking about Georgia and whether she would've approved of the changes that I made to the house she loved. Many people asked if I worried about ghosts or negative energy because she died in the home. I had a few doubts crop up here and there, but I set them aside. Walking into the home felt right, as if I belonged there; it was exactly how I felt when Gabe held me tight against him.

The house would be our home and our story. Yes, it would include grim stories from the past, but all homes and relationships had that. The key to happiness wasn't to pretend bruised souls and broken hearts didn't exist because you couldn't build something solid on a foundation made of pretense, no matter how well-intended. Instead, own it, embrace it, and grow past it. Build that life brick by brick with mortar made of sweat and tears of both joy and sorrow to act as the glue that holds it all together.

Our friends showed up in full force to help us unpack and set up our new space. Chaz and Mere showed up after the salon closed, but Harley showed up bright and early as did Kyle, not that Kyle and Chaz were an item. Yet. No way in hell that *wasn't* going to happen. The blush on Chaz's cheeks when he showed up and saw Kyle told me that *something* had already happened and it was damned hard not to drag him off someplace and demand to know the details.

"Stay out of it," Gabe whispered in my ear as I watched the two guys interact. "They obviously don't need your help. Okay, any more help," he corrected when I raised a scornful brow at him. I had pushed them toward each other a little bit, but he was right that additional interference wasn't warranted.

"I wasn't going to do or say anything," I assured him then

turned to give him a hug.

Gabe bounced back quickly after talking to Bonita the first time. It didn't take him long to reach out to her again, and they'd become friends quickly. He had told her he was gay during their second conversation because if she had a problem with it, then there'd be no need for a third. Bonita had already known based on the information that the private investigator gave her and she was very accepting. I had talked to her a few times on the phone, and I found her to be warm and funny. I looked forward to meeting her and Gabe's sisters. In fact, Gabe decided to invite Bonita, her husband, and his sisters to our wedding after discussing it with Martina and Al.

My favorite part had been listening to Gabe speak to each of his younger sisters on the phone. He hadn't even met them yet, but he was grilling them about having boyfriends or girlfriends in their lives. We had seen pictures of them, and they were stunningly beautiful. They all had similar coloring to Gabe, but their eyes weren't as dark brown. In fact, each lovely woman had a shade of brown unique to her.

We had quickly moved to Skype so we could see the girls instead of just hearing their voices. Selena was in graduate school at Vanderbilt studying to be a doctor, Marisol was a sophomore at the University of Tennessee studying to be an environmental engineer, and Arianna was a senior in high school. All of them had been home for the summer and eager to drive north to meet us in person and attend our wedding.

"I can't believe I have sisters that are twenty-three, twenty, and seventeen years old," Gabe had said the night we first chatted with them. "It seems surreal," he said, stroking my back as I lay beside him in bed. "In a good way, though." I knew what he meant. "We'll be meeting them at our wedding in four weeks."

That had been two weeks before our move, so that meant our countdown was half as long. Oddly enough, I wasn't stressed about it at all. We had everything under control—as best we could—and I focused on what was right in front of me, which happened to be my very sexy fiancé.

"As happy as I am that our friends are here to help us, I can't wait until we're alone tonight," I told him. I hoped to project how eager I was to break in our new bedroom properly—and judging by the glimmer in his eyes—I had hit a bullseye.

"Me too, Sunshine. Me too." Gabe kissed me quickly and patted my ass before we separated to get our tasks done.

We couldn't expect our friends to work for free so we ordered pizzas and salads that night and promised them an amazing barbecue the following day. By the time twilight moved in, the crowd had gone home. It was just Gabe and me on our front porch with cold beverages and anticipation of the night to come building between us.

I wasn't eager to toss back my lemonade and run up the stairs because I knew that every second we waited would make the loving that much sweeter. I could tell by the crooked smile Gabe sent my way that he was hatching a plan. He wasn't the only one. I saw that burgundy silk tie when I was hanging his suits in our massive closet and remembered that I hadn't been tied up with that sucker yet. The thought of it had me wiggling in my seat, which prompted Gabe to chuckle warmly beside me.

I set my glass down and turned to look at him then noticed a black car slowing down in front of our house. The windows were tinted so I couldn't see who was driving the car. Irritation and fear jockeyed for first place in the emotional upheaval competition going on inside me when the car pulled into our driveway. Gabe turned his head and looked to see what had put the damper on my "take me upstairs" look.

"Government plates," he said like that made me feel any better.

"Internal Affairs," I said smartly, in an attempt to calm myself with bad jokes.

"Wiseass," Gabe said then rose to his feet.

A man got out of the car wearing a serious-looking black suit and an even more serious expression on his face. He reminded me a lot of the main agents in *Men in Black* although I doubted this had anything to do with aliens. My breath hitched in my throat when the man didn't so much as offer a smile when he stepped onto the porch. I rose and went to Gabe's side because I had a strong feeling that this man was the one Emory had seen in his vision. Whatever this lawman had to say wasn't good.

"Are you Gabriel Wyatt?" he asked Gabe.

"I am," he responded in an equally serious tone.

"I'm Deputy U.S. Marshal Hayes Matthews with the United States Marshals Service field office," he said, pulling out his badge for Gabe to see.

"What can I do for you, Deputy?" Gabe asked.

"Have you been in contact with Jimmy De Soto?" Deputy Matthews asked.

Gabe flinched slightly when he heard the man's name. "No, sir, I haven't. What's this about?"

"New evidence was presented to a grand jury in the homicide of Ace Dixon that points to De Soto not only knowing the kid would get killed, but that he instigated his death. The grand jury issued an indictment, but someone must've tipped De Soto off because he had fled his home by the time Marshals Services arrived to take him into custody."

"I'm the last person he would look to for help, Deputy," Gabe told the man.

I had no idea what the hell was going on, but it sounded serious. Gabe had never mentioned that guy to me, but I figured it had to do with his first IA investigation that he wasn't allowed to discuss. He had seen someone from his past when he took me to Miami to meet his parents, but he hadn't said much about it.

"Him seeking you out for assistance isn't what I was worried about, Detective. It's well-known among his friends and family that he holds you responsible for losing his job. We worried that this might've pushed him into looking for you rather than running to avoid jail." The man pulled a card out of his jacket pocket and held it out to Gabe. "Here's my contact information, including my cell phone number. I want you to call me if you have any reason to believe De Soto is near. You need to consider that he'll be armed, dangerous, and not interested in talking. I mean it, Detective, you call me no matter what time it is or day of the week."

"Will do," Gabe solemnly replied as he accepted the card. The deputy nodded and returned to his vehicle.

"What's this about, Gabe?" I softly asked once we were alone again. I was scared out of my mind and trying so hard not to show it. *Armed. Dangerous. Not interested in talking.* The guy blamed Gabe for what happened to him. It was terrifying and I was certain it was the vision Emory had seen.

"Let's go inside," he said, scanning the neighborhood as if he was looking for any signs that something wasn't right.

I took our empty glasses to the kitchen sink while Gabe locked up and set the alarm. I could see that he was struggling to decide what he could or should tell me. I wanted him to tell me everything, of course, but understood that he legally might not be able to share some things with me. Gabe tipped his head toward the staircase indicating that he wanted me to follow him. I wasn't too surprised when he turned on the taps to run a bath for us. It was one of the places we felt comfortable enough to unburden our souls.

I lowered myself between Gabe's legs and reclined against his muscular chest once the bath was ready. The hot water worked wonders to ease my tense muscles and frayed nerves as I waited for Gabe to open up to me. When he did, I was horrified by the things his former partner allegedly did, and my heart broke for the kid's family.

"He was just a kid, who was mixed up in serious shit. I didn't see evil when I looked into Ace's eyes when I questioned him. I saw a scared kid who pretended to be smug. The only evil I saw was in Jimmy's eyes when he told me the kid would've died anyway. Who thinks that way? Who doesn't want these kids to have a chance at changing their lives? Who just thinks that a person deserves to die because he fucked up?"

"Not you, baby," I said, hoping to comfort him.

"It's about time that he stands trial for what he did," Gabe said adamantly. "Early retirement wasn't enough. He needs to be in prison."

"Hopefully he'll screw up and get caught," I told Gabe. "Surely his face is being plastered all over the media and internet as a wanted fugitive."

"I'm going to make sure his photo gets hung up around town so people can call if they see him. If he is coming after me, then everyone could be in danger." I loved the fierceness in his voice because it helped me get past my fear. I reasoned that the man would be stupid to come after Gabe, but when has logic ever applied to revenge schemes? Still, sitting around and waiting for him to strike made no sense where reasonable action did.

"That sounds like the time you hung up the picture of Buddy all over town," I said, smiling at the memory. "I think you left them up for a few hours before you yanked them down."

"It was a full twenty-four hours," Gabe replied while tweaking my nipple. "I wanted to give someone a chance to claim him if he escaped their yard, but I wanted it to be quick before I got attached to him. They didn't call me within a day and I tore the signs down."

"He was meant to be your dog," I told Gabe. "Of all the windows he could've cried beneath, he chose yours."

"How'd you know about the posters anyway?" Gabe asked.

"I saw them hanging up and recognized the tile pattern on the kitchen floor, and I already had your phone number memorized, even though I didn't want any part of you," I confessed.

"You wanted *some* parts of me," he countered.

"You mean the part that's poking me right now?" I asked, wiggling my ass against his erection. "Truth is, Gabe, just like Buddy was meant to be your dog, I was meant to be your husband. No owner was going to come forth and claim him regardless of how long you left the posters up. No amount of my posturing and resisting was going to do anything but delay the time that I finally gave my heart to you."

"That's beautiful," Gabe whispered thickly.

"So is your cock," I said, unable to behave for too long. "I have big plans for it too, so what do you say we focus on the things we can control and worry about the rest later."

Gabe wrapped his hand around my dick and began stroking it. "I think you're the smartest man I know."

Later, I lay in the darkness of our new bedroom that we broke in properly. The perfect name for our house occurred to me. It was okay to give our cars and each other cutesy names, but the place where we lay our heads at night needed a name with special significance. "I think we should call this place home," I said out loud. Homes were more than just shelter; they were the walls that housed your dreams, kept you safe, and the place you slept beside the person you loved. It was a word that encompassed so many things.

"Home, it is," Gabe agreed.

# SEVENTEEN

## Gabe

THE NEXT SEVERAL DAYS FELT LIKE I WAS LIVING IN AN ALTERNATE universe; an unending dream-like state that would drop me into the happiest days of my life before yanking me out and throwing me into the scariest. When I was in high school, I was forced to read "A Tale of Two Cities" by Charles Dickens like every other kid in America. It was classic literature at its finest our teacher said, but it seemed like a bunch of confusing nonsense to a teenager who was coming out of his darkness to discover healthier, hornier ways of dealing with the grief from losing his brother.

I found the book boring and depressing at the time, yet certain lines stuck with me two decades after reading it. Deputy Matthews' visit to our home was a prime example of how something could be the best and worst of times. He implied that a fugitive on the run could be heading to kill me, which qualified as the worst part of that day. What came after though was the best time, not just because Josh was wet, naked, and open to my body, but because his heart was wide open and willing to share all the secrets it held.

The days that followed had the same pattern. There were moments that were so brilliant and beautiful that they couldn't possibly be real; like Josh blaring Barry White's "Can't Get Enough of Your Love, Babe" and trying to teach Savage and Sassy to dance to it. Yeah, I had that on video and would cherish that for the rest of my life. The darkest moments came when I realized that the rest of my life might not be as long as I wanted. I projected confidence that everything was fine and that there was no way Jimmy would be stupid enough to come after me, but I couldn't shake the feeling that he was waiting for the right time to pounce.

I did the only thing I could to make the people around me aware of the threat by distributing his Most Wanted poster all over town. I also made arrangements to take care of Josh should Jimmy get the best of me. I didn't wait until after the wedding to change the beneficiary on my life insurance policy or the accounts where I had the rest of my inheritance tucked away. I woke up each morning sure that I would have a long, happy life with Josh and went to bed certain that he'd feel my love for him in other ways if I was wrong.

Of all the things we planned for our wedding, a bachelor party had never been one of them. Somehow this shocked and outraged our friends. Instead of a cornhole battle, they began planning our parties without our input. Josh and I sat beside one another listening to them talk over each other as they tried to come up with plans that could involve both of us, but it became quite obvious that we didn't always enjoy the same hobbies.

"Golf," Adrian suggested, which Sally Ann vetoed with a scowl.

"Day spa," she countered, earning equal scorn from Adrian.

"Reds game," Dorchester suggested.

"Dinner and theater," Deanna countered.

Okay, so Josh and I weren't the only couple with totally opposite interests. The debate went on for a while; I had no hope that we'd find a suitable compromise until Kyle spoke up.

"Why does it have to be one or the other?" he asked. "Why can't we start out with two separate outings then meet up later to celebrate as one large group?" No one said anything right away, so he continued. "One group plays golf in the morning then goes to a Reds game afterward. The other group does the day spa, dinner, and theater thing. All of us meet later at Vibe to dance and celebrate. We'll stay at a hotel and use a cab or a car service so we don't have to worry about driving."

It was the perfect compromise, but we only had one weekend before our wedding so I wasn't sure we could pull it off. Ha! Our determined friends said otherwise. Once everyone decided which outing they were going on, they whipped out their cell phones and began booking hotel rooms and spa treatments, buying tickets for the game and theater, and made reservations for golf and dinner. Neither the Dorchesters nor the Goodes worried about finding a babysitter since Adrian's and John's parents lived close and were always wanting time with the grandbabies.

The couples—and should-be couples—were split between both groups. In my opinion, we could have compromised even more so that the groups could've stayed together. It wasn't that I was crazy about going to the theater, neither was Josh excited about the ballgame, but each day that passed without Jimmy's apprehension felt like borrowed time with Josh. I couldn't very well tell him that without freaking him out, so I kept my mouth shut and agreed to the plan.

Jockeying back and forth between deliriously happy and scared out of my mind was catching up and wearing me down. I did my best to smile and laugh when it was appropriate on the afternoon we set out on our separate excursions. I kissed Josh goodbye in the hotel lobby and got in the car that Silver hired to drive us around. Emory seemed to accept his presence better once Silver followed him home the night of our barbecue, but I could see that he still wasn't completely comfortable around him.

I was off my usual golf game, which made Adrian happy. He could see that he was going to beat me for the first time since we started playing together not long after I moved to Blissville. He laughed and lived it up, which lifted my mood and made me smile. Not only was Adrian my best friend, but he was also a damn good detective, so I wasn't at all surprised when he and Dorchester pulled me off to the side.

"I can't pretend to know what you're going through right now, Gabe," Adrian said. "I know that my words and assurances aren't enough to erase your worry about De Soto targeting you, but the department is going to do everything they can to protect you both."

"Thanks, Adrian," I told him. "One minute I'm convinced he's long gone then the next I'm sure he'll attempt to take me out before he's captured."

"He's not going to get close enough," Dorchester said firmly.

"Thanks, John," I told him, wishing I could be as confident.

"Whoa," he said, eyes wide with surprise. "You just used my first name."

"Asshole?" I asked.

"No, that's what you call him when he's not around," Adrian said.

"Oh, I'm sure it's much worse than that," Dorchester quipped.

"I did ask you to stand up with me at my wedding, so it's only right I stop being so formal when I talk to you," I told John.

"You only did it so you'd have an even number of attendants,"

John scoffed. "Who else were you going to ask? One of your past hookups? Oh, wait, one of them was implicated in the death of the other, which leaves your former lover, or the guy who waved his dick at you, or me. I'm pretty damn sure which one of us Josh would prefer."

"Silver," Adrian and I both said at the same time, drawing ire from John and pulling Silver's attention to our group.

"I was just telling John how I'm going to replace him with you as one of my attendants if he didn't stop smarting off. I can't have someone up there trying to upstage me on my big day," I told Silver. I couldn't very well repeat what John had said since it was Silver's brother that was my past hookup whose death could've been prompted by the other hookup's negligence. It was obviously a good thing that my days of hooking up were over since I made such crappy choices.

"We're about the same size so I'm sure I could fit into his tuxedo if I need to step in," Silver said good-naturedly.

"Not so sure about that," John fired back. "I consider myself to be well-endowed, but even so, there are places the tuxedo pants might be a little too snug for you."

"What can I say?" Silver replied, shrugging. "Some of us are just blessed."

"Or cursed," John mumbled, then tilted his head toward Adrian as if he might not be so fortunate.

"Hey," Adrian said. "I'm blessed just fine and how the hell would you know anyway?"

"Wives talk." John laughed and walked away with an irritated Adrian right on his heels.

"No damn way my wife is talking to your wife about my small dick," Adrian said loud enough for everyone waiting their turn at the fifteenth hole to hear.

"Aha, so you admit it," John said then burst into laughter when Adrian realized what he'd said.

"You tricked me into saying it, asshole," Adrian said but struggled to keep the heat in his voice. He looked over at me and Silver laughing our asses off by that point. "Suit up, Silver, you're going in."

"I've heard that plenty of times too," Silver fired back. "I'm the man for the job."

It went downhill from there, and everything became a dick or stamina joke to the point that our last three holes of golf were so pitiful that I came back from last place to win. Of course, Adrian thought it was all a conspiracy on my part and ribbed me off and on during the baseball game.

The other group had an early dinner at a fancy restaurant before going to the theater, but we ate greasy, tasty ballpark food instead. Josh and I agreed to focus on our group of friends rather than texting one another, which was harder to do than I thought. I found myself wondering how he liked his massage, then I got more than a little possessive when I thought about another man's hands on Josh's body. I was ready to growl like a beast when my mind went there, though I knew damn well he'd never allow someone to touch him as intimately as the massages we gave each other.

"What's the name of that massage parlor again?" Adrian asked.

"Happy Endings," John said because he never missed a beat.

"You do realize that your wife went there too, right?" Kyle asked John.

"And the rest of our significant others," Harley mumbled, not at all happy with the way the conversation was heading.

"Yeah, but that's why John's wife was the first one through the door. She's not used to a happy ending," Adrian informed us.

Their banter entertained our group and everyone around us for the entire nine innings. I was more than eager to get ahold of my guy by the time the game was over. Silver let us in through the private entrance in the back of the club. The place was alive with thumping music and thrashing bodies, but our table was easy to find beneath the big banner that read: CONGRATULATIONS,

162

GABE AND JOSH!!!!

I had an amazing day with my friends, but nothing came close to making me as happy as when I saw Josh smiling and laughing at the table. He was wearing a sparkly crown on his head, and a sash across his chest with the word GROOM printed on it. Meredith and Chaz had similar sashes, but theirs said BEST WOMAN and BEST MAN on them. Josh was so beautiful that I stopped in my tracks and just stared at him. I wasn't the only one enthralled by the happiness at our table because the other men stopped and smiled at their significant others—or their heart's desire in the case of Kyle and Silver.

I turned to Kyle and said, "Don't blow your chance at real happiness. Shake off that reserve, take a chance, and grab life by the balls." Of course, I had to practically shout it over the music for him to hear me, which meant the other guys heard it also,

"Or him by the balls," they all chimed in encouragingly.

"Yeah, okay," Kyle said, his face red with embarrassment. "Maybe I should start with a drink first."

Josh looked over then and saw us all standing there. The smile that spread across his face was enough to obliterate the fear that clawed at my gut for the time being. He waved, and all eyes turned to us. The couples exchanged hugs and kisses and the four people who hadn't made that leap yet shared what I called longing glances.

"Don't worry, Adrian and John," Chaz said once the little reunions were over, "we got you sashes also."

John and Adrian began arguing over which one of them was going to wear the BEST WOMAN sash. I knew their ribbing was going to go on for a while, so I led Josh away from the crowd and onto the dance floor. I didn't need alcohol to loosen up that night because I had one mission on my mind: keep Josh smiling. We danced for so long that I lost track of where everyone was or what they were doing because my whole world was in my arms, grinding his pert little ass against my dick. There were a few slow dances peppered between the hard-thumping club music, and I loved the opportunity to slow things down and kiss Josh like it could be the last time.

"This time next week I'm going to be your husband," he said after a long, sexy kiss.

"I can't wait," I told him honestly.

"I can't either, but tonight I'm going to take you back to the hotel room and fuck you like a stranger." Josh nibbled on his bottom lip as if he was hesitant about my reaction.

"It's time to say goodnight to our friends, Sunshine."

It turned out they were nowhere in sight and our waiter told us they'd paid the tab and left some time ago. I didn't feel bad because we'd spent the better part of the day apart and the night was supposed to be about celebrating our upcoming nuptials. What better way was there than dancing with my guy for hours before we went back to our room, where Josh pounded me hard enough to wake the rest of the hotel.

# EIGHTEEN

## Josh

I HOPED, PLEADED, AND PRAYED FOR AN EASY, CHAOS-FREE WEEK leading up to Gabe's reunion with his birth mom, meeting his sisters for the first time, and a not-so-small event in our lives called a wedding. Our parents were scheduled to arrive on the Thursday before the wedding and stay with us in our new home since we had enough guest bedrooms to accommodate them. Bonita and her family were arriving in Cincinnati on Thursday also, but we weren't meeting them until Friday morning for brunch at their hotel. We would have our wedding rehearsal Friday evening followed by a catered dinner for our wedding party and parents. I wasn't sure if Gabe was going to invite Bonita, Miguel, and the girls but I made sure there was enough food for them should he extend an invitation. I figured he was waiting to see how things went Friday morning first. If it went well, I suspected he'd want them to feel included and I was positive that Al and Martina wouldn't mind if he did.

As exciting as all of that was, it took a lot of work and preparation to make it happen. Oddly enough, I wasn't even worried about the wedding part. The caterer had everything under control, Gabe hadn't changed his mind about marrying me, and Judge McDonnell was ready to officiate the event. We only needed one person to show up to make it official, and I was fine with that. It was everything else that had me tied in knots. I had to make sure there were plenty of towels and food on hand for our parents' stay and set aside time to spend with them, which meant I needed to rearrange my work schedule that week.

I had become more flexible and relied less on routine once I found harmony in all parts of my life, but I quickly realized that my laid-back attitude was harder to hold onto with so many big, exciting things looming in front of me. I fell back on my old routine to feel in control of my life and the myriad of emotions that fought for dominance in my brain. Which explained why Chaz and Meredith found me sitting on the floor in the supply closet of the salon taking inventory the Monday afternoon after we returned from our bachelor bash weekend.

Chaz crossed his arms over his chest and looked down at me with an amused expression on his face. "I thought that was supposed to be my job now. Am I not doing it good enough?" The crooked smile on his face told me that Chaz knew exactly why I was there and that it had nothing to do with being short on hair or nail products. That didn't mean I wasn't going to give him a hard time.

"If you start sucking more in other areas of your life and less at your job," I said, zinging him, "you could use those lips for something more satisfying than grinning at me like a lunatic." Instead of getting his feelings hurt, Chaz only smiled broader. He knew how much I loved him and saw through my snarktastic comment.

Meredith snorted then said, "He's worse than I thought, Chaz."

"His eyes are looking a little wild," Chaz said to Mere. He unfolded his arms and offered his hand to assist me off the floor. "He looks a little hungry too."

"I bet his nerves are making it hard for him to eat," she replied, nodding her head.

"Good thing we picked up his favorite foods from the diner on the way over," Chaz added, as they continued to talk about me as if I wasn't in the room.

"Then feed me instead of fucking around like clowns." I grabbed Chaz's hand, and he groaned while he helped me to my feet like I weighed a half ton. "You better start working on your strength and stamina for when you and Kyle stop dicking around and really get to *dicking* around. What do you authors call words that are spelled the same but have multiple meanings?"

"Homonyms," Chaz said patiently.

"I would've guessed versatile," I paused for effect, "like Kyle." I casually tossed that out there as I walked around my friends in search of food. I expected a big gasp or response from Chaz that didn't come, which meant I shocked him silent, or he already knew. The blush on his face when he entered the kitchen told me he already knew, but how? Did he assume, did he ask, or perhaps he had firsthand knowledge? I was more than a little curious, but that took a back seat to my ravenous hunger.

I at least used utensils and a napkin as I devoured the pot roast dinner they brought me rather than just shove my face into the container or use my fingers. I hadn't lost complete control of myself even though my riotous emotions had me in a tailspin.

"Let us help you work through some of this, baby," Meredith

said. "Maybe if you get it off your chest you can sort it all out and feel better. Normally, we'd let you internalize your feelings until you either work them out on your own or talk to us and let us help, but this is too important for us just to sit back and wait."

"Really, dude," Chaz said, sitting across from me at the small, round table in the kitchenette. "Get it all out so you can enjoy your week."

"What has you worked up the most?" Meredith asked. "Is it having overnight guests at your house? Do you need help getting the bedrooms ready or anything?"

"Nah, that's done."

"You want us to help you plan meals while they're in town?" Chaz asked. He could barely boil water, but I loved him for his offer.

"No, that's under control too. We stopped at the store on the way home yesterday to stock up. We're keeping it pretty simple because neither of our parents would want us to make a big fuss about them coming," I told them. Mere and Chaz exchanged a look that said it was too late and the ship to Stresstown had already set sail.

"Okay," Meredith said patiently, "are you nervous about meeting Gabe's birth mom and his sisters?"

"A little," I admitted. "I want Bonita and the girls to like me."

"They're not going to like you, honey; they're going to love you," Mere assured me.

"I do hope so, but I know it will be okay if they don't," I replied. "That's not what has me worked up in knots."

"Is there something wedding related that Mere or I could take off your plate? Do you need us to make phone calls to make sure that everything is going smoothly?" Chaz asked.

"No, I already did that this morning."

"Then what is it?" Mere asked, sounding confused.

Up until that moment, I probably couldn't have pinpointed what had me on edge until my friends helped me cross reasons to panic off my Reasons to Panic checklist. The real source of my struggle wasn't related to the reunion, overnight guests, or even the wedding. It was something so far out of my control that I felt helpless and weak, which in turn made me want to control everything that I could in place of the things that I couldn't.

"This is going to sound crazy," I said in warning, but instead of looking leery they placed their elbows on the table and leaned in closer.

"We were born for crazy," Chaz told me.

I could tell by their expression that they were expecting something a bit more lighthearted than Emory's background and the reason he believed he was in Blissville. I felt sick inside for betraying Emory's trust, but I had to explain why those "Wanted" posters hanging all over town scared the fuck out of me. My confession regarding what I knew about Emory received the same non-response as my announcement that Kyle liked to give and receive cock.

"But apparently, you both already knew that," I said.

"Emory said he wanted to write books, but he knew shockingly little about the process," Chaz told me. "I got the feeling he was covering something. I quietly did an internet search and read some articles about his past. I didn't say anything because it was obvious he wasn't here to hurt anyone, and I didn't feel right gossiping about him."

"Same," Meredith answered. "He was too vague about some things, and I wondered how he could afford to move here when he obviously wasn't working and said he hadn't published a book yet."

"Gabe would be very proud of your sleuthing skills," I told them.

I too wondered how Emory could afford to travel from city to city to help solve crimes. I seriously doubted that the police departments he helped paid much, nor did I think the television shows that featured him would shell out much cash for his appearances. He was either independently wealthy, inherited some money, or worked from home doing something he didn't share with the rest of us. Even though I was curious, I would never ask him.

"What does Emory's background have to do with you looking like a cat on its eighth-and-three-quarters life?" Chaz asked. "Oh," he said. "He's had a vision about one of you."

Mere gasped and sat straight up in her chair then covered her heart as if she was trying to protect it from the truth. "Jazz, is that true?"

"Yes," I admitted then told them the rest. "I just can't shake the feeling that something bad is going to happen."

"Honey, this guy has been on the run for weeks. He would've shown up here already," Meredith said calmly.

"Maybe," Chaz said. He didn't sound nearly as confident as Meredith that Gabe wasn't in trouble. "A guy like him would know how to avoid detection from law enforcement agencies. He's probably changed his appearance and is using cash he kept squirreled away if this day ever came." Chaz tipped his head while he thought some more. "Probably even money he'd taken from the evidence locker they'd collected from drug busts, searches, and seizures. Billy did that, and I bet it's not that uncommon. I mean, here these cops are eking out a living while that money sits in an evidence locker. Hell, I bet most of it never gets tagged into evidence. I think the temptation to resist making their lives a little better would be too great to pass. I doubt he's fled the country and he'll be looking for revenge."

Meredith nudged Chaz with her elbow to get him to shut up after glancing in my direction. Either my thundering pulse was visible beneath the skin of my neck or the veins in my forehead were popping out as my blood pressure soared, maybe even both. Chaz didn't even notice Meredith's attempts to get him to shut up and he sure as hell didn't see me stroking out across the table from him because he was staring off into space instead of looking at me.

"If he thinks Gabe is responsible for ruining his career then he won't go down without trying to take Gabe with him," Chaz said.

"Or, if he truly wanted to hurt Gabe he'd kill the one Gabe loves most in the world. He'd turn his attention on Josh when everyone focused on protecting Gabe."

"Charles Bailey!" Meredith yelled. "What-the-ever-loving-fuck is wrong with you?" She followed up her question with a smack to the back of his head, which forced him back to reality.

"Huh?" Chaz asked. "What did I say?"

"Look what you did to Jazz." Meredith pointed to the tears that ran down my face.

"Fuck! What did I say?" Chaz asked.

"You basically implied that there's no fucking way that Jimmy De Soto hopped on a dinghy and headed to the Bahamas and that he's most likely hiding out nearby so he can kill Josh to get back at Gabe," Meredith recapped.

"I said that?" Chaz asked. "Oh man, I was just plotting for my book out loud more than anything. Damn, Jazz, I'm so sorry I said that to you."

"Book plotting?" Meredith scoffed. "What, you have a Gabe in your book who also happens to be a cop with an ex-partner on the run from the law who may or may not want to kill him for ruining his career?"

"No, not really, but that's what I would do if I was writing this scenario in a book. I would have De Soto come after Josh, and I'd do it in a big way, but this isn't fiction this is…"

A knock at the back door scared the hell out of us and interrupted Chaz before he could finish. In fact, we all squealed high-pitched, girlie noises and jumped in our seats.

"Oh my God!" Meredith exclaimed. "It's him!"

"De Soto wouldn't knock, Mere. He'd just kick down the door like Oscar did last year," Chaz said calmly.

"Like that makes us feel better," Meredith said hotly. "What's the matter with you? You start writing some sexy suspense novel with a serial killer and BAM, you turn a little creepy yourself. I can't imagine what your search engine must be like on your laptop. That's probably the feds looking for your disturbing ass."

"Josh, you guys okay in there?" Emory asked through the back door as if he didn't just hear us all scream like little girls. Meredith was still giving Chaz an ass chewing when I opened the door and let Emory inside the kitchenette. "Is this a bad time?" he asked, looking over at my friends.

"Meredith is ripping into Chaz for misbehaving; same speech, different ear," I told him, putting a spin on the well-known phrase of same song, different tune. "What's going on? You sound upset."

"I have some bad news, I'm afraid," he said.

"Oh my God! What is it? Did you have another vision? Is Gabe in danger?" I fired one question after the other at him.

Emory placed his hands firmly on my shoulders, and the weight of them kept me grounded when the panic rose so high that I was in jeopardy of floating away. "No, Josh. My visit has nothing to do with Gabe or the vision. I came over to tell you that I'll be leaving town for a few days, but I'll be back in time for your wedding."

I finally got control of myself enough that I saw Emory, my friend, instead of Emory the bearer of bad news. The dark circles under his eyes indicated that he wasn't sleeping very well. "Is everything okay?" I asked him.

"No, not really," he admitted, "but I'm going to see if I can change that. I plan on returning Friday in case you need my help before your big day." Emory pulled me to him for a hug and whispered, "You've been a great friend to me, Josh. You can't possibly know how much that means to me."

I pulled back and looked into his sad, green eyes. The hug felt like a goodbye despite his promise to return in time for my wedding. If he had plans to run, I wasn't going to make it easy for him. "Running won't change anything, Emory. Sometimes we must accept that fate—or a higher power—knows what's best for us when we aren't smart enough or brave enough to see it for ourselves.

Sometimes you just need to have a little faith."

Emory nodded subtly and offered a small, uncertain smile before he left without another word. I closed my eyes and took some cleansing breaths to clear my mind and body of the toxic fear and hysteria that had bubbled up. I decided that I was going to take my own advice. I was going to accept that I wasn't in charge of the universe and I was going to have a little faith—in myself, in Gabe, and in our future.

# NINETEEN

## Gabe

"ARE YOU GETTING NERVOUS ABOUT THE BIG DAY?" ADRIAN ASKED during our lunch break on the Wednesday before the wedding. It was my last work day for more than two weeks and I was happy that things were blissfully quiet in Blissville for the time being and we could enjoy a nice lunch at the diner.

"No," I said honestly. "I'm excited about the wedding and looking forward to the two weeks in Hawaii with my husband." Yeah, I didn't bother hiding my smile over the images that came to mind just then.

"I sense a but," Adrian said, "and not the kind with two T's either." The smile slid from Adrian's face, and the expression in his eyes grew serious. "You're worried about De Soto, aren't you?"

My mind went back to Monday evening when Josh told me about the conversation he had with Chaz and Meredith over lunch. He laughed nervously when he got to the part about Chaz plotting a future book out loud and how it scared the crap out of them, but I wasn't laughing. Chaz had very valid points—ones I had considered myself. There was absolutely nothing Jimmy De Soto could do that would destroy me more than killing Josh. If I were playing the role of a villain that was exactly where my mind would go, and I had to put myself in the brain of a villain frequently as a cop to outsmart and apprehend them.

Josh said something that shook me to the core that night. "Gabe, I'm doing better at realizing there are only so many things I can control in this life. I can't control what other people do, but I can control how I react to it. Today, I was paralyzed by fear when Chaz talked about some lunatic that wanted to exact his revenge by killing one of us. Then Emory stopped over, and I saw how hard he was struggling to resist a future event with Jonathon Silver that he doesn't want to happen. I told him that sometimes we have to stop thinking that we know better than fate and have some faith. If I'm only going to have one more minute, one day, one week, one month, or even a year with you, then I'm not going to waste it worrying about when it's going to end. Regardless of how long we have, I'm going to love you for a lifetime. I am going to marry you on Saturday, and no lunatic with a B-movie plot for revenge is going to ruin that, Gabe."

We made love that night like it could be the last time, but it wasn't the beauty of our joining or his positive words about having faith that followed me into my dreams. Instead, I lived out that horrific B-movie plot in HD color with surround sound so crisp that it felt like I was really in my dream. I could even hear the thoughts dream me had running through his mind; it was the most frightening thing I'd ever experienced.

*Twenty seconds. That was how long Josh was my husband before all hell broke loose. One minute he was smiling at me after we shared our first kiss as husbands and the next he was in my arms with a bullet wound in his chest. I had removed my suit jacket and tried to staunch the flow of blood while Josh fought to breathe and to speak.*

*"Don't say anything, Sunshine. Save your breath. Where's that ambulance?" I shouted, but I heard the sirens faintly in the background, just as I heard Josh's mother, and mine, sobbing. They had wanted to rush to his side, but I made them stay back because crowding him was the last thing he needed and I wouldn't let anyone take him from me until the squad arrived.*

*I looked down to where I held his limp hand in mine in the back of the ambulance as it sped toward the county hospital where a Care Flight helicopter would meet us. Dried blood marred the perfection of the diamonds in our matching wedding bands. The only thing louder than the screaming sirens was the pounding of my heart as I prayed for him to live.*

*"Don't leave me," I begged Josh.*

*Twenty seconds. I saw every dream I ever had come true in Josh's eyes before...*

*"Mister..." The EMT wasn't exactly sure what to call me.*

*"Roman-Wyatt," I informed him.*

*"Mr. Roman-Wyatt, don't give up hope. Mister...." He nodded to my husband, unsure what to call him also.*

*"Roman-Wyatt," I said. It was something that we easily agreed on. We were going to be equal partners—in name and everywhere else.*

*"Mister Roman-Wyatt has a lot to fight for, and it helps. He'll arrive at the University of Cincinnati Hospital in minutes and they'll rush him into trauma surgery. It's the absolute best place for him to be*

*right now." I nodded my head because I knew he was right. "You won't be able to ride with him because there's not enough room onboard the chopper." I knew I could hitch a ride with one of the many people who would make the trip to Cincinnati.*

*I just needed to be with him as long as I could. Arriving at the hospital and seeing the helicopter waiting was bittersweet. It was the only way to save him, but it also meant that I had to let go of his hand, not knowing if I'd ever look into his beautiful eyes again.*

*I ran alongside the gurney until the last minute when they needed to load Josh onto the helicopter. "Don't you leave me," I said firmly. "You promised me forever and twenty seconds isn't forever. You hear me?" I dropped a kiss on his forehead and prayed it wasn't the last.*

*The EMTs pulled me away from the helicopter so the flight crew could strap my husband down for transport and liftoff.*

I came out of the dream the minute the helicopter lifted off the ground. I sat up in our bed with my heart racing and lungs pumping, and the sound of those chopper blades echoing in my ears. I was so relieved to see Josh sleeping peacefully beside me that I cried, but not loud enough to wake him.

I called Deputy Marshal Matthews the next morning and asked for an update on the search for Jimmy. The man didn't owe me anything, but he told me everything he knew as a professional courtesy. They knew from the camera at his bank that he cleaned out his safe deposit box hours before the grand jury issued his indictment, which meant that the secret proceedings were anything but, and someone tipped him off.

"Do you think he fled the country?" I asked hopefully. If he prepared to bolt for this possibility, then maybe he also had a fake ID and passport. It was obvious he was corrupt as hell and would have connections to someone who could procure quality fake documents. *As well as guns.*

"It doesn't look that way, Detective Wyatt," Marshal Matthews said. "He ditched his car a few hours north of Miami and stole one

177

parked outside a convenience store that a guy left running while he went inside to buy cigarettes. We later found it abandoned near the Georgia-Florida state line when he stole a different car. We've been able to track him by this pattern but could never get ahead of him, even knowing that he was most likely on his way to pay you a visit."

I liked the way Deputy Matthews made it sound like Jimmy was coming over for a barbecue. "Where was his last known location?" I asked.

"We lost his trail in Tennessee," Matthews said. "A park ranger found the last known stolen car in the parking lot at one of the Great Smoky Mountain National Park visitor centers. De Soto didn't steal a car from that parking lot or the immediate area which means he hitched a ride or…"

"… Had help," I said, finishing for him. "Any known family, friends, or colleagues in the area that might be helping him?"

"We're working on it, Detective Wyatt. Has something happened to make you think he is in the area?" Matthews asked.

I couldn't very well tell him about Chaz's ramblings and my scary dreams and expect him to take me seriously should I need to call him again in the future. Instead, I said, "I'm getting married this weekend, and I don't want any surprises."

"I understand your concern. Would you feel a little better about the situation if I sent two deputy marshals undercover as wedding guests?" Matthews offered. "Do you have extra pieces of cake to spare?"

"We'll have enough cake for each guest to have five pieces," I said, thinking about the massive cake we ordered. I smiled when I thought about the topper Josh had custom-made to look like the two of us. The thing was hand painted and freaking precious.

"I'll work out the details and be in touch," he said before he hung up. He called me back the next day to let me know that two of his deputies would be present for both the rehearsal and the wedding.

"Gabe?" Adrian asked, pulling my attention to him. "I asked if you were worried about De Soto."

"Yeah, of course, but I feel better after talking to Matthews." Then I told Adrian about the extra guests that would be attending the rehearsal and ceremony. "I'm going to try and let it go and enjoy time with our families and the wedding festivities."

"It's not easy to do under these circumstances but trust us to have your back," Adrian said.

"Don't forget the two weeks in paradise," I added. I definitely wanted to live long enough to see Josh in those sexy Speedos he bought. I asked him to model them off, but he refused.

"Yeah, I can tell by the look on your face where your mind just went," Adrian said then snorted. "Keep thinking those thoughts, and you should be just fine." Adrian snatched the checks up when Daniella dropped them on the table. "My treat, and there are to be no arguments." He laughed on his way to the register after he evaded my attempt to snatch them back.

I shook my head and checked my email on my phone to make sure I had the confirmation for the rental car I reserved for our parents. I wanted to pick them up from the airport, but they didn't want to "trouble us" and said they'd rent a car. It did make sense for them to have their own transportation to come and go as they pleased but not at their expense. I rented the car and refused to listen to their arguments, sort of like Adrian did with me. I wanted my parents to accept my gesture, so I did the same with Adrian.

"Excuse me, Detective." I snapped my head up and met the timid gaze of Felicity Wallace, wife of the jackass county commissioner. "Can I bother you for just a minute?"

"You're not bothering me, Mrs. Wallace," I told her. "Have a seat."

"Well, you don't know what I'm about to say," she replied uneasily. "Um, it's about your house and the vandalism that happened after Georgia died."

I sat up straighter in my chair. That vandalism was my only unsolved case, and one I wanted to solve since it involved the house I called home. "What do you know about it?" Adrian turned from the counter and started heading our way until he saw who sat across the table from me. I exchanged a brief look with him that asked him to give me a minute. He nodded and headed outside to wait for me.

Tears filled Felicity Wallace's eyes, and she said, "I know who vandalized your house and why. I should've said something after it happened, I should never have covered for him, but he was just so hurt about what he learned." I knew who she was talking about and the identity of the vandal.

"It was your son, Christopher, wasn't it?" I asked gently.

"Yes, Detective," she said then looked around to see if anyone was paying attention to us. It was late enough in the afternoon that the usual lunch crowd had mostly passed through already. "I know about Rocky and Jack; I've known for quite some time. I kept thinking that it was a phase that Jack was going through but it's not a phase, is it?"

"No," I said softly. "Is Commissioner Wallace aware that you and Christopher know?"

She shook her head slowly before she replied, "If I acknowledge it out loud to him then our marriage will be over; I'm not ready to do that, Detective. Anyway, Christopher overheard Jack talking to Georgia or Rocky—he wasn't sure which one—about the photos. He heard his father say that he hoped the truth came out that he was in love with another man. He came to me, and I told him that I had known for a long time and I was trying to find a way to come to terms with it before I decided what I wanted to do. After Georgia died, Christopher broke in and ransacked her house looking for the pictures, but he never found them. He confessed to me what happened and was going to turn himself in, but I wouldn't let him. Maybe it was the wrong decision, but we were dealing with so much at the time."

I felt sad for Felicity and her son, but there wasn't anything I could say that would make her feel better. Well, except for one thing. "This won't go any further than between you and me, Mrs. Wallace. I wish you and Christopher nothing but the best."

"But not my husband?" she asked with a crooked smile that said she knew there was no love lost between Jack Wallace and me.

"I'm not a big fan," I admitted to her. I knew that coming out was hard for people but cheating on his wife the way he did was unforgivable in my eyes. However, it wasn't my life, so I had no say. "Anyway, tell Christopher that I'll give him this one pass." I rose slowly to my feet and offered her a kind smile. "Take care, Mrs. Wallace."

"Thank you, Detective. I hope you and Josh have a happy life."

"We will, Mrs. Wallace, and you deserve the same."

I left the diner with a sense of closure. I felt better knowing the identity of the vandal, even if the police department never would. The kid was looking to protect his family and was no threat to Josh or me. Adrian raised his brow in question when I approached him.

"What was that all about?" he asked.

"I'm not telling you anything until you get off my car," I said, gesturing to where he leaned against the hood. Adrian rolled his eyes but straightened away from my car. "It was her son who broke into the house after Georgia died." It would seem to some that I broke my promise to Felicity Wallace, but Adrian was my partner and I didn't keep secrets from him.

"Christopher?" Adrian asked in surprise. "Did he find out about the affair and blackmail attempt?"

"Yeah," I confirmed. "I can't blame the kid. He was just trying to protect his mom."

"Well, at least now you know it wasn't something seedier that could come back and cause problems for you guys later," Adrian said. "Let's head on back to the station and see if there have been any new calls. If not, you should just head on home and enjoy your last night of peace before the chaos arrives."

As much as Josh and I loved our folks, it would be an adjustment to having overnight guests under our roof. There'd be no sex on the couch or up against the foyer the second I got home. In fact, their visit would probably put a damper on our sexcapades, so I thought Adrian had a damn fine suggestion.

When I got home, I discovered that Josh was of the same mind. "Quick, in case they show up a day early," he said, leaping into my arms.

"No damn way I'm going to rush anything." If it was going to be the last night I could love him without inhibitions until our wedding night, then I was going to take him as often as I could, starting with the foyer wall.

# TWENTY

## Josh

"HOW MANY TIMES ARE YOU GOING TO FLUFF THAT PILLOW?" GABE asked from the doorway of the room his parents would occupy for their visit. I looked over my shoulder at him and caught him staring at my ass. "Besides, I see you bent over near a bed, and I get all kinds of ideas," he said, earning a snort from me He didn't need a bed nor did I need to be bent over to entice that man. "Okay, you just need to be breathing," he said, repeating words I'd told him once.

I straightened from the bed and turned to him. They were due to arrive any minute, and I wanted things to look perfect. "I just want your parents to be comfortable and have a nice visit," I told him. It sounded logical to me.

Gabe cocked a brow and said, "I haven't seen you fluffing the pillows in *your* parents' bed ten times already this morning."

"That's because they're my parents and they'd love their visit even if I put them in a tent in the backyard," I said casually.

Gabe straightened from the casual lean he'd perfected, and the amused expression slid from his face. *Uh oh.* "And you think my parents are somehow different?" he asked, sounding insulted. "Do you think their love is dependent on a mattress that's 'plush, but not too plush' and pillows that are 'firm, but not hard'?" Gabe walked toward me in what I'd call purposeful strides, but they weren't angry; his body language and expression were that of a disappointed man. I thought it would be at least a week into our marriage before I earned that reaction from him. "Do you think my parents' love is that superficial or do you still not know how much you are loved?"

"Um." How does one answer that question without looking bad? Gabe thought it was one or the other, but it was simply me being me. And shouldn't a man recognize a fellow pleaser when he saw one? Gay men are supposed to have a radar that lets us know when another gay man is in the vicinity, shouldn't that be the case with other things also? It takes a pleaser to know one? Wouldn't that be handy? "Neither," I said honestly. "I'm doing this for the same reason that you went to two different liquor stores looking for my dad's favorite scotch and you had the florist order special flowers for my mom because they're her favorite. It's not as if they'd yank their support away for our nuptials if those things were not in the house," I told him. "We're both making sure our parents feel welcome and comfortable in our new home as we begin our lives together. We're just expressing it in different ways."

Gabe placed his hands on my neck and stroked my jawline with his thumbs. "You're right."

"Yes, I am," I boasted proudly.

"And so fucking adorable." Gabe lowered his head until our lips nearly touched. The intensity and adoration in his dark eyes nearly made me melt into a puddle at his feet. I thought it was an absolute travesty that people lived without having someone look at them the way that Gabe looked at me; and not just in that mushy moment either. I always saw respect and admiration in his eyes. "Only forty-eight hours until you become Joshua James Roman-Wyatt." Then he pressed his mouth fully against mine, and I lost myself in our kiss.

"And you become Gabriel Allen Roman-Wyatt," I told him once we unlocked our lips and tongues.

"I do," Gabe said like he was practicing for the big event.

"Wow, you've got that part down perfectly." An excited shiver worked its way through my body, and I wondered how I was going to react when he said those words for real.

"I've been practicing in the mirror," Gabe said playfully. He regaled me with ten different ways of saying those two words—from the serious to the hilarious. My favorite was his attempt at a British accent; it wasn't half bad, and I thought maybe we could have fun with that one someday. I opened my mouth to suggest it, but I was interrupted by the doorbell ringing. "Uh oh," Gabe said, his eye sparkling with mischief, "your future in-laws are here."

"Yours are too," I said, matching his tone and expression. Our parents lived only an hour apart and had become great friends once we introduced them at dinner in February, so they flew together and drove to our house together. "Last one to the door is the worst son-in-law," I yelled before I bolted for the door.

"Oh no you don't," Gabe said. He caught me before I left the room and playfully shoved me out of the way. Gabe had a strength advantage and agility from years of playing sports, but I was fast as lightning when I had nothing but open space in front of me, so I did what any man would do once he cleared the staircase and had the front door in his sight. I tripped my future husband and leaped over his body as he fell to the floor so I could get to the door first. Gabe grabbed for my shorts while I was in the air and managed to pull them down to mid thigh, which slowed me down a little but didn't stop me.

I laughed in exalted pleasure when I reached the door first and yanked it open. I just didn't realize how it would appear to the parents when I stood there red-faced and panting from exertion with my pants hanging low around my hips like I'd just yanked them up, which I had, but probably not for the reasons they thought.

"Gabe's coming!" I said between ragged breaths, adding to the impression that they'd just interrupted sex. "Behind me," I added, making it worse. My face flamed in embarrassment as soon as the words left my mouth. Our dads' lips twitched as they fought to keep the smiles off their faces—probably to spare me further embarrassment—but my mother wasn't feeling quite so generous.

"Yes, I imagine that happens frequently. Had we known we were interrupting we could've circled the block a few more times," she said, pushing past me to enter the foyer. "Oh my lands, this house is beautiful, Joshy."

"We weren't having sex," I told them. "It was a race to determine the best son-in-law. Here I am, the one to greet you while Gabe," I looked over my shoulder to see my man standing there with a huge smile on his face, "laughs at me behind my back."

"Darling," Martina said, looking at me then her son, "we're all adults who know what it's like to be in love and have sexual urges." Gabe started to retch by that time, and it was my turn to grin smugly. "Save your excuses for when your future children catch you in the act."

"Yeah, like that time the kids came home early from the pool," Al said then started to laugh. "Dylan wanted to know what we were doing beneath that blanket, and your mom told him we were wrestling."

Gabe plugged his fingers in his ears like a child and said, "Not funny."

"My parents told me they were hiding Easter eggs when I caught them going at it in the kitchen pantry," I told Gabe, hoping to make him feel better.

"Is that the same little room where you whip up your hair potions?" Gabe asked.

"The one and the same," I said. I could tell he fondly remembered the two times we fooled around a little in that same room. "That's also how I found out there was no such thing as the Easter Bunny."

"Josh demanded to know why we were hiding the eggs when the Easter Bunny was supposed to be hiding them. I panicked," my dad said then laughed at the memory. "He was really pissed when he made the connection later in the year that no Easter Bunny also meant no Santa Claus."

"Wait, you didn't make that connection right away?" Gabe asked. His tone was curious, not scornful, so it didn't hurt my feelings.

"Some people believe only in what they can see while others cling to the belief that the fantastic and implausible must be true—or at least attainable—on some level," I told Gabe, aware that all eyes were on us. My parents weren't the ones who pissed all over my dreams of fairy tales and fantastic things, but I lost them for some time. It got so quiet that you could've heard a pin drop. I wanted the moment to remain lighthearted, so I said, "You should've seen how pissed I was when I found out that Mary Poppins wasn't real." It got the laughter I wanted to break up the emotion building inside me. "How about a tour of the house that starts with the kitchen so I can feed you. I know damn well you didn't eat much on the plane."

"Yes," the parental units said exuberantly.

"My peanuts were stale," my father said.

"My Coke was flat," Martina added.

"They gave me two little cubes of ice in my cup," Al said. "You know how I like a lot of ice."

"They wouldn't give me a mimosa," my mom complained. "Hell, I offered to pay for it."

I looped my arm through my mom's and said, "I got you covered, Mama." I had squeezed the orange juice that morning and made sure Gabe picked up champagne when he bought the scotch. "Follow me if you want to eat," I said in my best *Terminator* voice. I glanced at Gabe on my way to the kitchen, and his shrewd gaze said that he saw I changed the subject, but he winked at me instead of commenting.

I didn't realize how ravenous our folks were until Gabe had to pull me to safety when I set the platters on the kitchen island. I wasn't sure what everyone would like, so I made chicken, tuna, and egg salad sandwiches using a variety of bread for a nice selection. I had a second platter with various veggies and dips.

"Put the potato salad on the island with your right hand because I'm going to need your left hand later," Gabe said.

"He's ambidextrous, sweetheart, so play time would still be okay," my mom said between bites of chicken salad on a buttery croissant. "Get the potato salad, and I promise no one will get hurt."

"Oh my God," I muttered quietly on my return trip to the refrigerator. "I can't believe my mom just implied I could jerk you off with either hand."

"She was telling the truth," Gabe said humorously. "I wasn't thinking about sex for once; I was referring to the hand that will wear the ring that marks you as mine." There was a touch of growliness in his voice because he still didn't like that we took off our rings. I tucked them away in our sex toy drawer with another type of ring until our wedding day.

"What's the status on the potato salad?" Al asked a little frantically, not at all sounding like his usual calm self.

"Coming right up," I replied before I pecked a kiss on Gabe's lips quickly then returned to the island with the covered bowl. "Holy crap!" I looked at the platter of sandwiches and saw there were only two out of the dozen I'd made left. It was a damn good thing that we'd eaten before they arrived. "How long were we at the refrigerator?" I asked out loud.

"For the love of God! Bill, use a fork," my mom demanded when my dad acted as if he was going to eat the mound of potato salad on his plate with his hands.

"Baby, I made a list of things to pack in our carry-on luggage, but I think I'm going to have to amend it," I told Gabe. "That's a long flight."

Gabe leaned over and pressed his lips against my ear. "Don't forget the lube." His breath tickled my ear, and his words delighted other parts a little lower.

"I was talking about snacks," I whispered back.

"You're my favorite snack." Gabe nipped my ear with his teeth to demonstrate the validity of his words. Then he growled and made me laugh by nibbling on my neck. "Much better than some granola bar you plan on feeding me."

I looked up when I realized how quiet the kitchen had become and found four sets of smiling eyes locked on us. Our fathers beamed with pride while our mothers looked at us with joyful tears in their eyes. Emotion rose inside me so swiftly that my head felt like a balloon, but the weight of Gabe's confident hand on my hip tethered me to him so that I couldn't float away. It wasn't an oppressive kind of feeling, he made me feel safe.

"Protein bars," I corrected, "and I planned other things too." I honestly hadn't put any food items on the list, but I was going to remedy that right away. "I'll come up with a new plan," I promised him. My first act as a nurturing husband would be to make sure Gabe landed in Honolulu with a full stomach and empty balls.

We took the parents on the grand tour and told them about the renovations we'd made. They fell in love with Savage and Sassy who'd turned into a freaking comedy routine by repeating the lines from movies we watched. I saw the wistful looks on the moms' faces when I showed them the empty bedrooms we hoped to fill with kids. The looks on their faces when they saw their guest suites made all my fussing worthwhile.

"This room looks like something I'd expect to find in a hotel," Martina had said. "It's beautiful."

"Oh, my favorite flowers," my mother had exclaimed. "Thank you." She moved to hug me, so I pointed to Gabe because a glory hog wasn't an attractive trait in a human being.

We went to dinner after the parents had a chance to rest for a bit. I had wanted to cook but our moms overruled me, insisting that I had enough going on and needed a night of fun. Gabe pulled the keychain for Charlotte off the hook and handed it to me. I just stared at him for several minutes because he'd indicated that no one except him, and maybe his dad, would ever drive her.

"What's mine is yours," Gabe said softly. "I want to see you behind her wheel." There was an emotion I couldn't quite place in his eyes, but it disappeared behind a brilliant smile when I accepted the keys and his gesture.

I was overly cautious at first because she drove nothing like a modern car and I was terrified of putting a scratch on her. Gabe made fun of me and said that the kid down the street was pedaling his Big Wheel faster than I was driving. I relaxed a bit once I got used to the steering and had a lot of fun.

Dinner with our parents was a riot, and like last time, our fathers squabbled with one another over who should pay. I snatched the bill and paid it without them realizing it until it was too late, like Gabe had done in Miami. I was starting to get suspicious that the geezers were pulling a fast one on us. I meant to bring it up with Gabe once we were alone but forgot all about it when he convinced me to practice how I was going to "quietly pleasure" him on our flight to Hawaii. He returned the favor, of course, and I discovered that trying to keep quiet enhanced my orgasm.

Once we finished, I rested my head over his heart and thanked him for giving me back the joys of fairy tales. Gabe had turned the fantastic and implausible into reality, and made me believe once more.

# TWENTY-ONE

## Gabe

THE BRAIN IS A STRANGE ORGAN CAPABLE OF BOTH AWESOME AND terrifying things. I considered myself a calm and cool guy, but I was overwhelmed by a case of nerves the next morning. It started when reality invaded my dreams again, but instead of Jimmy shooting Josh, my birth mother and sisters rejected me. I had no logical explanation for the path my brain chose in my sleep, yet I woke with an aching heart in the early hours of the morning.

The sun hadn't fully risen yet, so I silently pleaded with my brain to let me get back to sleep. It didn't take me long to realize my begging was futile. I rolled over onto my side and watched Josh sleep instead. I loved the play of light and shadows on his face as the sun rose higher in the sky. I wanted to touch him but knew where it would lead if I did, and he needed the rest. Instead, I slipped out of bed, pulled on some pajamas, and went downstairs to make a pot of coffee.

My mom had always been an early riser, so I wasn't surprised to find that she was up and made coffee already. "I think I love this room the most," she said when I joined her in the sunroom in the rear of the house. It was my favorite place to read the paper and drink my coffee on Sunday mornings because it reminded me of the porch at my childhood home. "I imagine it will get chilly in here during Ohio winters," she said.

"I don't think it will be too bad," I replied after my first sip of coffee. "These are triple pane windows, we upgraded the heaters, and added a fireplace." As much as I hated snow, the thought of watching it fall silently to the ground while cuddling with Josh beneath a blanket while a fire crackled was very appealing to me.

"It's going to be beautiful," my mom said.

"Yes, it will." She was talking about the winter landscape, but I was talking about what would happen when cuddling with Josh became something more.

"Are you ready for today?" she asked softly. I knew she wasn't talking about the wedding rehearsal or dinner.

"I think so," I said honestly. "I don't have a reason to feel nervous..."

"... But you are anyway," she finished for me. "I think that's pretty reasonable, Gabe. You're only human after all." She smiled softly, but it didn't quite reach her eyes, which didn't make sense to me. She had encouraged the reunion from the very beginning. Why did she suddenly look as nervous as I felt? "Don't you go loving her more than me." *Ah, that was it.* "I'm sorry, son; I should never have said that to you when you're already nervous about meeting Bonita."

Her words were the jolt back to reality that I needed. "There's no way in the world that I could ever love her more than you. It doesn't matter that she was the one who gave birth to me; you will always be my mother. I'm hoping to be great friends with Bonita, and I want to know my sisters, but I'm not looking to replace you or the memory of my brother. They're not mutually exclusive, and it's because of your unwavering love that I know I don't have to choose. I can have it all."

"I have been proud to call you my son every single day of your life, but moments like this just take my breath away. Gabriel, you are a remarkable man, and I love you so very much." She swiped at the tears that streamed down her face. "Oh, I promised not to get too sappy this weekend, and here I am squalling already."

"I plan on getting super emotional this weekend, so I think it's okay if the mother of the groom cries a little also." I had no intention of holding back the joy that swelled inside me when I saw Josh standing across from me at the altar in his tuxedo, or when I slid my ring on his finger and heard the judge pronounce us as married. I knew that I would shed some tears and I didn't care what anyone thought.

Mom covered my hand with hers and said, "You chose well, Gabriel. There's no one better for you than Josh Roman. I have never seen you look as carefree and happy as you are when he is near. Seeing you like this makes my heart so happy. Your father and I adore him."

"Thanks, Mom. Your support means a lot to me." I was glad to have their approval, but I didn't need it to marry Josh. I knew he was the best thing for me and nothing and no one was going to get in my way. *Except maybe Jimmy De Soto.* I stomped down that thought as soon as it popped into my head. There was no way I'd let that asshole ruin my weekend or my life.

"Dylan would adore him too," my mom said quietly. "He'd love the way Josh jabs at you, but mostly he'd love the way that Josh looks at you as if you alone created the universe."

"I think about Dylan every single day of my life, but his loss is felt even stronger on certain days. Tomorrow will be one of them," I told her. I was thrilled to have found friends like Adrian and John in my life, but no one replaced the big brother I adored so much.

"He's with us, baby. We can't see him or hear his laughter any-more, but he's looking down on us. He'll be with you every step of the way, and you'll feel him in your heart." I hooked my arm around her shoulders and pulled her against my chest. She tucked her head under my chin, and we cried quietly together for a few minutes. My mom wiped her eyes, cleared her throat, and said, "Today is not about being sad; it's about welcoming your birth mom and sisters into your life. I want you to tell Bonita that I'm looking forward to seeing her again. Will you do that for me?" she asked.

"Gladly," I replied, kissing her on top of her head.

The early morning chat with my mom helped me push away any lingering nerves that remained. I focused on the important things like kissing Josh awake and luring him into the shower for some wet, naked fun. Neither of us wanted to abstain from sex leading up to our wedding nor would we spend the night apart. We were doing things our way because it had worked well for us up to that point. Why fix something that obviously wasn't broken?

I was my typical calm self when I pulled into the parking garage at the hotel where Bonita and her family were staying. We had arrived fifteen minutes early, so I was surprised to find them waiting for me outside the doors of the restaurant. I observed their family dynam-ics as we walked toward them because they hadn't spotted me yet. Bonita looked as anxious as I had felt that morning after my dream, but my sisters practically vibrated with excitement. Dear Lord, their beauty was more captivating in person than on Skype. I felt my big brother instincts kicking in again as I saw more than one guy checking them out. I thought it was too damn bad my gun was locked in the glovebox of my car and not on my hip.

"Gabe, do you really want to be growling when you meet your sisters?" Josh asked beside me. "Plaster a smile on your face before you scare them! We can hunt those pervy bastards down after brunch."

"Good idea, Sunshine."

"I hope he likes us," Arianna said as we neared.

"Well, he might not like *you* since you're a spoiled brat, but he's going to love Marisol and me," Selena told our youngest sister.

"You're such a…"

"Girls, please," Bonita said, interrupting them before an argument could start. "Do you want his first impression of us to be the three of you arguing?"

"They were only playing around, Mama," Marisol said. I already knew that she was the most laid back and practical of the three sisters. "He wants to get to know the real us, not the Stepford Sisters that look and act perfectly at all times."

"She's right," I said.

"Gabe!" All three sisters yelled my name at the same time as they launched themselves at me. Then they proceeded to talk over one another.

"Girls, one at a time," Miguel said patiently.

"Oh my goodness, you're more handsome in person," Marisol said.

"And tall," Arianna said.

"And broad. You look like you bench press buses for a hobby," Selena said.

"Just small cars," Josh commented, "and only every other day."

"I like you," Selena said before she threw her arms around Josh's neck for a hug.

"It's a good thing," I told her, "because we're a packaged deal."

"A few months ago we didn't know we had a brother and now we're about to have two!" Arianna exclaimed excitedly.

Marisol cocked an eyebrow high at Josh and asked, "On a scale of one to ten, how protective are *you* going to be?"

"That depends on the situation," Josh said, keeping his answer vague. He spent a lot of time around women and seemed to sense a trap when it was near. He once told me that women never forgot a damned thing and would recite something a person said verbatim ten years after it was spoken. He wasn't about to back himself into a corner.

"I like you too," Miguel said. He extended his hand to Josh first and then to me and introduced himself. He didn't seem to find anything awkward about our situation, and in fact, looked to be a proud father of three amazing young women and a doting husband who wanted to make his wife happy. If I hadn't already run him through every background search system available to me, I would've known at that moment that Miguel Gutierrez was a good man.

Bonita quietly watched everything unfold as if she was just happy to take it all in, but I could see the glimmer of wanting more in her eyes. I knew she hesitated because she wasn't sure what I was comfortable with, so I took the first step. I opened my arms, and she stepped into my embrace. I heard her crying softly against my chest and felt her tears soak my shirt.

"You look just like your biological father," Bonita said when she pulled back and looked up into my face. "You have my coloring, but other than that you're the spitting image of him. If you ever want to know more about him, I'll gladly tell you what little I know and show you his yearbook pictures."

"I'll give it some thought," I told her.

Bonita hugged me again and cried a little more.

"Gosh, Mom," Selena said. "You act like you haven't seen the guy in over three decades."

"Oh hush," Bonita replied, waving her hand in Selena's direction as she battled to keep her expression serious. "Can't we at least try and trick him into thinking we're a normal family for the weekend. I'm not expecting the three of you to keep up the charade forever, but at least until after the wedding."

We all laughed when the three of them said, "Okay," in unison.

"Are we ready to eat?" Miguel asked.

"Always," Arianna said. "I looked at their menu online, and I have my heart set on that big breakfast with the bacon, eggs, home fries, and pancakes."

"Quit bragging about your metabolism, skinny bitch," Selena said affectionately to our sister.

"It'll catch up to her when she goes to college," Marisol said. "She'll be eating pizza and Chinese takeout and gaining the freshman fifteen like the rest of the world."

"I gained twenty," I told them, "maybe even twenty-five pounds because I wasn't burning off the calories like I had in high school while playing football."

"I tried to gain fifteen pounds but couldn't do it," Josh said, earning glares from everyone else.

"You two skinny bitches," Marisol said, pointing her finger at Josh and Arianna, "can sit at a table by yourselves while the rest of us eat egg white omelets and wheat toast."

"I'm ordering the same thing as Arianna," I announced.

"I'll eat the egg white omelet and toast," Josh said. "I don't want to rip out the seams of my tuxedo pants tomorrow." Josh ate like a fucking bear coming out of hibernation, so I knew damn well he was just saying that to please my sisters, who were perfect, beautiful, and healthy women.

Brunch was a wonderful experience; there wasn't an awkward lull in the conversation and we never ran out of things to discuss. I was enjoying myself so much, and I hated to leave their company, but there were things we needed to do to prepare for the rehearsal.

Then it occurred to me that our day didn't have to end at all.

"I'd love for you to come to the rehearsal tonight. We're having a barbecue afterward with the wedding party and our immediate families. My mom and dad are looking forward to seeing you again, Bonita, and meeting the girls and Miguel. What do you say?"

"Yes!" my sisters exclaimed.

"Are you sure?" Bonita asked, but I saw the hopefulness in her eyes. "We don't want to intrude."

"Speak for yourself, Ma," Arianna said. "I want to spend as much time with my brother as I can, and I don't mind being pushy about it."

Marisol nodded. "Yeah, what she said."

"See, Ma," Selena added. "You said more than once that you wished we could all agree on things and now we do."

I laughed at their antics and said, "I'm positive that we want you there and that you won't be intruding."

"Okay, if you're sure," Bonita said.

"We are," Josh affirmed. "Rehearsal starts at five so how about you guys show up around three thirty or four?"

"We'll be there," Bonita said.

We exchanged hugs all around before we headed to Marla Henderson's boutique to pick up our tuxedos. I was shocked that Josh waited until the day of rehearsal to pick them up, but he had absolute faith in Marla and her team. They had met when they filmed the wedding series for Channel Eleven News and became fast friends. In fact, each of his former cast members was involved in our wedding day.

Marla was excited to see Josh and even happier when our matching tuxedos fit us perfectly. Of course, she wouldn't let us see each other. Waiting to see one another in our tuxedos on our wedding day was the one tradition we decided to keep. I had to admit that the charcoal gray color Josh insisted on looked perfect with my tan skin. I was positive it would be just as flattering against his fairer skin.

Josh and I stepped out of our dressing rooms at the same time and smiled. We looked happy and excited that our wedding was a little over twenty-four hours away, not hesitant or nervous. "What's next on our errands list?" I asked Josh, knowing damn well he had one.

"A fast food drive-thru," he replied. "How can anyone live on that pathetic amount of food? Baby, I need a juicy cheeseburger right away or I might not make it to the rehearsal dinner."

"I know just the thing." I took him to his favorite drive-thru and ordered him a burger, fries, and a milkshake.

"We're going to be very happy together," Josh said between ravenous bites of food. "I love a man who produces meat when asked."

"Anytime, Sunshine. Anytime."

# TWENTY-TWO

## Josh

OUR REHEARSAL AND DINNER THAT FOLLOWED WENT OFF WITHOUT a hitch. A psychotic man with a revenge plot didn't crash our event, and no awkwardness existed between the Wyatt and Gutierrez families. The two women didn't try to outdo one another, and neither of them challenged the other's right to be in Gabe's life. It was wonderful that there wasn't the female equivalent of a pissing contest over Gabe's attention. It was just a beautiful night.

I woke up the next morning to find that Gabe was out of bed

before me for the second consecutive day. He rarely woke before me and two days in a row had never happened. I was usually up and finished with my workout before he was up and moving. In fact, I typically woke him by holding a cup of coffee near his nose and lured him into joining me in the shower for his morning jolt of caffeine and cum.

I wondered if his early rise was due to his excitement about our big day, or because he wanted to spend as much time with his parents as possible. Another option might've been that he was trying to resist my charms and temptations. We said we weren't abstaining from sex leading up to our wedding, but it felt right to save a little something extra for our wedding night.

*Wedding night.* Those were two words I thought would never apply to me, yet they did. I was hours away from marrying the man of my dreams, and I couldn't keep the smile off my face as I dressed, brushed my teeth, and headed downstairs. I expected to find him in the kitchen or the sunroom with his mom like yesterday morning, but instead, he was in the garage wrenching on Charlotte with his dad. They hadn't heard me come in the door and continued to talk.

"You've taken great care of her, son. I'm very proud of you," Al said to his son. The pride I heard in his voice made me smile, and it looked like Gabe puffed his chest out a bit more than usual.

Every child born into the world wants to please their parents and make them proud; it is hardwired in our DNA. Some people have parents who love them unconditionally, and are their kids' champions in every part of their lives. Others have parents who only love them if they meet certain criteria. Gabe and I both had parents who set amazing examples for us in case our kids turned out to be straight.

"You need to dedicate yourself to giving the same amount of care to all the wonderful gifts in your life," Al told his son. I backed out of the doorway and eased the door shut when I realized that they were having a special moment.

"There's my boy," my mom said when I reentered the kitchen. "I thought I'd make your favorite crepes and sausage for breakfast unless you're too nervous to eat."

"I'm not nervous at all," I replied then realized that I meant it. "There's absolutely nothing to fret about." I couldn't recall a time in my life where I'd felt calmer. "Sausage and crepes sound amazing."

I tried to help her, but she smacked my hands away and shooed me to sit on an island stool. My dad joined us a few minutes later when he returned from taking Buddy on a walk. We chatted about anything and everything just like we had my entire life and it was a beautiful way to spend the morning of my wedding. I realized how much I missed my parents and decided that seeing them once or twice a year just wasn't enough, especially after the grandbabies came.

My mom sent me to round everyone up when breakfast was almost ready. I found Martina in their bedroom steaming non-existent wrinkles out of the dark teal dress she chose to wear to the wedding. I could tell by the number of pressed and steamed clothes hanging up around the room that she'd been at it for a while. I figured it was her way of working through her excitement and making the day pass faster.

I tapped lightly on the doorframe so that I didn't startle her. "Breakfast is ready, and then it's time for your pampering."

"What pampering?" she asked.

"Oh, did I forget to tell you what I had planned for the mothers of the grooms?" I extended my arm out so I could escort her to the kitchen.

Instead of looping her arm through mine, she reached for my hand. "Yes, I believe you did, but I'm intrigued. What do you have in store for the mamas today?"

"I think I'll wait and surprise you instead."

"You shouldn't have gone to so much trouble," Martina said an hour later when she settled into the pedicure chair with her feet soaking in the jetted basin and a mimosa in her hand.

"Josh, this is your special day, not ours," my mom said. "You should be the one getting pedicures, manicures, and massages."

I closed Curl Up and Dye to the public, but my special ladies were getting the works that day. Despite their words, I saw the pure enjoyment in their eyes when Dee and Josi worked their magic.

"Hair and makeup will follow after your massages," I told them.

"You spoil us too much," Martina half-heartedly protested as Josi massaged the arch of her right foot.

"Not enough," I replied. I dropped a kiss on top of both our mothers' heads and went off to find my two best friends who were on hand to help me.

Chaz looked me over from head to toe with narrowed eyes. "I expected to find you wild-eyed and crazy," he told me. "I'm happy that I don't have to talk you down from the ledge."

"I'm feeling great," I told them. "I can't wait for five o'clock."

"I'm so happy for you, sugar." Mere threw her arms around my neck and rocked me back and forth. "I am so proud to stand beside you on your wedding day." She pulled back and smiled up at me. "You're going to return the favor, right?"

"I wouldn't miss it for the world," I replied.

"That goes the same for me," Chaz told her

"Does that mean you think Harley is 'the one' for you?" I asked her.

Meredith smiled happily and said, "I do."

"That's Josh's line today, Mere," Chaz said. "Wait your turn." I hoped it wouldn't be long before it was her turn to recite those words.

The day passed by quicker than I expected it to, and before I knew it, I was in our bedroom about to get dressed for the main event. The door opened just as I reached for my tuxedo. Gabe entered the room carrying his garment bag. Our original plan had been to dress separately and meet our parents in the sunroom so they could escort us down to the altar, so his appearance surprised me.

"I want to get dressed in our room," Gabe said.

"Oh, do you want me to use the spare bedroom then?" I asked.

"No, I want to get dressed in our room with you," he said huskily. "I don't want to spend another second of this day separated from you."

"Not even if I have to poop?" Come on; I couldn't be expected to lose my snark and sass overnight. Besides, it was better to let my mouth run amok privately when my emotions soared rather than at the altar.

Gabe laughed hard before he hooked his finger in the elastic on my aqua blue bikini briefs that I bought for the special occasion. "I'm going to dress you now then undress you later." His eyes held so much sensual promise that I worried we might be late to our own wedding.

"That's much better than doing either of them alone," I told him.

"Indeed."

"I think we should remove some of your clothes to level the playing field," I told Gabe, who had his clothes on while I stood in my new undies. "I should be aggravated that you get to see my something blue before I was ready to reveal it to you. It's also my something new," I told him. Okay, we were guilty of following that tradition too. "I'm wearing the cufflinks that my dad wore on his wedding day as my something old and borrowed." I was pleased that two items counted as four.

Gabe smiled broadly at me, and I wasn't sure I understood what was so damn cute until he pushed his sweats down to reveal he was wearing the same underwear as me. "I guess we are starting to dress alike after all," he said. "Here's my something new and blue."

"What's your old and borrowed?" I asked.

Gabe reached inside the garment bag and pulled out a baseball card. "Chipper Jones rookie card from 1991; it was Dylan's prized possession. I asked my mom if I could borrow it for the night." Gabe swallowed hard and cleared his throat before he said, "I thought it would be awesome to have a piece of him with me at the altar."

I fought back the tears and said, "It's perfect, Gabe."

"Let's get this show on the road, Sunshine."

Gabe finished stripping down until we stood across from each other wearing nothing but our undies and sappy smiles. "This is the opposite of strip poker," I told him. "Asking you to get dressed is the opposite of what I normally want to happen, but I'd rather not say our vows in our skivvies."

"I'll go first," Gabe said then proceeded to pull on the dark gray dress socks.

I put on my socks then waited while Gabe pulled his tuxedo pants up his long legs. I fastened them for him and he did the same for me once I put on my pants. We tried buttoning one another's shirts simultaneously, but we kept getting in each other's way. I buttoned his shirt first—making sure I got a sweet kiss each time the button slid through the opening—then he did the same for me. I tied his necktie for him next then giggled when he turned me to face the mirror so he could tie mine.

"I have to be looking in the mirror," Gabe said in my ear when he stood behind me. I wasn't complaining because I took the time to study our reflections while he reached around me and tied my tie. I loved the difference in our height, build, and coloring. He was dark where I was light, the yin to my yang, the night to my day, and the sky to my sun—opposites, but equal and you couldn't have one without the other. He was mine, I was his, and we were us.

Our jackets and shoes were the final touches to complete our look. Once they were on, Gabe turned us to face the mirror once more. He wrapped his arms around my chest and rested his head against mine. I glanced at the clock on the dresser and saw that we were expected downstairs in three minutes. That was plenty of time for me to say what needed to be said.

"Thank you for loving me," I said simply.

"Thank you for letting me," Gabe replied. It might've sounded odd to anyone else's ears, but it rang true in mine because I fought him and his affection for months.

I turned to face him, linked my hands with his, and said, "Let's do it!"

Gabe widened his eyes in surprise. "Now? Our parents are waiting for us downstairs, Sunshine. I don't think they're going to believe that we're up here hiding Easter eggs or wrestling," Gabe said.

"I can be quick," I said, playing along.

"Where the hell is the fun in that?" Gabe asked. "I'm going to take my time unwrapping the greatest gift I've ever received."

"Hey, you two," Al hollered through our bedroom door. "There are people waiting downstairs who want to see a wedding. You coming?"

"I was close, Al, but not anymore." I covered my mouth when I realized that I had just made a sex joke with my future father-in-law and was about to faint when I heard his hearty laughter thundering in the hallway.

"Damn, I'm getting the best son-in-law in the world," he said once he could speak again. "Oh man, that's awesome. You better get down here before one of the mothers comes looking for you." That was exactly the words we needed to hear to get us moving.

Gabe and I followed Al to the sunroom where our moms and my dad waited. Our moms burst into tears and took turns fussing over both of us. Al and my dad pulled handkerchiefs out of their pockets and handed them to our moms. I had a vision of Gabe doing the same for me someday when our kids got married.

"Good thing you scheduled ten minutes for our moms to cry

and fuss," Gabe whispered in my ear as they were starting to wind down. He pressed his forehead to mine and asked, "Are you ready to become Joshua James Roman-Wyatt?"

"I am. Are you ready to become Gabriel Allen Roman-Wyatt?"

"I am," Gabe said tenderly then dropped a sweet kiss on my lips. "After you."

I pulled back from him so I could join my parents who waited for me at the door. I fixed the smudge of mascara under my mom's left eye then joined hands with my parents. I looked over my shoulder at Gabe who stood watching me with smiling eyes filled with so much love and happiness that I was sure I had to be dreaming. No one had ever looked at me the way he did. "It's not too late to run," I said teasingly.

"I'll see you down there," Gabe assured me.

The music started the second we stepped around the corner of the house, and the altar came into view. I didn't have the urge to look back to see if Gabe followed because I knew damn well he did. I faced forward to a gathering of people who loved us and a future I couldn't wait to begin.

# TWENTY-THREE

## Gabe

I PAUSED WITH MY MOM AND DAD AT THE CORNER OF THE HOUSE to allow Josh and his parents time to reach the altar. I wished that I could watch him walk between the aisles of seats where our closest friends and family gathered to share the day with us, but I stayed hidden so that I didn't detract from his attention. Besides, I'd get to watch the video recording as many times as I wanted later. Perhaps, watching it would become an anniversary tradition for the two of us.

Josh and I had talked at length about the music we wanted to represent us as we walked, first as individual men then later when we became one. The songs we liked weren't unique, but we found a way to make them our own. The second verse of an acoustical version of Train's "Marry Me" was the cue to begin my walk. I inhaled deeply and exhaled slowly to calm my racing heart while searching for the center that Josh was always trying to find.

"Keep breathing, and it will be all right," my mom said, squeezing my hand.

"You're right," I told her then plastered a huge grin on my face for my guy and our guests to see. "Let's not keep him waiting any longer." Then the three of us took a step forward at the same time.

"Would you look at that," Dad said once we rounded the corner of the house and could see across the expanse of the yard. We had practiced the walk the night before, but it looked completely different with smiling people filling the chairs, and the man at the altar wore a matching tuxedo to mine instead of shorts and a T-shirt.

"I'm looking," I told him. My ingrained protectiveness urged me to keep an eye out for a potential threat, but my soul whispered *don't look away from Josh*. I placed my faith in the universe that brought Josh into my life and my trust in the extra men on hand for protection. I refused to let Jimmy rob me of another moment.

I saw the same love and commitment shimmering in Josh's gaze that I felt in my heart. Tears welled in my eyes when he held out both hands for mine. Standing in front of me was a man who turned toward me instead of away from me, who reached for me instead of pushing me away. My Sunshine.

I never looked away from Josh's eyes and listened with half an ear as Judge McDonnell began to speak about why we had gathered and the meaning of life and love. I knew why we were there and I was looking right at the meaning of life and love. I knew from rehearsal that I'd be reciting my commitment to Josh first. The level of excitement inside me kept building as I waited for the part where I got to promise to love and cherish him for the rest of my life.

Judge McDonnell seemed to be more long-winded the day of the wedding than he was at the rehearsal. I was ready to jump out of my skin by the time he said, "Gabriel…"

"I do," I said eagerly. I winced with slight embarrassment when I realized what I'd done. The guests and judge chuckled over my exuberance, but the only reaction I cared about was from the man holding my hands. The joyous smile on his face said he didn't care that I jumped the gun a bit.

"I do too," Josh said just as eagerly.

"Fellas, this isn't how we rehearsed it last night," Judge McDonnell said good-naturedly. "Perhaps now that we've got that out of the way we can go back and do it right."

"Not from the very beginning though," Josh told him. "Start at the 'Gabriel' part."

The judge chuckled some more, and I could see him shake his head out of the corner of my eye. He cleared his throat and began again. "Do you, Gabriel Allen Wyatt, take thee, Joshua James Roman, to be your wedded husband, to have and to hold from this day forward, for better, for worse, for richer or for poorer, in sickness and in health, to love and to cherish, 'til death do you part?" Emotion clogged my throat, and it took me longer to respond than the judge expected. "Now you can say your part, son," he encouraged.

Laughing at my idiocy dislodged the lump in my throat. "I do!"

"Do you, Joshua James Roman, take thee, Gabriel Allen Wyatt, to be your wedded husband, to have and to hold from this day forward, for better, for worse, for richer or for poorer, in sickness and in health, to love and to cherish, 'til death do you part?"

"I do," Josh said proudly.

"May we have the rings?" Judge McDonnell asked.

I turned to Adrian and accepted the ring he held out for me. The man who'd become more like a brother than a friend winked and smiled happily. I placed the ring on the tip of Josh's finger and said, "I give you this ring as a symbol of my commitment to love, honor, and respect you." I felt tears sliding down my face as I pushed the ring the rest of the way home.

Josh's voice cracked with the raw emotion he felt while reciting those same words to me before he slid the ring on my finger. I raised my hand to brush away his tears just as he did the same for me. There were audible sighs coming from our guests when we smiled at one another.

"By the power vested in me by the great state of Ohio, I now pronounce you husband and husband." I had already planted my lips firmly against Josh's before Judge McDonnell could finish saying "You may kiss your husband." My eagerness earned whistles and catcalls.

I pulled back and stared into Josh's smiling eyes until a peppy ukulele version of "Somewhere Over the Rainbow" from the *Wizard of Oz* began to play. It was our cue to take our first walk as a married couple. In keeping with the desire to do things our way, we stopped at each row of seats and shook hands or hugged the guests as they exited the rows rather than walk down the aisle and wait for them to converge on us.

Our guests walked over to the ornate marquee that was set up for our reception while Josh and I posed for photos with our families and the wedding party. I wanted to tell my husband three very important words, but I was interrupted by Josh's photographer friend who kept saying, "stand here" or "look this way" or "smile."

I snagged Josh's hand to hold him back when the smiling and posing was over. "I love you."

"Still?" he asked like he was surprised.

"Forever," I promised then pulled him to me for a long, lingering kiss.

"I love you too, Gabe," Josh said when we finally broke apart. "Now, we better get in there before those damn deputy marshals eat all the food." At first, he caught me by surprise because I was so fixated on him that I forgot about the potential threat to both of us. Then I laughed because they did seem to enjoy the barbecue while they kept an eye on things at the rehearsal. Well, I thought his observation was humorous until he said, "I hope they didn't find the apple tarts in the kitchen."

Most men would question why two deputies from the Marshals Services office would be rummaging through his kitchen, but not me. "What apple tarts?" I asked as I began tugging Josh toward the reception.

"I got up after you fell asleep last night and baked tarts to take to the hotel. I knew you'd prefer it over the cake we ordered," Josh told me.

"How well did you hide it? My dad can sniff out apple, cinnamon, and pasty better than a bloodhound," I said, increasing my pace.

Josh tugged on my hand to slow me down and nodded his head in the direction of the marquee when I started to veer off toward the house to check on my tarts. "He already found them, but your mother threatened his life if he so much as stole a fleck of cinnamon sugar off the crusts."

"I'm going to trust you on this, Sunshine." I placed another kiss on his forehead before we entered the marquee.

"Let's hear it for Mr. and Mr. Roman-Wyatt!" the DJ announced. Cheering and clapping erupted when we walked to our table.

I was eager to get Josh alone in our hotel room that night, but I didn't want our reception to pass by too quickly. Our wedding was a once in a lifetime occurrence, and I wanted to savor every minute, every smile, kiss, and especially when we shared our first dance to Louis Armstrong's "What a Wonderful World." I'd relive that moment until the day I died. When the song finally ended, our guests clapped, expecting us to leave the mock dance floor or invite them to dance also, but we had a surprise. Instead, we struck a pose in the middle of the floor until "It Takes Two" by Rob Base and DJ E-Z

Rock started to play. Josh had created a fun, easy dance that even I could pull off to entertain our guests. I had been nervous about it, but we laughed, and they cheered, not caring if I missed a step.

"It's time for the grooms to dance with their mothers," our DJ said once Josh and I finished busting a move. We had something more than a simple dance planned to honor our parents. As Celine Dion's "Because You Loved Me" began to play, the screen behind the DJ showed a video we comprised of pictures of us as kids with our parents. There were photos of them holding us for the first time, holidays, birthdays, sporting events, and spelling bees. As we spun our sobbing mothers around on the floor, our guests saw our prom, graduation, and pictures of us at college. As the song worked to a close, the individual photos turned into group photos of all of us taken when we visited them in Miami. I doubted there was a dry eye beneath the marquee by the time the song ended.

"Our greatest blessings," my mom said to me. "I cannot wait until you experience it for yourselves."

Later, I shared a dance with Bonita and my three beautiful sisters and so did Josh. I spun Meredith around the floor and then sweet, feisty Mama Richmond, who assured my mother that she watched over me like she did Josh. I was able to find moments with both fathers, my friends and coworkers, and even Captain Reardon. I smiled when I saw Kyle and Chaz take a few spins on the dance floor and the way Emory and Silver tried not to watch each other. It was the most precious night of my life, and I knew when it was time to steal my husband away to consummate our union properly.

We said our goodbyes to our guests and thanked them for being part of our special day then headed to Cincinnati in the back of a hired car. We decided to stay closer to the airport when we booked a flight that was scheduled to leave CVG at seven forty in the morning. I would've booked a room even if our flight didn't leave until noon because I had no intention of being quiet or holding anything back and some things parents didn't want to see or hear.

"Here comes your favorite part," Josh said once we were inside our hotel room.

"Third favorite part," I reminded Josh as I backed him up toward the bed.

"I brought something special for our night," Josh said.

"Toys?" I asked in surprise.

Josh snorted and said, "Hell no. With our luck, we'd be 'randomly selected' for a luggage search and the TSA would have a grand ole time waving our dildos around."

"We have dildos?" I asked.

"I was just using that as an example. I do have lubricant in our luggage, but no sex toys. Oh," Josh said with a crestfallen face, "the FAA doesn't permit us to have liquids in our carry-on luggage," he said. "No lubricated hand jobs for you on the flight unless you want me to use spit?"

"We'll worry about tomorrow's orgasms tomorrow. I want happily-ever-after sex," I told Josh.

"I brought just the thing too," Josh said excitedly. He left me standing by the bed while he fiddled around in the suitcase. When he returned, he held a bottle of lube in one hand and my burgundy silk tie in the other. "We're tied together now, baby, so let's do it right."

I'd wanted to wrap that tie around his wrists every time I wore it, but I would always forget later in my haste to have him. Josh was right; there was no better night to slow it down and love him properly. I took the tie and lube from his hands and placed them on the bed then we proceeded to undress one another until we wore nothing but our matching bikini briefs. I'd made love to this man as his boyfriend and fiancé, but that night I was his husband. I felt the enormity of the moment in my soul and swore that I'd make it the best night he ever had because I'd never get another first time as his husband.

Josh held his hands in front of him and said, "You'll just have to tie my wrists together since there's no way to anchor my hands to the bedframe. I would expect these pricey hotels would think more outside the box and at least have some discreet rings disguised as decorations or something."

"I'll ask next time before I book a room," I told him while I wrapped the silk around one wrist then the other. "Excuse me, sir," I said pretending to talk to the concierge, "does your establishment offer beds where a man can tie down their husband for sex?"

Josh chuckled briefly, but all traces of humor faded from his face when I pushed his briefs down his long legs. I removed mine also then helped him get comfortable on the bed. I saw nothing but trust and desire in his eyes when he rested his bound hands above his head on the pillow. I wondered if my faith in him those two times he bound my hands was as big of an aphrodisiac as it was for me. I had to close my eyes and breathe deeply to stifle the urge to take him instead of drawing out his pleasure.

"I can't wait to taste you," I told him.

"You just had my dick in your mouth yesterday," he said, already impatient.

"You might taste different now that you're a married man," I said before I licked the thin line of pre-cum that dribbled from the tip of his cock to pool on his stomach. "Yep, sweeter." I worked his cock until he was a quivering ball of nerves then moved to tease his ass open with my fingers and tongue.

"Fuck me, already," he yelled, probably louder than he intended. Not that I gave a flying fuck what the people in the room next to ours thought.

"I'm just warming up, Sunshine," I said, fighting the urge to give into his demands. All I had to do was remember how he tormented me and I found the resolve I needed.

"Gabe, please. I want to feel you inside me."

"I am inside you," I replied, twisting my two fingers up to massage his prostate.

"I want your cock!" His eyes were wide and pleaded desperately for the relief that only I could give him. He pitifully moaned when I removed my fingers from his ass, which left him empty and hungry for more.

I pressed my lubed cock against his puckered entrance. "I don't think the people across the river heard you, Sunshine," I said, then pushed in until I was buried balls deep inside him.

"Fuck me, Gabe!" He was beyond desperate by that point, and it felt cruel to draw out his torture for another second.

I captured his lips in a searing kiss and began to love him in earnest, catching his every groan and sigh in my mouth. The sound of our flesh slapping together echoed in the room and spurred me on. Josh lowered his bound hands and looped them around my neck like he needed to touch me.

He slid his fingers in my hair and tugged seconds before he broke our kiss. "Yes, Gabe!" I only had to peg his prostate a few more times before he came apart beneath me and all over me. His ass put a stranglehold on my cock, sending me over the edge after him.

I collapsed on top of him, careful to keep the bulk of my weight on my elbows, while I labored to suck oxygen into my lungs. I slid out from beneath his looped arms and untied his wrists. "You know what I want to do now?"

"Recharge and do it all over again?" Josh asked hopefully.

"Eat apple tarts!"

"Never change, Gabe," he said.

"Some things will never change," I assured him. "My love for my man, my family, my country, and apple pie."

# TWENTY-FOUR

## Josh

I WASN'T REMOTELY CONCERNED ABOUT THE LACK OF SLEEP THE next morning when we set off for our honeymoon because I knew there'd be chances to nap on the flights. I worried less about people's opinions about the matching shirts Gabe and I wore on our first full day of marriage. My mom had them custom-made for us, and we fell in love with them. The white T-shirts had kissing caricatures that looked just like the two of us in our tuxedos with the words "Just Married" beneath them. We wouldn't know what other wedding gifts we received until we returned from our vacation and opened them, but I knew those shirts would be my favorite.

The layover at LAX was longer than the flight there, but I was too happy and excited to be bored. Plus, our T-shirts became a conversation starter with a fun couple we met at the airport restaurant.

"Can you imagine if Gram had shirts made for us, babe?" Ben asked his husband.

"They probably couldn't be worn in public," Xavier replied.

We learned that Ben and Xavier had been married for a few years and spent as much time traveling as they could before they started a family. I figured by the sweet smiles they exchanged when they talked about their future children that it might happen sooner rather than later. Laughing and joking with them while we had breakfast made the layover pass by faster and took the sting out of paying fifteen bucks for an omelet, two pieces of toast, and orange juice.

Before we parted ways, Ben asked me to find out where my mother purchased the shirts. "We're going to be making a special announcement soon that calls for custom T-shirts." My mom was happy to help them.

"They're a fun couple," I told Gabe as we boarded the plane.

"Yes, they are," he agreed. "Does that mean you're going to invite them to Sunday dinners from now on?"

"I would invite them if they lived closer. My food is good, but I'm not sure anyone would drive from D.C. to Ohio for it," I replied.

"I would," Gabe said with a warm smile.

I had never been one to fall completely asleep on a plane, but I did take a few catnaps during the long flight to Honolulu. My husband didn't have any problem falling asleep and staying that way. He snored softly through at least half the flight while I read an advanced copy of Chaz's next book release, but I thought the sound was more endearing than annoying. I had hoped for some mile-high action, but neither of us took that risk.

Needless to say, Gabe's steps were a bit peppier than mine after we retrieved our luggage, but that changed the minute I stepped outside the airport and into the brilliant sunlight. We might've traveled for more than twelve hours to get there, but it was only five o'clock in the evening due to the time change. The sunshine and the smell from the flowers in the lei I wore around my neck revived me.

We decided that we didn't want to stay in a touristy part of Hawaii, so we rented a home that afforded us a lot of privacy. The house was a short drive from the beach and surrounded by lush landscaping, trees, and waterfalls that made us feel like we were in a private oasis. I had big plans for that waterfall, but it had to wait until after we returned home from dinner and grocery shopping.

I made a pitcher of sangria and carried it out to our private swimming pool where Gabe waited naked for me. I plopped my bare ass down on the chaise lounge chair beside his and poured us both a tall glass. "This is stunning," I told him, looking at the pool that picked up the rays of the setting sun.

"Most beautiful thing I've ever seen," Gabe said huskily. I turned my head and found him watching me.

"Charmer," I said.

"Honest," he replied. "I'm looking forward to skinny dipping with my husband."

"When can we expect his arrival?" I asked.

"I also have big plans for that sassy mouth. Drink up, Sunshine." Gabe took a sip of his sangria and said, "Whew, that's strong!"

I would've made fun of him, but he was telling the truth. I must've fucked up my measurements because that drink was going to my head quicker than Gabe's kisses. My eyelids started getting heavy, and my body was warm all over by the fourth sip.

Gabe chuckled warmly beside me, causing goose bumps to pop up all over my skin. "Lightweight," he said softly.

I fell asleep before I could argue and didn't stir until Gabe lifted me off the lounger. I had no idea what time it was, but the sun had set completely, and the stars were out in full force.

"Okay, I'm ready," I told him.

"For bed," Gabe said humorously.

"It's our first night here, and we need to have sex," I protested when he laid me on the bed and covered me.

Gabe got in bed beside me and pulled me against him. His body heat was lulling me back to sleep already. "We'll make up for it tomorrow," he promised.

"K," I said sleepily. "I'm going to ride your ass all over this bed."

"Aw, you should've put that in your wedding vows," Gabe remarked.

"Your level of snark is getting out of control," I told him, but couldn't keep the smile off my face.

"I learned from the master," Gabe said.

"So did I," I replied. We both knew I wasn't talking about our personality traits. Gabe was the first man I topped and he'd be my only.

"Get some sleep because I have something special planned for us after you ride my ass all over the bed," Gabe said, dropping a kiss on the top of my head.

We woke early the next morning feeling rested, and horny. I rode Gabe's ass hard as promised then he took me on the most amazing day adventure after breakfast. The Big Island was known for having beaches with three different colors of sand—green, white, and black.

"I've planned day excursions to all of them," he told me excitedly.

I didn't know there was such a thing as green sand until I saw it with my own eyes. It was a damn good thing that Gabe fixed a hearty breakfast because getting to the green sands of Papakōlea wasn't easy, but damn it was breathtaking.

We parked our rental car at a small harbor and hiked for a little over two miles before we reached the lava cliffs above Green Sand Beach. Our journey didn't end there because we had to walk down the lava cliff on one side of the bay to reach the sand. It wasn't a steep climb, but it was fucking exhilarating. I stripped down to my skimpy swim briefs—I mean the fabric was barely enough to cover my junk—and hit the water with my husband fast on my heels.

He tackled me in the water when it was deep enough, and we splashed around trying to pull each other under water. I soon found something more interesting to do with my hands than splash water at Gabe. I stroked his erection through his swim shorts and smiled at him in a way that projected my wicked intentions. We were alone on the beach that morning, and I decided to take advantage of it by looping my arms around his neck and pulling myself up until I could wrap my legs around his waist.

Water might be sexy and do wonderful things for your libido, but it's not your friend when it comes to having sex and should never be confused with lubricant. I loved Gabe more than life itself, but unless he wanted to backpack me to the car after he wrecked my ass, we would have to settle for some good old-fashioned frotting.

Gabe gripped my ass hard and held me tight against him like he feared I would swim away. There was no chance in hell of that! I tangled my hands in his hair and gave him a slow burn kind of kiss, the ones that start out with just a hint of tongue then eases into a sexy glide. I sucked his tongue into my mouth wishing it could be his dick but settled for the insane thrill that raced up my spine when I began grinding our erections together.

In the grand scheme of things, getting off by rubbing our dicks together through our clothes seemed innocent and immature, but the landscape and the emotions involved elevated it to an erotic encounter like nothing I had ever experienced when I was young and innocent. The intensity of our kisses matched the activity going on beneath the water. The closer we got to our orgasms, the harder we kissed one another, and they slowed to savoring sips as our bodies came down off our climactic high.

"Did we break any environmental laws by unloading spunk into the ocean?" I asked Gabe once we dropped down on the towels he laid on the sand.

"Nah," he said calmly. "It's just basically salt and water, so the marine life won't notice the difference."

"Oh, I bet there's a sea turtle out there appreciating that you ate cinnamon muffins and drank pineapple juice with breakfast," I said.

"Breakfast of champions to help you choke it down like a champion," Gabe said. He tilted his head to the side like he was thinking about putting that slogan on a T-shirt.

We lay on the beach for a while longer before Gabe pulled out bananas, water bottles, and granola out of his backpack. "What else do you have in your bag, Mary Poppins?"

"I guess you'll have to find out," Gabe said smugly. "You about ready to hike back?"

"I guess," I said. I wasn't very eager to leave that piece of paradise.

"I have more surprises for you," he said cajolingly.

I used to hate surprises but not when it came to Gabe. His surprises were the absolute best. I hiked back on sex-weakened legs and talked Gabe into stopping for a Hawaiian ice that was way better than the versions we got back in Ohio. The sugary cold treat was what I needed to fuel the rest of our adventure.

Gabe's surprise that night was taking me to a luau where we were served amazing food and drinks while we watched stunning performances by musicians and dancers. The men were virile and strong during their muscle dancing, and the women were fluid and graceful during their hula dancing. I even managed to stay awake long enough that night to recreate some of the moves with Gabe.

"There's no way you can top the magic of this day," I said into the darkness before I fell asleep. I should've known that Gabe would see that as a challenge.

# TWENTY-FIVE

## Gabe

I READILY ACCEPTED THE CHALLENGE MY HUSBAND THREW DOWN and the rest of our trip became a fun contest where we tried to outdo each other. We both came out as winners, regardless of who picked the adventure for the day. It was hard to consider it "losing" when we went on helicopter rides, snorkeled with sea turtles, or made love against the black, slick rock behind a waterfall. No one was keeping score and Josh's laughter and smiles were the best part of it all.

There were also days that we spent being lazy by the pool or strolling through an outdoor mall holding hands while buying souvenirs, or trying to make some of the Polynesian recipes in the cookbook Josh found in the kitchen of the rental house. There were seamless days of adventure and nights of passion, peacefulness in my soul, and more joy in my heart than I ever dreamed possible. There were times I felt it so acutely that it took my breath away and I knew I had to be dreaming. I was certain that at any moment I would wake up gasping for air like when a person wakes from a dream about falling. I'd reach for Josh to pull him closer only to find that he wasn't there. I'd sit up and look around only to discover I was back in that rental house alone, not in the new house I bought with my husband. But I wasn't dreaming; Josh was real, and so was our marriage.

Away from our everyday worries, which often included a threat of some kind, I could relax and enjoy our time without looking over my shoulder or trying to split my attention between loving Josh and protecting him. The likelihood that Jimmy found a way to follow us to Hawaii was slim, so I let my guard down and just soaked in the good stuff while I could. Being on vacation, however, didn't mean that I ignored my responsibilities as an officer of the law and ignored trouble when I saw or heard it.

One day, Josh and I were sitting at an outside café sharing lunch when I heard a woman shouting for help. I leaped from my seat and saw the woman pointing to a fleeing young man who'd stolen her purse. I chased that punk for two blocks, but I finally caught him—well, tackled him—in someone's front yard.

"Get off me, fucker!" the punk demanded.

I heard the screen door open quickly and slap the side of the house. "What the hell is going on here?" a woman asked angrily.

"Ma'am, can you please call the police? This punk stole a woman's purse from the market," I told her.

"Is that true, Raymond?" she asked angrily, ignoring my request.

"Ma, I don't know what the hell he's talking about," the punk said from beneath me since I had him pinned to the ground.

"Oh, yeah?" she asked, sounding angrier with every word she spoke. "Is a hot pink Coach purse what you're carrying these days? I wasn't aware you'd become such a queen."

"Get off me," Raymond demanded, "unless you want to use my asshole to get off. Will that make you forget what you saw because I can make you forget that twink you were with at the café." Raymond tried to push his ass against my crotch to entice me, but that only pissed me off more.

I dug my knee harder in the back of his leg making sure I hit a nerve that would render it numb for a minute. "That's no twink," I told the dipshit. "That's my husband, and there's not a damn thing you could do to make me forget him."

"You think?" Josh asked from behind me. "'Cause I'm not so sure from where I stand, Gabriel." I didn't know that he'd followed me.

"Quit busting my balls and help me out by calling nine-one-one," I told him.

"Please don't," the woman said. Her tone of voice caused me to snap my head up and look at her. It was more than sadness; it was desperation. "He didn't steal the purse for something bad like drugs," she told me. "Well, I guess it's for drugs, but they're legal." She removed her ballcap and exposed her smooth scalp. "He was only trying to get money for my chemo pills this month. My social security wasn't enough, and they cut his hours at work. He's a good kid." She turned her gaze back to her son and said, "This isn't the way, Ray Ray. I've completed the paperwork the social worker at the hospital gave me, and we need to have faith that the Lord will provide."

"Yeah, he's done a great job so far," Raymond said bitterly.

Raymond's mother let out a long-suffering sigh, and I had a feeling they'd had that same conversation more than once. "That doesn't mean I want you to snatch purses, Raymond. If I've learned one thing these past few months, it's that there are no guarantees on time. I don't want to spend the time I have left visiting you in jail, Ray Ray."

All the fight left the kid, and he released his grip on the purse that we'd been fighting over like it was the after-Thanksgiving sale at Macy's or something. I grabbed the purse and rose to my feet then offered my hand to Raymond to help him up. He hesitatingly accepted, which was smart because I grabbed him by the collar of his shirt once he stood in front of me.

"Do what your mother says, Ray Ray. Stop making things harder on her and spend some time with her. And don't ever insult my husband ever again." I used my most menacing voice, which seemed to work because he swallowed hard and nodded his head sharply. I turned loose of him and faced his mother. "Ma'am, I'd be happy to help you if you'd let me."

"You've helped me enough," she said proudly. "Thank you." I wanted to insist that I could help her, but I saw in her eyes that she wasn't receptive to the idea. "Just make sure that purse gets back to its rightful owner."

"I promise," I said. "Good luck to you, ma'am."

"Bless you," she said to me before she turned her attention back to her son. "Get your ass in here so we can Netflix and chill."

"Ewwww, Mom. That's just gross," Ray said. His face turned a flaming red color when Josh laughed so hard I worried something would rupture. "That doesn't mean what you think." Ray shivered hard and walked into the house with his mom.

"What does it mean then?" I asked Josh who still hadn't stopped laughing.

"Oh, Gabe, you're so damn funny!" Josh wiped the tears that were streaming down his face. "When teenagers tell their parents that they're going to someone's house to Netflix and chill it means they're having sex." It was the first time in my life that I felt... old. I considered myself pretty hip on terms kids were using since there were plenty of times I had to interview them in my line of work.

"Does everyone talk in code now?" I growled when I reached him on the sidewalk. "I feel like I should start taking notes for when we have kids."

"Oh, these codes will be replaced long before then. I'll make sure you stay on top of things though." Josh nodded to the purse in my hand. "What are you going to tell the woman when we get back to the café?"

"I'm going to tell her the kid dropped it and I stopped to pick it up instead of continuing after him," I replied. I would never condone Raymond's behavior, but I'd been around long enough to know that bad deeds didn't always equal a bad person.

"You're such a good man, Gabe," he said tenderly.

"You didn't think so five minutes ago. You called me by my first name, Sunshine. You only do that when you're pissed."

"Well, I didn't expect to find my brand-new husband grinding against another man's ass so soon," he said smartly.

"I wasn't grinding; I was apprehending," I argued. "So soon?" I asked, needing clarification. "Don't tell me you actually think I'm going to stray sometime down the road?"

"No," Josh said immediately. "That was a slip of the tongue. You have too much integrity to fool around behind my back. You would tell me if I stopped doing it for you." He said it as calmly as if he was talking about a new pair of shoes he wanted to buy while my heart hurt just hearing those words leave his lips.

"I'm happy that you believe in me so much, but I'm a little worried that you think there could come a time when you wouldn't be the one I wanted. I figured there'd be times that we argue, and possibly moments that we don't like one another, but I am certain there'll never come a day that I walk this earth and don't want you by my side." I leaned down and kissed his lips softly. "I'll prove it to you," I said, knowing that I would need to show him and not just tell him.

The police had arrived at the café when we got back. I returned the purse to the grateful lady, who introduced herself as Carol from Rhode Island. I felt guilty for lying to the police, but I also knew it was the right thing to do. Hopefully, it was the break that Raymond needed to turn his crap around.

As our time in paradise came to an end, I began thinking of ways to put an end to the situation with Jimmy. I couldn't continue to live with the threat hanging over my family. I put the planning and plotting on the back burner until it was the final night of our honeymoon and I could no longer ignore the danger waiting for us to return.

I held my husband in my arms and made a crucial decision. I needed to find a way to draw Jimmy out of hiding and get him on my turf, so I could take him down.

# TWENTY-SIX

## Josh

RETURNING HOME AFTER TWO WEEKS OF LIVING IN OUR LITTLE private oasis in Hawaii was bittersweet. I was excited to see our friends, our pets, and to sleep in our bed again. I was eager to resume filming at the news station and looking forward to the grand reopening of Curl Up and Dye after the renovations. I wasn't looking forward to the unpleasant intrusions into our life—namely Gabe's concern that Jimmy De Soto was still planning to strike.

I felt the tension rising and growing stronger inside him the closer we got to our departure day. He was thinking so hard that I could almost hear the gears grinding and I knew he was working out a plan in his head. He was great at covering it up, but the stress lines around his eyes gave him away. I don't think he slept more than a few hours the night before our flight home and he didn't sleep at all on the plane. I expected him to crash hard once we finally walked through the door, but he kicked into Josh gear and started channeling his emotional restlessness into physical activity. Hell, I'd have been okay with that if *I* was the physical exercise he'd chosen as his energy outlet, but he chose to unpack the suitcase and sort laundry.

The way I saw it, there were two ways to handle the situation: old Josh would've pouted, but new Josh joined in and waited for Gabe to come around because he always did. I just needed to be patient and wait for him to talk *or* jump him in the laundry room when his guard was down.

"I need to help with laundry more often," Gabe said, leaning on the dryer to catch his breath. "Those clothes were clean." He pointed to the clothes basket beneath him that caught a different type of load. I smiled at Gabe's splattered cum on the top of the formerly clean, dark clothes.

I couldn't resist his pert ass in the air while he was bent over to pull the clothes out of the dryer. "Good thing you have lube stashed in nearly every room," I told him.

"Damn good thing," Gabe agreed.

I could see fatigue from lack of sleep and a long day of travel moving in fast and hard like the pounding I'd just given him. "Baby, why don't you go upstairs and start the shower. I'll join you as soon as I toss these clothes back in the washer." I smiled wryly at him.

"Don't be too long," Gabe said then dropped a lingering kiss on my lips before he left.

Telling me to hurry was completely unnecessary because I never missed an opportunity to get wet and naked with Gabe. I tossed the clothes and detergent in the washing machine then fired her up before I snagged two beers out of the refrigerator and headed upstairs.

"We need a mini-fridge in…" The words died in my throat as my eyes locked on my husband through the glass shower doors. He was sliding his soapy hands up and down his ass crack to clean away the remnants, and it had to be in my top five list of hottest things I'd ever seen.

Gabe looked up when I didn't finish my sentence then smirked when he saw where my attention had gone. That smirk grew into a full-on wicked smile as he switched to washing his cock and balls. "You just going to stand there or are you going to bring me one of those beers?"

"Maybe they're both for me," I said, tipping one back for a long drink.

"I got a longneck for you to drink down," Gabe said causing me to nearly choke on the beer. "Sorry," he said when I sputtered. "Too cheesy?"

"A touch perhaps, but still adorable," I told him.

Gabe opened the shower door and crooked his finger at me. "Get in here." There was no point being stubborn when being with him in the shower was where I wanted to be, and I saw no point in denying myself what my heart, and his, desired most. I expected him to reach for his beer right away, but he took both from me and set them on the shelf. Gabe cupped the back of my head with one large hand and said, "Thank you."

"For?" I was being deliberately obtuse to force him to come clean with me.

"Pulling my head out of my ass again," he said with a wry smile.

"Is this about Jimmy?" I asked, even though I knew the answer.

"Yes," Gabe admitted. "I want him captured and out of our lives, Sunshine." The determination I heard in his voice concerned me.

"You have a plan to do that, don't you?" I asked.

Gabe inhaled deeply and released his breath slowly, but I wasn't sure if it was done to calm himself or delay the freaked reaction he was sure to get from me. "Okay, don't freak out…"

"No conversation that starts with those words ever goes well, husband of mine," I told him. The constipated face he got when he was concentrating faded into a beautiful smile. "What?"

"I'll never get tired of hearing you call me your husband or hearing you say that you're mine," Gabe told me. He pressed his lips to my forehead, knowing damn well what a sucker I was for those kisses. He was trying to disarm my defenses before I fully erected them. "I love you so damn much, which is why I just can't sit back and allow Jimmy to strike whenever it's convenient for him. I need to go on the offensive."

No amount of forehead kisses was going to prevent the shiver of fear that worked its way through my body after hearing those words. "How do you plan on doing this?" I asked.

Gabe's eyes took on a faraway look when he said, "I need to find a way to draw him out of hiding."

"Baby, have you given serious consideration to the possibility that Jimmy was heading north for Canada and not Ohio? It's been more than a month and what would be the point of waiting? He's had plenty of opportunities to hurt us and hasn't taken them," I said softly.

"I wish you were right, but I saw his hatred for me when we locked eyes in Miami. Escaping to Canada is a lot less probable than escaping by boat to the Bahamas. He didn't just disappear into the Smokey Mountains either. I want him on my turf and on my terms, but I need to do it in a way that doesn't jeopardize you or anyone else in this community." Gabe blinked, and his eyes met mine. "It's the only way."

I wasn't keen on the idea at all. Gabe made it sound like he wanted to paint a large red target on himself and parade around. The idea terrified me, and I wanted to argue that there had to be a better way, but I saw the determination in his dark gaze and the resolution in his firm jaw. The only thing I could do was give him the support he needed and hope Jimmy was captured soon.

The next morning, I decided to head to the grocery store by myself when it looked like Gabe might sleep until noon. I figured he needed the rest so he could go Clint Eastwood on Jimmy, but Gabe wasn't amused when he woke up, and I was gone. I had discovered some new music while in Hawaii and smiled when my new ringtone for Gabe went off. I just loved the peppy music and words in Anuhea's "Simple Love Song." He was surly on the phone when he demanded to know where I'd gone, then annoyed that I didn't wait for him.

"I wasn't aware that you liked to grocery shop so much," I said to him as I looked through the assortment of green apples. I could tell I was going to have to bring out my big guns to calm him down. "Or are you mad that you didn't get your morning blow job?" A startled gasp reminded me that I needed to keep my voice down. "You should try it some time," I said to a retreating Mrs. Adams, whose back was as stiff as her unfortunate-looking helmet hair.

She was one of the few openly hostile people in my town that weren't afraid to tell me what they thought of my "lifestyle." I hated that terminology. I couldn't change who I was any more than she could change herself. I'd never make her understand that I was born to love Gabe. I preferred people show their true colors, rather than be nice to my face only to cut me behind my back. I normally just ignored her attitude, but I wasn't in the mood that day.

"Josh," Gabe said in a warning tone.

"Gabe, I'll be extra cautious, but I won't be a prisoner to fear. I'm going to buy groceries so we can have a fun time catching up with our friends when they come over for dinner tonight."

"Dinner?" Gabe asked.

"It's Sunday," I told him using my *duh* voice.

"I know what day it is, Sunshine. I just figured you'd want to take tonight off since we just got back from our honeymoon."

"Never," I said like it was the most shocking thing I'd ever heard. "Our friends want to watch us open the gifts they bought us for our wedding, and they want us to feed them." I had the text messages from Chaz, Kyle, Deanna, Mere, Emory, and Sally Ann to prove it.

"Okay, we'll just keep it simple with hot dogs and hamburgers or something," Gabe said.

It was my turn to gasp like Mrs. Adams. "Our friends have come to expect nicer food than hot dogs and baked beans."

"Our friends love us regardless of what we serve," Gabe said. "I bet they won't even know if there's any meat offered at all if you make your baked macaroni and cheese." I ignored the door he opened with his meat comment and got to the heart of his meaning.

"Gabe, do you want me to bake macaroni and cheese to go with the pork chops I picked out?" I asked.

"Maybe, if it's not too much trouble," he said. "I don't want you to spend all day working on a cheese sauce."

"I promise you that it's no problem," I told him as I headed to the frozen food section in the store. He already learned my truth about my quick fix for mashed potatoes on a weeknight. It was time he learned the secret to my macaroni and cheese. A marriage built on lies was destined to fail.

"Be careful, Josh. Be alert to everything around you," he said, but I was only partially listening because I had locked eyes with Laura Sampson. "I will." Then I told Gabe that I loved him and disconnected the call. "Hey, Laura," I said when it was obvious from her expression that she wanted to speak to me.

"Congratulations on your marriage," she said sweetly. "I hope you both will be truly happy together." I had only seen her a few times since Billy was arrested, and although we were always cordial,

I felt awkward in her presence. Gossip about the status of her marriage to Billy was practically nil, and I didn't want to know anyway.

"Thank you, Laura. I appreciate that very much." I offered her a wide smile and hoped that was the only thing on her mind so I could get going, but I wasn't so lucky.

"He's sorry for what he did to you, Josh," she said softly while looking at her feet.

"For which time, Laura?" I asked, unable to keep the bite of temper out of my voice.

She snapped her eyes up to meet mine again, and I saw so much sorrow in her expression that I regretted my tone immediately. "I'm pretty sure all of it. Billy wrote you a few letters from jail, but they detained them before they were mailed to you."

"You think?" I asked her. "He admitted to stalking and harassing me. I'm no expert on our penal system, but I'm pretty sure that it's frowned upon for inmates to reach out to their victims." Laura flinched, and I was reminded just how much of a victim she was also. She wasn't my enemy. I moderated my tone and said, "Laura, I hope that Billy is truly sorry for the things that he did to both of us, but my happiness isn't contingent on it. I made my peace with the past and the things he did, and I don't care if he's happy or not. I do care about your happiness and that of your children. If you ever want to talk about you and your kids, I'm game, but discussing Billy—past or present—is off-limits." There was one thing that nagged at the back of my mind that only she or Billy could answer. "Except for one thing," I amended.

"Okay," she said hesitantly.

"How'd you guys live here for six months without me knowing it? I own the business that's at the epicenter of gossip."

"Billy was adamant about not living in Blissville," she told me. "I knew he was trying to avoid seeing you. We rented a house that was far enough in Carter County that it had a Goodville zipcode. I don't know why Delaney never talked about Billy to you during her visits; maybe she suspected there was something between you." That wasn't likely because publicly Billy had treated me like shit. "We did all of our shopping in Goodville, and he had no reason to come to Blissville until the time he dropped the kids off to Delaney at your salon. He deteriorated quickly after that. Josh, I'm…"

"Please don't say that you're sorry." I could see the apology in her eyes and hated that she thought any of it could be her fault.

Laura nodded slowly and pasted a trembling smile on her lips. "Anyway, I won't keep you. I just wanted to tell you that I'm happy for you."

"Thank you," I said again. "I'll see you around." We didn't attempt an awkward hug or anything; we just continued with our original destinations.

My mind wanted to stray to the conversation I had with Laura and the things that were left unspoken at my insistence, but I promised Gabe that I'd be alert to what was going on around me. As much as I hated whatever scheme he, Adrian, and John would come up with that evening, I agreed that we couldn't keep looking over our shoulders every two seconds.

Gabe helped me pack the groceries in the house once I got home. The look on his face when he saw the box of frozen macaroni was priceless. His jaw practically hit the floor like a cartoon character. "You've been serving me frozen macaroni and cheese *all* this time?" he asked. "I can't believe it."

"Gabe, we've been a couple for less than a year," I told him. "I might've served this to you three or four times." His crestfallen expression seemed extreme compared to my crime. I stood straight and put my hands on my hips. "What did you do?"

"What makes you think I did something?" he asked, but the guilty expression in his eyes gave him away.

"Spill it, Husband Hot Lips," I demanded.

"Dorchester and I might've entered you and Deanna into a macaroni and cheese contest," he said sheepishly.

"Why would you do that after Deanna was humiliated last time?" I asked in stunned belief. "Oh my God, now it's my turn to be humiliated."

"Well, I…"

"Maybe she'll show me the same mercy I showed her," I said to Gabe. "You better hope so anyway," I told him. I debated putting the frozen pasta in one of my baking dishes but decided against it. That kind of devious behavior would only encourage the jackasses more.

It turned out that I didn't have anything to worry about because Deanna unpacked an identical aluminum foil pan to the one I bought from the store. We shared a glass of wine and a good laugh over the incident before the other guests arrived. Gabe looked at me hopefully when he popped into the kitchen to get two more beers out of the refrigerator. He thought all the laughter meant that I forgave him. I narrowed my eyes that let him know he could expect retribution later that night. Unfortunately for me, he seemed more excited about his *punishment* than sorry about his actions.

# TWENTY-SEVEN

## Gabe

I KNEW WHAT THE LOOK THAT JOSH SENT ME IN THE KITCHEN meant. I loved how he thought I would be intimidated. Instead, my head went into hyperdrive wondering what he'd do to torture me once he got me alone upstairs, or anywhere in the house for that matter. We had free range fucking until we decided to have a family.

"Why're you looking so damn happy suddenly?" John asked when I returned with his beer. "You went in with your tail tucked between your legs and came back out... Ohhh." He winked playfully.

"Not that," I told him. "I wouldn't be back so quickly if that was the case." I handed his beer to him and said, "Our spouses have duped us both when it comes to the macaroni and cheese." I shook my head sadly then told John what I saw in the kitchen.

"What?" John asked. "Do I even know my wife at all?"

I could've let the silly competition between spouses go and look forward to my *punishment*, but I found that I liked giving John a hard time. "I bet Josh makes better potato salad than Deanna."

"Without a doubt," John said, not taking the bait. "I'd say baked beans, but I know for a fact she buys those in a can." He thought for a minute and said, "Chili cook-off. Technically it's fall, even if the temperatures are warmer than normal."

"Halloween party slash chili cook-off," I countered. "Anyone can enter their chili for judging."

"Who's going to be the judge?" John asked.

"We'll find impartial judges," I told him. I freaking loved the idea once it took root. "I think we should have a costume party too so that you guys stand a chance at winning something."

"You're a boastful son of a bitch when it comes to Josh's cooking, aren't you?" John asked.

"It's not boasting if it's the truth and I've asked you to stop calling my mother such harsh names," I said good-naturedly. "It's Martina, Mrs. Wyatt, or Mom; never bitch."

John threw his head back and laughed heartily. "Okay, I won't make that mistake again."

I wasn't excited about having the Sunday dinner when Josh first told me it was still on, but once I saw our friends' smiling faces, I was glad that he insisted. It seemed like Adrianna had grown so much in the two weeks we were gone.

"Hi, pretty baby," I said to her. "Did you miss Uncle Josh and Gabe?" She smiled up at me, and I felt my heart squeeze tight in my chest.

"Um," Sally Ann said, "Adrian and I would like to talk to you about something tonight after everyone leaves."

"Is everything okay?" I asked nervously.

"It's fine, honey. I'm sorry if I sounded so serious, but we do have an important question to ask you."

"Name it," I said. "Blood, money, or John's kidney."

"Hey!" John hollered. "My kidney is already promised to someone else."

"Who?" Deanna asked. "Busty Buxton?" My eyes widened at the mention of John's ex-girlfriend until I saw the grin on Deanna's face.

John just rolled his eyes and said, "Nah, I bargained it away to the crossroad demons so I could have you."

"Awwww," our friends all said.

"They didn't want your soul, huh?" Deanna asked.

"What soul?" he fired back.

"Good point," she said, nodding. "You made a good deal, babe."

"We don't want blood, money, or anyone's kidney," Adrian said. "We'd like you and Josh to be Adrianna's godparents and stand beside us for her christening in a few weeks."

"Oh," Josh said, his eyes were as wide as saucers. "We're not ready for a baby. We have a road trip planned for next summer before we get serious about babies."

"We'll try not to die until you get back from vacation," Adrian said dryly. "We'll try not to die for four or five decades while we're at it."

Josh's cheeks flamed red with embarrassment. "That's not what I meant," Josh said in a rush. "I don't want anything to happen to either one of you." Josh looked at Adrianna then back at me. "She's not quite housebroken, yet, but what do you say?"

"We'll take her," I told Adrian and Sally Ann.

"This conversation didn't go according to plan," Sally Ann told Adrian.

"It never does with Gabe," Adrian said. "He goes off the rail all the time."

"Hey, you're the one who wants me to raise your daughter," I told Adrian. "What's that make you?"

"Uhhhh," he said when he couldn't think of anything else.

"That's what I thought." I left my best friend grinning like an idiot at his precious daughter and went to circulate amongst our guests.

I was glad to see that Emory was still around, but I wished he looked happier. Josh and I had become that annoying couple that wanted everyone else to be happy too—like Kyle, Chaz, Emory, and even Silver. It was nearly a painful experience to see people looking at one another longingly but doing nothing about their situation. Silver would watch Emory when he was busy looking away, and Emory would do the same when Silver was engaged in conversation with someone else. I had no clue what the hell was going on between Kyle and Chaz. They looked chummy and on the verge of taking the leap during our wedding reception, but they looked like they'd rather be anywhere other than our barbecue that night.

*Stay out of it. Stay out of it. Stay... Oh fuck it!* I headed over to the corner where Kyle broodily sat nursing a beer. "What did you do?" I asked.

"Me?" Kyle sounded shocked that I'd think such a thing. "Me?"

"Yes, you," I said. "You looked like you were so close to getting everything you deserved and now... Well, it looks like everything went tits up."

"Tits up?" Kyle asked.

"It's a saying that Josh is prone to use on occasion. That one and 'calm your tits.' So, what did you do?" I asked again.

"It's not me," Kyle said, holding his right hand up like he was swearing in before giving testimony. "I thought we were finally heading in the right direction, but he put the brakes on when I asked him on a date. He turned me down flat."

"You asked Chaz on a date, and he turned you down flat? No

explanations or nothing?"

"Nothing," Kyle said, shaking his head like he still couldn't believe it. "One minute he was looking at me with eyes that begged me to kiss him again, and the next he was telling me that he couldn't go out with me, but didn't say why." *Kiss him again?* I caught that part, but I bit my tongue instead of saying anything. "I think I'm just going to give up."

"Don't do that, Kyle," I said firmly. "If you weren't upset about it, then I'd agree with you, but you are upset. That means you do care and brushing away your feelings isn't the right thing to do." I thought back to the times I could've given up on Josh because Lord knows he tried my patience something fierce. I looked across the expanse of the family room and saw him laughing with Mere and Harley. I couldn't imagine a day without Josh in it and fighting for him, and with him, was the best thing I ever did. "I promise you that it's worth the battle."

Kyle inhaled deeply and released his breath slowly. He turned his head and looked over to where Chaz was sitting next to Emory. Chaz looked up just then, and their eyes met and held for a few seconds before he looked away again. If Kyle couldn't see how much Chaz wanted to be with him, then he was a lost cause. Kyle looked back at me and the crooked smile I always associated with him appeared on his face. "Yeah, okay."

"Good man," I told him.

"You guys going to open your presents?" Mama Richmond asked. "It's getting late, and some of us have to work tomorrow."

"Yeah, okay," I said, echoing the words Kyle had just used.

Josh and I took turns opening our gifts, which were thoughtful and perfect. There wasn't a single dud or gag gift in the bunch. Josh loved the cast iron cookware he received, and I loved my grilling stuff. We received some beautiful picture frames for our wedding photos.

"I'll walk everyone out then come back in and help you clean the kitchen so we can go upstairs and get some sleep," I told Josh.

"No sleep for a while," he said in what he probably thought was a menacing voice.

It sounded promising to me, so I didn't linger outside for too long. I said goodbye to everyone and returned to the house. "I'm ready for my punishment, Sunshine. We can clean up the mess later," I said as I came through the kitchen door. Josh wasn't in the kitchen, he didn't answer me, and I didn't hear him moving around anywhere on the first floor. I wanted to think that he'd gone upstairs to wait for me, but the hairs standing on the back of my neck told me that danger awaited me instead.

I wanted to charge through the house and find Jimmy and Josh, but I had to be smart. Adrian and Dorchester probably hadn't made it down the street, but I couldn't risk their families becoming involved. I dialed 911 and whispered into the phone my name, location, and that I needed backup right away. I asked them to come in quiet, so they didn't tip Jimmy off. I set the phone down on the kitchen island and went in search of my husband. Maybe I was overreacting, but I didn't think so.

I pulled my backup gun from the tea and spice tin in the kitchen cabinet and turned the safety off. "I know you're here, Jimmy," I yelled as I eased toward the family room where I last saw Josh. "There's no point in playing games with me." Buddy wasn't barking, and that scared me. If that sick bastard hurt my husband or my animals...

"Who's hiding," he responded smugly. I rounded the corner, and sure enough, Jimmy De Soto stood in our family room with one arm tight around Josh's neck and held a gun to his head with the other. He had dyed his hair and eyebrows black, but the hatred in his pale blue eyes was the same. "Put the gun down, or I'll blow his head clean off. Well, I plan to do that anyway, but not before I finish destroying your life. Put. Your. Gun. Down." He jabbed the barrel of the gun in Josh's head with each word.

"Okay," I told Jimmy. "Easy, Jimmy. Let's talk about this." Adrian and Josh always joked about television and movie villains talking so much that they gave the hero a chance to save the day. I never considered myself a hero, but I desperately wanted to be that for Josh. "I'm the one you want, not him. Let's take a drive and settle this away from here." I would do anything to protect my husband. I didn't chance looking into Josh's eyes because I had to concentrate on Jimmy and the hand that held a gun to Josh's head.

"Where the hell is the fun in that?" Jimmy asked. "Kid, I'm going to strip you to the bone then I'm going to take away everything you love. You might get the drop on me, but not before I destroy your life like you did mine."

"Jimmy, I didn't do anything to you. I only testified to what you said to me about the situation with Ace Dixon. I never implicated you in any wrongdoing," I told him, hoping I'd have enough time for the cavalry to arrive. "We were partners, Jimmy. We were friends—more like family. You took me under your wing when I was just a young pup and taught me everything you knew."

Jimmy snorted derisively. "You were only my partner so I could keep an eye on you. I couldn't let an overeager little bastard like you ruin my career. I guess the joke was on me after all."

"What do you mean?" I asked. "The only case I was eager about was my brother's shooting." The wide, evil grin that spread across Jimmy's face turned my stomach, and I thought I might throw up all over Josh's fancy schmancy area rug. "You knew who killed my brother all along, didn't you?"

"You could say that," Jimmy answered mockingly. "I see his killer's face every time I look in the mirror." Jimmy laughed when he saw my horrified expression. "He was in the wrong place at the wrong time. I was shaking down the store owner for Big Saul. I thought the clerk was reaching for a gun beneath the counter and I put a bullet in his chest. I didn't even know Dylan was in the store until I looked up in that big round mirror up on the wall. He was cowering behind a row of chips and snacks with a tub of ice cream in his hands. He refused to look up at me and kept saying that he didn't see any faces so he couldn't tell the police anything. It wasn't a chance I could take."

"I don't believe it," I said. "You went out of your way to help me investigate leads on his case in your free time."

"No, I was making sure you never learned the truth. I might've recommended you for promotion as my partner for purely selfish reasons, but along the way, I came to love you like a son. I didn't fake my affection for you, but then you went and stabbed me in the back. I'm not sorry that I killed your brother anymore. In fact, I'm going to kill your husband with the same gun I used to kill him." Jimmy jammed the gun in Josh's head again for emphasis.

He was right. His words cut me to the bone. I hated the thought of my brother afraid and scared. Had Dylan known he was going to die? Did he die instantly or did he linger slowly in a pool of blood and melted ice cream. "I fucking hate you."

"Good, and now for my final act…"

"Put your hands up, you dumb son of a bitch, and I won't blow your fucking ass away!" Sassy said loudly, repeating a line from a movie she'd recently heard. Her voice was so clear that it sounded like a person and it was the distraction I needed to go for my gun. I dropped to my stomach and aimed at Jimmy, but I wasn't the only one Sassy spurred to action.

I watched in awe as Josh elbowed Jimmy in the stomach, stomped down hard on his foot, rammed his head back into Jimmy's nose, and brought his hand back and tagged Jimmy hard in the balls. Jimmy had dropped his gun in the middle of Josh's assault, and Josh kicked it out of Jimmy's reach like a pro. Once Josh got free from Jimmy, he turned around and kicked him in the ribs. The air in Jimmy's lungs loudly expelled as he collapsed writhing on the floor, unsure of where to put his hands. I'd seen a bit of Josh's skill when he took down Billy, but the moves he used on Jimmy were something spectacular.

I scrambled over to Jimmy and pushed him down face first into the carpet. "Josh, go get my cuffs from the bedroom."

"Don't let him bleed all over my rug. Drag his sorry ass to the hardwood floor so I can mop it up later," he said as he ran from the room.

"Where the fuck is my dog, you sick bastard?" I demanded to know.

"He's just sleeping," Jimmy said. "I couldn't hurt an innocent animal."

"But innocent people like my brother and my husband, are okay?" I asked him. "Never mind, don't answer that question. Save your breath for your attorney."

"I can't go to prison, kid. I won't last a minute there. It doesn't matter if they keep me out of general population either and you know it. The inmates will pay off a guard to slip them inside so they can kill me."

"You're going to die anyway," I said. "Isn't that what you said about Ace Dixon? Am I supposed to feel sorry for you after what you confessed to doing before my husband took you out?"

"Detective Wyatt," Officer Wen hollered from the kitchen.

"In here, Wen," I yelled back. "I've apprehended the fugitive."

"Are you taking credit for my work?" Josh asked when he ran back in the room and handed me the cuffs.

I secured Jimmy and jerked him to his feet. "Check him for secondary weapons, take him to the station, and phone Deputy Marshal Matthews." Then I told them about Jimmy's confession about killing my brother and his claim that the gun they took into evidence was the murder weapon.

I heard toenails on the hardwood floor and looked up to see Buddy walking groggily into the room. "Josh, please call Kyle and ask him to come back to check on Buddy. I don't want to take any chances."

"We're going to need you to fill out a report," Wen said with a crooked smile once I finished barking orders.

"I'll be there first thing in the morning," I promised Wen.

Kyle came right away and listened to Buddy's vitals. "He sounds good, but I'd like to pump his stomach, flush him with IVs, and keep him overnight as a precaution if that's okay with you," he said.

"Whatever Buddy needs," I told him.

"I'll call you guys in the morning and let you know how he's doing," Kyle said.

I carried Buddy out to Kyle's truck and promised I'd pick him up as soon as possible. Kyle smirked at my puppy dog voice but didn't comment. I returned to the house and breathed my first real sigh of relief since the police hauled Jimmy out of our house. The threat to my family was over, and I could focus all my energy on good things. Then I saw the thunderous expression on Josh's face and stopped in my tracks.

"What did I do?" I asked, knowing that I was in trouble but not knowing why.

"What the fuck was that 'let's take a ride' bullshit?" Josh demanded. "You thought it was okay just to let him drive off someplace and shoot you?" He was so angry that his voice cracked and tears threatened to spill. Chaz once told me to avoid making Josh mad enough to cry or risk having him rip my arm off and beat me to death with it. I scoffed then, but I wasn't when faced with snapping hazel eyes that had turned brown with rage.

"Sunshine, I was just buying us time. I remembered what you and Adrian said about yapping villains, and I just thought I could buy some time for the BPD to arrive." I was hoping that my praise got me out of trouble a little bit. "It turned out we didn't need them because you used badass moves to take down a gunman and..." *Oh my God! Josh could've been killed!* "What the fuck were you thinking?" I yelled, suddenly angry at the risk he'd taken.

"Me? What about you?" Josh yelled back.

248

We argued back and forth for several minutes until we both wound down once we realized that we were wasting energy on fighting when we could be loving. "Where'd you learn those moves?" I finally asked once I pulled him into my arms, relieved that we were both okay.

"*Miss Congeniality*," he replied.

"Who?" I asked.

"We need to talk about your movie preferences, Gabe. You've learned nothing valuable." He then told me how he learned about the S-I-N-G defense moves in a movie about an FBI agent going undercover as a beauty pageant contestant. "It's hilarious," he added after I didn't immediately respond.

A wave of exhaustion washed over me as soon as the anger, fear, and adrenaline stopped pumping through my veins; in their place was sadness and grief that someone I had once loved and trusted killed my brother. I thought that I would feel a sense of closure once I learned the identity of Dylan's killer, but I didn't. I grieved all over again.

"Baby, sit down before you collapse," Josh said, pushing me onto the sofa. "What can I do for you, Gabe. How can I make this better?" My guy was a doer and had no intention of sitting idly by while I struggled through my grief.

I passed up the opportunity to make a snarky comment about what Josh could do to make me feel better, but it was a good sign that the chance to do so penetrated through the mental anguish I experienced. "I have to tell my parents, Josh. It feels like losing Dylan all over again. I thought knowing the truth would help me and provide closure. The pain is still there; in fact, it's worse. My mom..." my voice broke, and I cleared my throat, "baked Jimmy cakes for his birthday. She made him all kinds of meals he could freeze and heat later after his wife left him. He joined us for Thanksgiving his first year alone." I closed my eyes and shook my head. "How could he sit at my parents' table and eat the food my mother made all the while knowing he killed their son? Who does something like that?"

"A psychopath," Josh said calmly.

"Did you learn that in psychology classes?" I asked, finding a bit of humor after all.

"Yes," he said smartly. "Jimmy could be a sociopath, but his complete lack of guilt and conscience makes me think he's a psychopath."

"Huh," I said, not sure what else to say. I looked at my watch and noted that it was getting close to ten o'clock. I knew my parents were still awake, but that didn't mean calling them was a good idea. What good came out of them losing sleep? On the other hand, they would want to know that Dylan's case would be closed if the ballistics test on the gun showed a match to the one used to kill my brother. What if Jimmy was lying? Did I risk upsetting my parents without solid proof?

"I can hear you thinking," Josh said.

"Do I tell my parents now or wait until I know for sure that Jimmy killed Dylan?" I asked my husband.

"What would you want to happen if you were in their shoes?" Josh asked me.

I picked up my cell phone and dialed my parents in Miami. Josh pressed himself tight against the left side of my body then squeezed my knee comfortingly. The heat of his body and the slight weight of his hand was just what I needed when my words shattered my parents' hearts all over again. Josh pressed his lips against my shoulder in a simple kiss when I couldn't hold back my tears any longer.

Josh led me upstairs after I was done talking to them and held me tight in the darkness of our bedroom. I knew there was no fucking way I was going to get any sleep that night. I was also just as certain that the sunrise the next morning would pale in comparison to the man who loved me.

"My Sunshine," I said, kissing his forehead.

"Always."

# TWENTY-EIGHT

## Josh

"Come out and let me see you," I said to Gabe through the bathroom door. "It can't be that bad."

"I'm not coming out," Gabe said, sounding more like a petulant teenage girl than a sexy stud. "I can't believe I let you pick out the costumes for the party."

"You didn't *let* me. That was your punishment for the asinine contests you and Dorchester set up again. Clearly tying you to the bed and fucking you stupid was only encouraging more stupid."

"Stupid is as..."

"No, Gabe. Now is not the time to repeat movie lines like Savage and Sassy do to get out of trouble. You agreed to let me pick out the costumes, and you're going to plaster a smile on your face when we go down there and kick some costume ass!"

"Can I wear my real gun in my holster instead of the fake one you gave me?" Gabe whined.

"No! Get out here."

Gabe opened the door so fast that I nearly stumbled in, but then I got a look at him and fell to the floor laughing. Gabe stood over top of me with his arms crossed over his broad chest. "I don't know why you're laughing at me. That wig makes you look more like *Joe Dirt* than James Crockett."

His ire only made me laugh harder. "That wig!" I said in between gasps of air. I'd gotten him a wig that was supposed to resemble the curly hairstyle of Ricardo Tubbs, but he was looking more like Lionel Richie.

"I look ridiculous," he said. "Can't we just cut eye holes in the bedsheets and go as a ghost or something?"

I stood up and faced my husband down. I was a firm believer in picking your battles wisely, and I discovered that I didn't want to back down from him that night. "No!" I looked down at my white pants, pink silk T-shirt, and open white jacket. "I think I look damn fine in this outfit."

"You'll look better out of it," Gabe grumbled, but at least his humor was starting to return. He looked down at his double-breasted suit jacket and matching trousers that were like a suit Tubbs wore on an episode of *Miami Vice*.

I pulled one side of my jacket open to reveal my cheap pleather holster and water pistol. "I'm still going to have a lot of fun if we don't win."

"Hey, why don't I get a water pistol?" The whining had returned to his voice.

"You can play with my pistol once the guests go home," I told him over my shoulder as I headed for the door. I had tons of things I still needed to do before our guests arrived.

"By then it'll be empty," Gabe argued.

That got my attention. "What kind of party do you think we're having and where exactly do you think I'm going to be expending my cartridges?"

Gabe's phone rang before he could answer me. He looked at the caller ID and smiled broadly. "Now you're going to get it," he told me before answering the phone. "Hi, Mama. Josh is being mean again. He won't let me have a water pistol." Gabe smiled smugly at me as he listened to what she had to say. I rolled my eyes because there was no way Martina would side against me. "Yes, I'll put you on speakerphone so Josh can hear what you have to say."

"Hello, my loves," Martina said. "I'm happy to hear that you're fighting over important things like water pistols and not boring crap like finances. I'm almost hesitant to intrude on the precious moment. Perhaps I should call back tomorrow."

"No!" Gabe and I said at once.

"What's on your mind, Mama?" Gabe asked.

"I know you are planning to wait a year before you adopt your first child, but an opportunity has presented itself. You see, there's a young woman in our neighborhood who is looking for a couple to privately adopt her babies."

"Babies?" we both asked in surprise.

Gabe recovered faster than I did. "How many babies?" I nodded my head because it was a great question.

"She's having twins—a boy and a girl."

"We'll take them," Gabe said as if he was talking about tickets for a concert that were up for grabs.

"What?" I asked in a near panic. "But our trip? Our plans? We aren't ready."

"Josh," Gabe said, his voice thick with emotion, "were you ready

253

for me? Was I a part of your plan? We'll move our trip up a few months and be ready when they get here."

Damn, but he was right. The best things in life were often ones you never saw coming. I saw the same hope and excitement in Gabe's eyes that I felt bouncing in my chest with every beat of my heart.

"We'll call you tomorrow morning once we make travel arrangements," I told Martina.

"I'm so excited about being a grandmother." Martina acted like it was a sure thing and I hoped she didn't have her heart crushed if the woman chose someone else. "Even if it's years instead of three months."

"Three months?" we asked her. It sounded to me like any road trips we'd be taking the next year would be done in a minivan instead of Charlotte.

"We can do this," I told Gabe. "Three months is plenty of time to plan for a baby."

"Two babies," Martina reminded us.

"Two babies," Gabe and I repeated, sounding like our birds.

"Lick my hole," I heard Savage squawk downstairs.

"Butt Breath!" Sassy repeated back.

Our eyes widened, and our faces turned red because surely Martina overheard the birds repeating an exchange they learned from her son and me.

"You have three months to get Savage and Sassy's language cleaned up," Martina said after laughing so hard she gasped for air.

"Yes, ma'am," we both said.

"Have fun tonight, Hole Licker and Butt Breath. Wait until I tell Bertie about this one. She'll have new T-shirts made," she said before she hung up.

I looked into Gabe's smiling face and said, "I will not be called Little Daddy by my children." Gabe threw his head back and laughed raucously. "I mean it, Gabe."

"Oh, Sunshine. I love you so hard."

# EPILOGUE

## Somewhere on a cloud, most likely over a rainbow...

"You did good, Bianca," Georgia Beaumont said to me. "Did you know that Gabe would fall for my Josh when you slipped that potion in his drink?"

"No," I answered honestly. "I don't even know if Gabe drank his coffee that morning, and even so, it might not have worked."

"What do you mean?" Dylan asked. Gabe's brother was such a sweet young man, and I loved watching over the guys with him and Georgia.

"Gabe had to believe that the spell was possible for it to have worked on him. I had no idea if he believed or not; I just knew I wanted to try," I explained to Dylan. "Even if Gabe believed, the potion only made it possible for him to see his true love. It didn't make him fall in love. As you saw, he still had to put in the time and effort."

"So, Gabe and Josh falling in love was all their doing and not the work of a spell, magic, or juju?" Georgia asked.

"That's right," I said. "I was just responsible for the shattered mirror."

"Too bad you weren't around to help me out," Georgia said somewhat bitterly. "Then again, maybe it happened the way fate intended. At least they're going to bring children into my home." I didn't bother pointing out to her that it was no longer *her* home, but *their* home. I thought she was going to have an angelic meltdown when they started remodeling the place, but she approved in the end.

"Oh man, I can't wait," Dylan said. "Gabe is going to be an incredible father."

"As will Josh," I said.

We enjoyed the Roman-Wyatt's Halloween party from up high. Dylan and I danced to the retro music while Georgia tapped her toes in time to the beat while she kept an eye on the activities below. Something good must have happened because she threw her head back and laughed boisterously.

"I was going to say it was too bad you didn't help the town vet with Josh two-point-oh there, but I can see that the strapping stud is taking matters into his own hands," Georgia said.

I peered down through the clouds and saw that Kyle had tossed Chaz over his shoulder and was heading toward the door. Chaz was wiggling to get loose, but the hunky vet slapped his hand sharp against the younger man's leather-clad ass.

"Get the popcorn ready," Dylan said. "This ought to be good."

**The End!**

# ACKNOWLEDGMENTS

First, I need to thank my husband and children for their constant support and encouragement. It's not easy living with a writer who often disappears into a fictional world for long periods of time. They do so many things to help me out so that I can realize my dream. I love you guys more than words can ever express.

Many thanks go out to my three best friends, Anne, Deena, and Kerry. They've stood by me, cheered me on, picked me up, and held my hand through some really rough patches. I love you girls so very much. I wish everyone had friends like you because the world would be a much kinder place.

To my creative dream team, thanks seem hardly enough for all that you do. Pam Ebeler of Undivided Editing thank you for your tireless work, feedback, and many laughs while editing. Wander Aguiar Photography for the incredible photoshoot that made these gorgeous covers and teasers possible. Jay Aheer of Simply Defined art is just an incredible artist, and I love how she brings my words to life. Stacey Blake of Champagne Formats is also an amazing artist who does incredible interior formatting and designing for e-books and paperbacks. Judy Zweifel of Judy's' Proofreading does an amazing job of finding the tiniest details that make a book shine.

I would like to thank my beta readers for all the honest feedback they give me on my storyline. I appreciate you guys so much. Aimee's ARC Angels are Anne, Kerry, Jason, Jodie, Kim, and Laurel. Thank you for all that you do!

# ABOUT THE AUTHOR

I am a wife and mother to three kids, four dogs, and a cat. When I'm not dreaming up stories, I like to lose myself in a good book, cook or bake. I'm a girly tomboy who paints her fingernails while watching sports and yelling at the referees. I will always choose the book over the movie. I believe in happily-ever-after. Love inspires everything that I do. Music keeps me sane.

I'd love to hear from you.

You can reach me at:

Twitter - twitter.com/AimeeNWalker

Facebook – www.facebook.com/aimeenicole.walker

Blog – AimeeNicoleWalker.blogspot.com